About the author

Maria Akhanji is a British Bangladeshi Muslim writer. She has completed her BA (Hons) in Child Development. She wrote her debut novel, *Salt and Pepper: Unearthing Taboos* due to the lack of accurate representation of the taboo issues embedded in this ethnic minority. She is currently editing the second volume in the Salt and Pepper trilogy, titled, *BrideMaids*.

She developed her writing on youwriteon.com and both her books were featured in the Top Ten Chart on that website. Her books explore issues such as child molestation, Asian in-laws, "family politics" and the double standards that often overshadow Asian culture.

Her books centre on the trials and tribulations of British Asian/Muslim women; however, her writing could give a male audience a quintessential insight into a realm that is commonly experienced yet often left unexplored.

SALT AND PEPPER
UNEARTHING TABOOS

Maria Akhanji

SALT AND PEPPER
Unearthing Taboos

Vanguard Press

VANGUARD PAPERBACK

© Copyright 2018
Maria Akhanji

A CIP catalogue record for this title is
available from the British Library.

ISBN 978 1 784654 36 8

Vanguard Press is an imprint of
Pegasus Elliot MacKenzie Publishers Ltd.
www.pegasuspublishers.com

First Published in 2018

Vanguard Press
Sheraton House, Castle Park, Cambridge
England
Printed & Bound in Great Britain

Acknowledgment

I would like to thank my husband who was the first in whom I confided my wish to be a writer, and who believed in me and made me believe in myself, that I was capable of writing a story. I cannot thank my friends enough, namely: Julaka Misbah, Asya Begum, Rasna Begum-Choudhury, Khatija Mohamed, and Jean Mohamed for they were the first Asian and/or Muslim readers who read the manuscript of my debut novel and reviewed it positively. I am also indebted to writer, Jim Baton, (author of the Peace trilogy) who read and reviewed my work willingly. And if it wasn't for the constructive criticism of the fellow writers from youwriteon.com, my book wouldn't have materialised to what it is today. I'd like to thank my sisters, cousins, Aunt (Chachi), and mother-in-law for praying that my book becomes successful.

Last, but not least, I'd like to offer my deepest thanks to my publisher and editors for guiding me through this journey with their continuing support; it has been a privilege.

For those who suffer in silence...

PROLOGUE

Amma, my mum, was an eccentric character. Most of the time she was driven by her whims and desires. Anger and arrogance were the propellers that sailed her across the sea of life. But then she'd have sporadic moments of wisdom. She was being rather gentle towards me in the last few days while Yasin Bhaiyya, my elder brother, was with us in Dubai. She persuaded me that I should lessen my time spent with him. When I asked her about this she replied that the change I'd experience upon my brother's departure back to London would be heart-breaking for me. So, to console myself, I should gradually move away from him. I took her advice and refused to be fed by Bhaiyya. It was hard. But it made sense. And it got easier too; I just didn't feel hungry any more. Gradually I weaned myself off the affinity with my brother and welcomed the onset of an eating disorder.

Normality was soon restored. Amma was back to her usual peevish mood; I feared her a lot. Childhood is that time when you understand to a profound level but are not articulate enough to comprehend. And such an incident occurred one evening. The scene was not as frightful as the day Bhaiyya was being beaten up but the magnitude of the fear and trepidation was equal, if not more.

I was playing with my beads with Abba, my dad.

He was in a jovial mood that day.

'Ranya!' Amma hollered, 'you need to have your shower, *now*!'

I got nervous and hurried like crazy; yet I never got to have a shower that evening. From the bathroom, I let out an ear-shattering cry.

Within seconds, although what felt like a lifetime, Amma and Di, my elder sister called Megha, ran towards the hallway. They found me standing wide-eyed, perplexed, terror-stricken. They looked relieved though, to see Abba already there, next to me, trying to calm me down.

'For God's sake! What's the matter, Ranya?' Amma and Di asked for the umpteenth time.

I only chanted, 'I'm scared! I'm scared! I'm scared! I'm scared!' in delirium. For all their heartfelt entreaties, I could give no answer, not even another word, no matter what or how they asked me. I just didn't know how or what to say.

I tried hard to forget this incident that occurred; like a felon, I fastidiously tried to bury this memory, ensuring that not a single clue was evident. It took me years to realise that though such things can be inhumed, they remain in a state of dormancy. I was incarcerated within its ubiquitous fortress. And gradually, I came to believe that I simply got carried away with my imagination. Because believing this, and *only this,* proved therapeutic to my *salt and pepper* perception of the world.

RANYA

From my earliest memories, Megha Di was always there. She ensured my needs were taken care of just as any mother would do for their child. She checked that I was clean every day and she was almost religious in helping me with my homework and mannerisms.

Di wasn't always kind; when I acted up, she was there with a quick and stinging hand to correct me. But she wasn't a harsh or a mean mother figure. When I needed love, she didn't hesitate to cradle me in the safe embrace of her arms. She wasn't perfect by far, but I was fiercely loyal to her. My mother, my sister; she was both of these for me.

We got to travel a lot with our parents. Both of them put their careers first and foremost. I'd been transferred to at least six different schools. Unlike my siblings, I was born in London. Our parents were selectively cultural too. When Bhaiyya and Di began to incline towards songs like Michael Jackson's *Bad* and Madonna's *Papa Don't Preach,* they decided to migrate to a more conservative country, like Dubai. Moving was hard and it was getting harder not having my elder brother around. But Bhaiyya had to go back to London for his education. I had to make sure that I didn't keep asking why he left and that I didn't cry. I was *salt and pepper,* in Bhaiyya's words. Di said that I was the youngest in the family and therefore didn't understand everything properly. Just because I was there, it didn't mean that I could join in the important conversations that took place. This used to make me very cross. So Bhaiyya would use that term for me. He'd say that I wasn't the main food like the rest of them, and neither could salt and pepper be consumed just on their own. At the same time, the main food would be tasteless without salt and pepper.

I always felt lonely so for company, I talked to myself. Di had to look after me and that was difficult, I could tell. If I ever needed something, I usually approached her first. I never quite felt accommodated to speak to my parents. Abba hardly spoke to me. He wasn't always grumpy but neither was he easy going. And I *always* avoided Amma. I never knew what to expect with her. Her capricious temper was more unpredictable than the toss of a coin. She could camouflage her persona like a shadow in a dark night.

Di was like Abba. Usually they were calm but once in a while they needed to pop like a cork in a bottle. She was very studious too. She loved English Literature and fashion.

Di and her friends wore door-knocker earrings and shoulder pads all the time. She read all the novels of Dickens, Austen, and the Brontë sisters. She would've read more but we had only the school's meagre library to explore. The bookstores didn't have a variety of books in the English language so the next best choice was to borrow books from friends or from friends' friends. Di would re-read the books when there was nothing else to read.

Abba and Amma were in the middle of another feud. Amma had locked out Abba for something she was angry with him about and so Abba broke the door. Amma kept calling

Abba and his mum vulgar names. In a fit, Abba hit her and ripped her clothes.

I was petrified. Nonchalant, Di carried on studying. I didn't know how she kept her cool at such times. Our final year exams were around the corner. Di was stressed because Abba and Amma could and perhaps would stop us from sitting our exams. Di was praying hard that nothing of that sort happened.

Amma still had no control on her waspish tongue and although silent, Abba was angry too. This was evident as long he ate out or ate bread with sugar, despite food having been cooked at home. The loaf of bread therefore finished quicker than usual as a result. He also didn't do any grocery shopping.

On the last day of our exams, Di filled a large metal container with raisins. She filled it entirely as we both would need to share. She told me to keep the container, as my exam would finish two hours before hers. Di fixed me a bowl of cereal that morning, as there was just enough milk for one person.

She had water and a handful of corn flakes. She ironed our clothes while I brushed my teeth.

At six, I still struggled with my shoelaces so Di had to tie them for me. She tried hard not to seem frustrated. I felt bad for her. I really wanted to thank her with a gift – *a solid gift*. But I had no money. My exam was over and from time to time, I went upstairs in the school building to see if Di had finished or not. I found Di in the same classroom in which Bhaiyya used to sit for his Maths lesson, two years ago. I used to be in kindergarten then and was finding it difficult to settle in. I'd cry every single day after Abba would drop us off before heading to work. Amma never came for she wasn't a morning person but my classmates' mothers used to be with them until they stopped crying.

The school was run by a Bangladeshi team; therefore, they weren't taken seriously by "influential people" like Amma. She'd say that her social status was too high to handle mediocre issues like me crying. The teachers were already there and being paid to handle that. For a whole month, Bhaiyya's kind teacher with crowded but clean teeth, allowed me to sit next to my brother and practise my alphabet.

It was getting dark and the temperature usually dropped at this time. My cardigan didn't feel warm enough. I took the container out and began to munch on the raisins. I reckoned that there were at least five hundred raisins in there.

As I played with my friends, the coach driver who always dropped us off home along with other children, called me. He was a young, good-looking man in his early twenties. He was Indian and on his own in Dubai. We used to call him Samir Bhai. All teenage girls in our school had a crush on him. Some of Di's friends would giggle without any reason for a long time on the bus. Di was unusually quiet whenever he was around and so was he. Often, he'd stare at her. My friends teased me that Samir Bhai fancied me since he was always getting me little gifts like chocolate bars or lollipops. I said I didn't mind for he was a very nice person. He listened to my stories, just as Bhaiyya used to.

That day he asked me a few important questions. He asked me what I'd like best as a gift to which I replied that I'd like a rose with its roots so I could plant it in a pot. He then asked me whom I loved the most in my family. Without a second's hesitation, I replied, 'Di.'

'And who does Di love the most?'

'Me. And books too.' I paused a bit before carrying on. 'Samir Bhai, can I do something for you? And in return, you could get me the book Di has been wanting to read.' He was curious so I explained briefly as to why I needed to buy something for Di.

He said he'd think of something. The bell went off so I bid Samir Bhai farewell and made my way to Di's classroom. Abba usually picked us up whenever Di had an exam this late. Di looked pale. She sipped water from her flask and told me to give her the raisins. My heart sank. I practically had nothing to do in those two hours after my exam. All my friends had been collected by their parents straight after their exams were over. Abba had work and Amma wouldn't trouble herself to pick me up, so, to kill time, I kept hovering about. As I hovered, I didn't realise that I kept eating the raisins, one after another. I looked at the container and saw only four raisins.

'You stupid, idiot!' I felt a hard slap on my head.

'I am so sorry, Di,' I cried. Di was seething and I felt wretched. Any other time, I would've hit her back. But not this time as I knew that I deserved it.

Abba was an hour late picking us up. From a distance, I saw Di's friend giving her a chocolate wafer. Di saw me looking at her as she bit into it. She came up to me and offered me a bite from it. Reluctantly, I shook my head and Di left without saying anything.

As promised, Samir Bhai gave me a task. We went to the compound called *Bahr*. A lot of Indians and Bangladeshis stayed there including bachelors like Samir Bhai. There was some sort of a function going on and Amma was going to perform a few songs. Amma took opportunities like this very seriously. She wore a yellow, silk saree that had block prints of black flowers. The temperature was cool so she draped a black woollen poncho, filigreed with gold thread, around her. For jewellery, she chose to wear my gold set. Di told me that that was an old trick Amma played with Abba. She'd get a new set claiming that she was saving either for Di, Bhaiyya's future wife, or me.

Her pixie haircut looked more like a bob now, which she brushed and set in perfect waves with hairspray. Her lips were hued in deep maroon, her eye shadow was gold and, her nails were painted in a shade of copper and gold glitter. The arch of both of her jet-black brows seemed to affix her look into a permanent startle. That, along with her prominent widow's peak reminded me of *Maleficent* from *Sleeping Beauty*.

Di was busy laughing and talking with her friends, while my friends played in the vicinity of their mothers. Amma was in the makeup room and the proximity within which I was permitted to be in was the sitting area before the stage. That's where Amma and the other artistes would perform. Abba was with his friends somewhere else so I was all by myself.

Amma made me wear a pair of lilac, *dhoti* style trousers with a short kameez. It was a hand-me-down from Di. I looked at my black pumps. The sole of my right shoe had come off a quarter of the way from the front. My feet didn't touch the floor if I sat back properly on the foldable chairs. To prevent the sole sticking out, I had to press down my right foot on the ground. I didn't realise this fiasco till a cabal of Di's friends pointed it out, laughing. And that's why I sat here by myself.

The hall was slowly but surely getting full but the seats on either side of me were still empty. I slouched on the seat and wished I had brought something along to keep me busy. I looked around and studied the people seated there. A particular lady with her daughter caught my attention. The lady was dressed in a simple pink saree with a beige cardigan. Her makeup was very minimal but her daughter was dressed up like a doll. She wore a red and black checked dress, a red cardigan, white tights and a pair of shiny red Velcro shoes. Her hair was parted in the middle into two neat French braids. At the bottom, her braids were clasped in white and red gingham bands. Their conversation was audible from where I sat. Every few minutes, the mother would ask her little girl if she'd like to eat something. Her daughter was plump, very cute, and seemed a bit younger than me. She was already eating a packet of crisps while her devoted mother had a carton of juice in one hand. She had her other hand inside the food bag, perhaps rummaging for some more food. It was a green apple flavoured juice. I had a taste of it once. It was an equal balance of tartness and sweetness. Saliva dribbled at the corners of my mouth.

Presently, the mother asked if she'd like to eat some biscuits. Chocolate biscuits. The whole packet of biscuits was in her hand now, and she was attempting to open it. Her daughter whinged and shook her head so the mother kindly asked her to sip some of the juice.

'Ranya.' I turned around and found Samir Bhai next to me. I was so happy that I hugged him. He gave me a bar of *Cadbury* chocolate and the joy I felt was the same as a nomad would feel after days of travel in the desert and then stumbling upon an inn with hospitable people. He gave me a carton of

Ribena too. I didn't want to sound spoilt and rude so I thanked him and decided to give the juice to Di later. I loathed *Ribena.*

He got a metal piece out which appeared to be something like a fancy key ring. He said that it was a puzzle. Two metal parts were connected and I'd need to separate it, within a week. If I could do that then he'd buy me anything I wished. I was even happier now. I loved it how Samir Bhai didn't ignore me. He treated me like I was as important as an adult was.

Amma sang away while people clapped and chanted *"encore, encore."* Usually I felt embarrassed and annoyed whenever Amma performed. To her fans, she was an idol worth worshipping. To me she was an imp mutated from an angel. But I wanted her to carry on singing today for I wanted to solve the puzzle while this function lasted. This could herald my victory in getting something for Di.

It was the sixth day and still I had no luck at cracking the piece into two. I was frustrated and disheartened.

'What are you doing?'

I told Di about the puzzle. 'I have one more day to separate it or else…'

'Or else what?'

I felt like kicking myself. 'Nothing. Can you help me?' I asked. She said that in return I'd have to tell her why I needed to separate this. I agreed. Within ten minutes, Di cracked the piece into two. I was overjoyed. But at once regretted for I had to confess. She hugged me and said that I didn't have to do that.

'Erm, did Samir Bhai say anything about… *me*?' Di asked. I looked at her. She wasn't looking at me. She was trying to fix the books on top of the desk in our room, which looked silly since they were already neatly arranged. Di was always dusting and tidying the house. I recounted the day of the exam when I spoke to Samir Bhai. Di looked at me and paid attention like she never did before. I felt very important. I wished there was something else to say for I didn't want her to lose interest in me.

'I think he likes you,' I said. Di blushed.

'Why do you say that?'

'He keeps looking at you and wants to know about you.' I stopped after this for I knew that I'd be stretching the truth more than necessary.

The following day, a couple of families from *Bahr* compound came around for dinner. Amma made Hungarian goulash, cooked chicken biryani, a meat curry, fish cutlets, and tarka dal. She also made salad and two massive desserts: a fruit custard and an egg pudding.

Samir Bhai drove the guests in his van. He wore a white linen checked shirt tucked inside black jeans and white trainers. His thick black/brown hair was back brushed as usual and complimented his tanned skin. While sitting in our living room, Uncle Minhaj told him that he would've been better off if he became an actor or a model in India. At five feet ten he was tall and athletic enough for the part. Samir Bhai smiled uneasily for he was under the supercilious gaze of Amma and wanted to get out of there. Amma wasn't happy that he was sitting with everyone as she felt his status was lower than us. Uncle Minhaj had two daughters: Jheenuk studied in the same class with Di and Jhumur was two years older than me. Both of them were snobs. Di was far prettier than Jheenuk but she crowed that all the boys in the school fancied her, including

Samir Bhai. She also bragged that, on the way to here, Samir Bhai kept adjusting the interior mirror to see her.

Her dress sense, however, was very good; it accentuated her lithe figure and compensated for her plain, rather boyish features. At the dinner table, she pointed out in front of Samir Bhai, that Di seemed to have put on more weight. I wished Amma and Abba spent a bit more on our attire since Di had so much more potential than Jheenuk.

'You have such ugly teeth.'

'Huh?' Jhumur was looking at me. 'What's wrong with my teeth?' I asked.

'You have buckteeth. Your mum was telling my mum that she regrets about how you turned out.' She giggled. 'You look nothing like your sister. Megha Di is so pretty.'.

Uncle Faris's three sons, who were similar age to us, joined in the laughter. I writhed in stifled fury. Amma always called us names in anger: Di was the elephant or donkey due to her weight or foolishness, and I was the rabbit because of my buckteeth. It didn't bother me. But the fact she had genuine concern about my looks, took me aback.

After all the children had eaten dinner, we went downstairs to play. A new game was being played. Everyone would yell "buckteeth." This would aggravate me and make me run after them and they would have to run and hide from me. Samir Bhai heard all this and told them off. They all got a piece of his mind and even apologized to me. I was still sad so he took me for a drive around the corner in his van. He told me that it was time for me to have my reward. He asked me what I wanted. I told him that it was actually Di who solved the puzzle. He said that in that case I could have two gifts.

'What gift will you give me?'

'It's your choice,' he said.

'I want twenty ice creams.'

Abba hardly allowed us to have ice creams. Now that I had the opportunity, I didn't want to let it go. Di would be so happy about the ice creams too. I chose twenty chocolate *Cornettos* and a *Sweet Valley High* book for Di. Samir Bhai smiled and paid for them. He didn't show the scorn Abba usually had whenever I wanted to buy something like ice creams or chocolates. Seldom Abba would treat us with chocolates. Usually he'd buy one *Mars* bar to share between Di and I.

He said it wasn't good for our teeth.

My buckteeth.

We came home half an hour later to find Amma and Abba and everyone else waiting for us. The look on their face was something between outrage and concern.

Suddenly I wasn't excited about the ice creams any more. The uncles defended Samir Bhai's innocence while Amma shouted at the top of her lungs. I didn't get to hear anything but I was sure that he was belittled and humiliated beyond my imagination. And all because of me. I went to our room looking for Di and was about to leave when I felt a hard slap on my back.

'You little scoundrel,' Abba muttered under his breath, 'how dare you go like this with another man without our permission?'

I cried the whole night. Di tried to comfort me. We were both squashed in her single bed but I was too scared to sleep next to Amma or by myself. Abba threw all the ice creams away. A week later I got to hear that Samir Bhai had been deported back to India.

'Di.'

'What?'

'This is for you.' I gave her the book. I had it hidden inside the pocket of my jacket and had forgotten about it due to all the commotion on that day. Di shed a tear and hugged me.

'What did Amma and Abba tell Samir Bhai that he had to go back home?'

'Don't worry 'bout it,' Di said. I ruminated that I was still *salt and pepper* to understand it fully.

RANYA

Summer was here. We didn't leave anything plastic-like pens or water bottles in the car or on window sills as the extreme heat would melt them. Often the sky was a royal blue with no trace of clouds. Di covered my English homework notebook in a calendar sheet that had the picture of a similar blue sky but with a flock of birds. I'd never forget this notebook for just as ink marked its pages, similarly the incident attached with it left an indelible realization about the heinous character Amma possessed.

Di used to make me study while she tidied the house. Next to the television there were artificial but elegant flowers in two large floor vases. They displayed conspicuous dust by the end of each month. It was Di's duty to wash them by hand, in detergent water, rinse them out, dry them, and then rearrange each flower respectively. It was a tedious job. She changed all the bedding in the house, every month too. Amma used to sleep most of the time saying she was ill. Di did all these extra chores so that Amma didn't call her to massage her legs. That was a cumbersome job we had to always do – just sit in one place and massage her for hours on end. Di was almost fifteen so she could use the excuse of household chores; being eight years younger than her, I could only use the excuse of my homework, for a short while. Today she was rearranging the flowers while I had to answer some questions from a comprehension. Di helped me to write them correctly and neatly. She told me to put the notebook in my school bag so that I didn't forget the next day.

The following day something out of the ordinary happened. My Indian friend, Rani, was sitting next to me as usual. We both had our English homework notebook in front of us. She showed me her work and silently, I appreciated that Di helped me with my task. Her writing was illegible and didn't meet the writing standard that should've been met. Our teacher, Mrs Shikdar, was very strict and no one dared to speak unless spoken to.

We both sat in the front desk so I could easily see when she was checking our notebooks. What followed next made me regret that Di had written my name in black ink directly on the royal-blue sky cover of my notebook. Rani scribbled her name on her notebook herself. Her mum was a nurse and hardly had the time to look out for her and her brother. I felt sorry for her. I was baffled when our teacher smiled at Rani and handed her *my notebook.* She was checking the last notebook. I figured out why she smiled at Rani when she was checking *my notebook.*

'What the hell have you written, Ranya?' Mrs Shikdar yelled. Our teacher shook my notebook like a ragged doll and showed it to the classroom. She said that the splay of a hen's feet dipped in ink and then pressed on paper would've been more legible than what I had written. And as for what I wrote, she said that the person who passed me for the admission test needed a revision of their alphabet.

Everyone laughed. I looked at Rani and wasn't sure if she was being stupid or sly. I was terrified. I was itching to open my mouth but my voice box seemed indefinitely out of order.

Would it be disrespectful if I tried to defend myself? I didn't know what to do. But Mrs Shikdar knew. She made me stand outside the classroom, holding my ears. I cried the whole day. Each second felt like an hour. I was still crying when we went home. Di told me off for not telling her about this at school. In the meantime, Amma heard us and wanted to know what was going on. The kettle behind Amma was boiling and the steam escaping its spout formed a festoon around her head. I was getting anxious. When enraged, Amma's manner of speech didn't quite conform to complaining regulations. I wished that my prediction sprinkled with the concept of *salt and pepper* would be wrong. But even at seven, I was right in this aspect. I couldn't sleep the whole night. With a cloak of arrogance, a crown of authority, and a sceptre of impudence, Amma harassed Mrs Shikdar in a way that'd be remembered for a long time. In the principal's office, the principal, all the main teachers and I witnessed Amma calling her a jealous, middle-class pauper who was trying to snub her daughter since she couldn't compete with Amma's beauty, social, and financial status. A tearful Mrs Shikdar was made to apologise to me. I wanted the earth to swallow me instead.

She was still my teacher but I was no longer her student. She never spoke to me like before and didn't acknowledge my presence. If I did something wrong, she ignored me, as though I was invisible. She was extra nice to the other students and had become a lot more laid back with them. It felt deliberate. Often, she'd draw pictures for the children except for me, to colour in. I didn't dare ask her to make me one. Deep down two things were clear to me: Mrs Shikdar's new attitude was because of me and Amma's bullish defence was *not* for me.

For days, I thought about this. Every time I went to school I had to live that moment of guilt. I blamed myself for crying in front of Amma which made Di tell her about the copies being swapped. Di assured me that Mrs Shikdar shouldn't have been insulted the way she was and neither was she supposed to mistreat me the way she did.

But Amma was Amma and we couldn't undo the incident now. At lunchtime, I saw Di speaking to Mrs Shikdar and since then she stopped ignoring me. She was back to scolding me when I deserved it. I was overjoyed as with this a huge burden was lifted off my chest.

Usually I hated to run errands like buying *khubz* from our local shop. At dusk, Di's friend, who lived next door, came around. Di wanted some snacks and fizzy drinks. She gave me some money and told me to get those and I was more than happy to do so. The shop wasn't too far but it wasn't close by either, and *Nahr* compound was a safe place. Abba was on call at the hospital, within the compound, and Amma went to one of the Arab houses outside the compound. Those Arab houses appeared like a shanty town and contrasted the contemporary flats where we lived.

There were hardly any Arabs living inside the compound and so the Arab boy must've been from the shanties. He looked like he was Di's age. He was tall, slender, and wore Arab-style clothes. They were light blue.

He had frizzy brown hair and an olive complexion. I was certain that I didn't see him in the shop. As I walked home, I felt that I was being followed and before I knew it, a hand cupped my butt-cheeks and squeezed them a few times before letting go.

I screamed as extreme fright impaled me. I fell on the ground and the contents in the shopping bag fell out. I turned around and caught a glimpse of the boy. He sprang over the wall that surrounded the compound and was joined by other boys. Their laughter echoed in the quiet evening air. I ran all the way home crying and both Di and her friend were shocked to see me like this. I didn't make any sense as I spoke through violent sobs. It was sometime before they were able to comprehend what I said.

Back then, our perception wasn't informed with this form of a nefarious assault. Di and her friend were therefore in stitches for at least half an hour about the part regarding my backside being kneaded. I left them to their mirth and went into the guest room to be alone. To cogitate.

There was a confounding lack of discernment in the incidents with Samir Bhai, Mrs Shikdar, and the Arab boy. I didn't know how to deal with them but I reckoned that the way they were looked at was an unfortunate case of misjudgement. I didn't mention this incident to Abba or Amma. Either they'd laugh too or deal with it in an obnoxious manner. I wouldn't mind if that was the case, but I somewhat felt embarrassed about it. Somehow this incident paralleled another occurrence in my life that I couldn't quite recall.

MEGHA (DI)

I was fifteen, getting more confused, and scared. Ranya got chicken pox and as usual Amma was not looking after her so I had to. She was very ill and emaciated. As usual, I was the only one who cared for her so after tending to her needs, I fell ill. Amma woke at two in the afternoon every day. After breakfast, which I made for her every weekend and holidays, she'd leave the house and return late at night. I was bedridden. Ranya didn't say it but I knew that she was upset, as she too had to miss school because of me. I was spiking temperatures and often fainted.

He looked after me the whole time. *He'd* come into our room, especially in the middle of the night. During the day, Ranya would have her back facing me when she studied at the desk. *He* didn't care; perhaps he thought that she was too young to grasp the gravity of the situation. I knew *I* wished that she was. In the night, *he'd* close the door and undress me, till I was stark naked. *He'd* rub a wet flannel all over me saying it was to lower my temperature.

I was too weak, ashamed, and in denial to put a stoppage to *his* morphed affection.

I diverted this trauma by making out with any guy in the block 'cos I didn't care. I felt good and happy so long I knew some other guy was touching me. To be with *any* guy who wasn't *my father* always abated my frustrations.

"But he's your father after all, and my husband," Amma would say. "Everyone has flaws. You have to overlook it and move on. We have our reputation to consider."

I knew that it was Amma's fault; she hardly did any wifely duties, provoked him, and constantly suspected him. At least Abba didn't beat me up like Amma did. I'd hit Ranya for the littlest mistakes she'd make. Just like how Amma would hit me after Abba would try to get intimate with me. I just couldn't control my anger. I felt terrible afterwards when I'd see her crying. I'd take a vow each time that I wouldn't take it out on her but I'd break it all the time. Ranya didn't understand what I was going through, and I didn't want her to either.

RANYA

One day, Abba announced that he'd been offered a very good job. Not only housing, education, medical care, and holidays for the entire family were of excellent quality, but they were also the perquisites of his fabulous job.

But – it was in Saudi Arabia. That signified a very big issue: Amma, Di, and later on I would have to wear the *hijab,* and possibly cover the face too with a *niqab*, a face veil.

'What?! You want the girls... *me* to walk around like a mummy?' Amma questioned and of course it was a rhetorical one. Amma was a narcissist. She was a dainty and stylish little woman, therefore covering herself other than with makeup was totally out of the question.

'Well, not that you aren't one already.' Abba winked. Abba was more than a foot taller than Amma, leaner, with a luscious mane of hair and beard. He reminded me of a cross between the *Lion King* and *Captain Haddock* from *Tintin.* Di and I looked at each other and burst out laughing. Amma glared and quickly attempted to reach for her sandal to throw at us but, in her rage, didn't realise that she was barefooted. This cracked us up even more. But Amma being the fighter she was, quickly rolled up the newspaper she found next to her on the side table and thrust it across us. Di ducked just on time but it struck me hard and knocked me off-balance. By now the situation wasn't comical any more. A fight and a fortnight later it was settled that we will move to London. Unsurprisingly, this decision got changed sooner than it was made. We stayed in UAE for another year but moved to another city and so to another school.

One sunny day, Abba returned from Friday prayers (from what I had seen, that was the only time Abba prayed). Amma didn't pray but ensured that Di prayed all her five prayers. He told us that he needed to discuss an important issue. Amma complained that he was reeking of *oud*, an Arabic musk she couldn't stand. Abba said that the bottle slipped from his hand and most of it fell on his garment. Amma twitched her nose and looked intimidating. Di discreetly scowled at Amma as she could never stand Amma mistreating Abba. She was a daddy's girl and Abba loved her just as much. We had lemonade, fresh hot *khubz,* and sheesh kebabs. Di made a tuna and *harissa* mix and Amma prepared a tomato, feta cheese, and olive salad. I picked the olives from the trees in the compound swathe the day before. We were all anticipating to hear the news.

As he ate, Abba said that we needed to leave Sharjah and settle in Bangladesh. Uncle Minhaj, and a few others had decided that too, due to the current political situation in the Middle East. Amma surprised Di and I by agreeing to this decision.

'I've already spoken to a family of four,' Abba said as he munched on his tuna baguette. 'They've agreed to buy everything for six thousand dirhams.'

'No way! I know people within and outside here. They will pay more if not the original price,' Amma said.

'Are you crazy? No one will buy anything if you haggle now. We'll just have to get rid of everything for nothing.'

'Leave it to me. Actually, I'll do a forfeit. I get to keep *all* the money if I can sell them for more than six thousand. But if I make even a dirham less than six grand then you keep it all. Deal?'

Abba looked at Di and smiled. 'Deal.' We were to leave by December. But by the end of November, Amma had auctioned everything, even the clothes that had become too small for me. I could see dollar signs in her eyes. One hot day after work, Abba asked where the water cooler was. Di told Abba that Amma had sold it. He shouted at Amma for giving the most essential item this early. Amma roared back that he was getting jealous since he knew that she was going to win the challenge. Secretly, Di and I agreed with Abba but remained silent since Amma would beat the hell out of us if we proclaimed this. Amma's acidic gaze alone could curdle milk.

Di had told her not to give it yet but Amma was on a selling spree. Di and I had to eventually go to the person to whom Amma sold the water cooler. Amma was infuriated and we were embarrassed, as we had to go to a sundry of people in the compound to get back other essential items and give their money back too. I asked Di if Amma would still win the forfeit. She said that only time would tell.

There were two days left till we left Sharjah indefinitely for Bangladesh. The almost empty apartment echoed. We borrowed two mattresses, four pillows, and two blankets from a neighbour. We were eating takeaways and drinking bottled water. From time to time, the Arab neighbours from the shanty gave us home-cooked meals. I was feeling very sad to leave

UAE. My memories were full of the sand dunes, the sun, the beach, my school, museums, my friends, neighbours, and olive trees. I felt like I was being uprooted. I shed tears like a tree shed its leaves.

Abba left early in the morning for work and Amma woke up almost immediately after he left. Di, Amma and I had some milk and bread for breakfast and soon after Amma told me to fetch her bag. She unzipped it and gathered several bundles of dirhams and began to count them. I'd never seen so much zeal and admiration in Amma before. Money and fame rendered an incandescent glow in Amma. After counting the money herself, she told Di to count it again. They counted three times altogether; she made a whopping thirteen thousand two hundred and twenty-six dirhams. Amma was euphoric.

Abba returned at lunch time, and while he had his back facing us, Amma declared, 'Seven and a half thousand dirhams. And it's all mine.'

'Huh? I thought it was...' The scowl and painful pinch from Amma made me stop midway. I made no noise whatsoever. Once Amma did this to Di and she screamed in agony. Abba knew at once what had happened. Amma got a slap for it. Amma avenged herself for this the following morning; after Abba left for work, Amma whipped Di with a thin bamboo stick. This taught me to remain absolutely silent should such a thing occur with me.

I looked at Di who chided my supposedly weakness in mental arithmetic. She took me to the other room to do my maths work. Sometime later Amma came in and slapped me hard on the face for almost blurting out the truth. Di explained to me that Amma didn't want Abba to know.

'Why?' I asked through sobs.

'Because Abba may not let her have it all.'

'Why?' I was confused.

'You're too *salt and pepper* to understand this.' Di sighed.

MEGHA (DI)

Bangladesh was hotter than I had expected. There was always a power cut, for hours on end. But when there was electricity, the fan kept circulating hot air. Abba didn't like the fan to be on when we ate, as the food got cold. Amma hated the heat so she ate in the living room and to pester Abba, she'd add extra chili powder to the curries. She knew Abba couldn't handle hot and spicy food yet the few times she made the effort to cook were always heaped with extra hot chili powder. She just wanted Abba dead so she did this deliberately. I just knew it. Poor Abba worked all day and all night long, away from us. He came once in a while and even then, couldn't have some decent food. Half the time he ended up eating bread with sugar.

The other day Amma came home with this lady. She seemed to be in her mid-twenties but looked older than Amma. She was tall and slender though. Abba was saying how he felt sorry for her since her husband deserted her and now she was knitting to make ends meet for her eight-month-old daughter and herself. Amma took this completely the wrong way. She accused Abba of having an affair with her. She insulted the lady the next time she came around to drop off the cardigans Amma had asked her to knit for us. Amma didn't take them and nor did she pay her.

'You ought to stop calling Abba names like that,' I said one day. I had to say something. The anger in me was bubbling to boiling point.

'Who the hell are you to tell me that, you fat whore. You probably sleep around with the guys in your school. Do you want me to tell your Abba about your boyfriend?' Amma said. She pulled my ponytail real hard when she said the last bit. I had to bite my tongue and take it in.

I thought she'd keep quiet if I didn't open my mouth. I was so wrong to think that she tried to hide this incident to save me from Abba. Recently she'd been blackmailing me a lot regarding this. She kept hitting me for anything and everything. She suspected Abba of having affairs with other women and, while she verbally abused him, she physically attacked me. She hit me with a cast iron candle stand last week. I got a big bruise on my left shoulder, which was going yellow now. Now she found another issue – accusing me of sleeping with Abba. She threw me on the floor and squashed her feet on my chest. Then, with a fork, she poked my breasts.

'Do you think I don't know what you do behind my back? I know what you and your Abba get up to in the middle of the night, you slut. You undress to let him prod your nubile breasts, don't you, you fucking bitch?'

My inner lip was cut and bruised after she punched me on my mouth. My mouth was bleeding and the pain was excruciating. Lulubu and Samia, our maidservants, were crying in the corner. Lulubu always tried to stop Amma and, in the process, she used to get beaten up too.

The month of Ramadan was here. Amma wasn't religious so she wasn't fasting. I fasted for I felt that there was someone up there who was the controller of everything. And I believed that asking him would give me what I wanted.

I came home from school with Ranya; she was too young to fast. There were only fifteen minutes left for *iftar* but Lulubu said that Amma hadn't given any money to buy food. There was no rice, lentils or any vegetables. Meat, chicken and fish were confined to my dreams only. Lulubu was crying, as she couldn't make anything.

'Where's Amma?' I asked.

'She's been out with that Rocky uncle since morning. She had a photoshoot first in the house and then she left. I asked her when she'd be back but she shouted at me saying, as a servant, it wasn't my job to ask that.'

I hugged her; she was fasting too. She worked for us for free and knowing her, she would've spent her own money to buy us food, if she had any. I opened the fridge and found three eggs. I fried them and toasted a few slices of bread on the gridle pan as we had no toaster. Ranya suggested that she could make potato chips. Lulubu cut the last four potatoes and, under her supervision, Ranya fried them. I looked at my eight-year-old sister and realized how time had flown. We broke our fast with that and just then, Amma walked in with several bags in her hands. She was dropped off by some wealthy producer, who promised to produce her recordings, and turn Amma into "a big star".

'Look at all these *sarees* I bought.' She showed us five of them. Each was exquisite and rich in taste and colour.

While she was being ostentatious, I thought about the underwear I wore. Amma told me last week that as Abba hadn't given enough money, she was unable to buy me a new set of knickers. I had to resort to cutting an extra piece of cloth from one of my old cotton shawls and sewing it onto my knickers – *that's* how tattered they were.

Amma brought some pizza as well. Ranya, Samia, and Lulubu devoured them but I refused. The following day, I spoke to a friend at school and asked her if she could arrange some students for me to privately tutor. Within a week, I had six students whom I used to teach after my English coaching classes. I lied to Amma that my teacher was teaching us an extra hour for free.

By the end of the month, I was given a total of sixteen hundred takas. I was thrilled and didn't know what to do with the money. I bought two lipsticks and two eyeliner pencils for Lulubu and Samia. I took Ranya out to one of the first fast food shops that had opened in our area. I bought her a burger, a hotdog, and a pastry too. I looked at her the whole time while she ate. She looked so happy. She could eat a lot and still remain so skinny. I wished I could be like that. I bought some burgers for Lulubu and Samia too. Later I took Ranya to a bookshop where she bought *Archie* comics. She loved those. I then popped into a clothes store where I picked up some essential stuff like undergarments. I dropped off Ranya and the food at home and then went out again, to meet my boyfriend, Tilak. He was tall, handsome, and very rich. His best friend, Sabbir had a crush on me too, I could tell. Ranya said that she thought Sabbir seemed a nicer person than Tilak. But Sabbir was only five feet seven whereas Tilak was six feet two. Short guys just weren't my type. All the girls swooned over Tilak but he only chose me. He was born and brought up in America and I just loved his accent.

I came home and although I knew that Lulubu would never betray me, somehow Amma knew that I was lying about the extra coaching classes. She beat me up and said that I wasn't allowed to go out on my own any more, and that Lulubu would have to escort me from now on. I guffawed inside; little did she know whose side Lulubu was on.

When I was going for my coaching class, Lulubu told me on the rickshaw that I shouldn't hang around with Tilak but I told her not to worry. She was like a mother to me. However, when I came home, Amma discovered the truth –from Ranya. She demanded to know where I got the money to buy her burgers and comics, and stationery stuff. Lulubu insisted that I was innocent since she was escorting me now. Amma couldn't say anything on that any more so she began to stir up old issues, like me being an overweight whore and fucking my dad. And on that note, she beat me up ruthlessly. She pulled my hair so hard that I could hear the strands snapping off my scalp. I had beautiful coffee brown hair. It broke my heart to see my thick locks being pulled out.

Amma grabbed my cheeks with just one hand; it was a tenacious grip and I felt her long fingernails dig into my skin. But I couldn't scream as my lips had taken the form of a goldfish. She called Abba names too.

'You want to know why I cook spicy food? It's so that it aggravates your faggot of a father's illness.'

That was the last straw and I made my plan. I decided to embark on an abominable and unimaginable deed. My face was covered in nail marks and when asked by my friends and teacher the next day, I passed them off as busting my pimples. I went to the local shop after school and purchased some rat poison. But when I came home, Abba was sitting in the sitting room.

'What are you doing here?' I asked.

'Why, aren't you happy to see me?' Abba asked.

I was glued to where I stood so he got up and kissed my forehead. I told him that I couldn't be happier but I was actually annoyed. I didn't want Abba to be held responsible; I had to postpone my plan.

Abba and Amma were frolicking the whole time and it vexed me to see that. Abba was too naïve to see the truth and Amma was too cunning for her own good. I couldn't sleep the whole night. I kept tossing and turning. Ranya complained so I got up. It was past three o'clock in the morning and the house was very quiet. I crept out into the kitchen to have some water when I thought that I saw something move in the room, where Lulubu and Samia slept.

Could it be burglars? I tiptoed into the kitchen and grabbed a wooden spoon. There was some light shining into the room from outside which was enough for me to see what was happening there.

Abba was sitting on the floor, next to where Lulubu and Samia slept. And he was groping one of them.

I recalled Abba telling me that he used to love me in that manner, as he felt sorry for me that Amma verbally and physically abused me. That it was okay for a father to do so and I should go with the flow. Abba saw me staring at him. I didn't care and neither did he.

RANYA

It was December. At this time the air in Dubai used to be cool. But as we landed on the soil of Bangladesh, humid air smacked our bare arms and faces. No sooner had we entered the airport than beggars started to throng us asking for money in dirham instead of taka. Amma chased them away in an apathetic manner since she knew they were acting. I felt sorry for them but supposedly begging was a business and they were all con artists who picked pockets like the *Artful Dodger* from *Oliver Twist*. The fact that we moved a lot was one of the second major problems in my life. The first, by far, was my parents' perpetual, annoying, and non-stop rowing. That dictated every other aspect that revolved in the galaxy of the roving Kuraishi household. One could possibly not imagine another couple so-not-made-for-each-other. Abba and Amma always convinced us after they made up that they loved us to pieces and that they'd never split because of their love for us. But Di and I gradually came to understand that we weren't the cause, but rather the society and culture were the reasons and pressure, as to why they stayed under the same roof.

Is this "reason and pressure" common in all families? This phenomenal question rose in my mind when I was around nine. Whenever we visited a relative or a friend, I used to observe our hosts and assess this matter privately to myself. I pondered the possibility of a darker and unknown side to their parents' personalities. My parents fought almost all the time for the pettiest of issues. They could be loud and equally as foul when they argued. At home, there was often a marital emergency, requiring our relatives to intervene. They had to stop my parents from humiliating themselves – or maybe I should say the relatives themselves, any further. I used to constantly worry that they might separate. Although we were non-practising Muslims, I'd always implore Allah that they remained together, no matter what happened.

At times, I couldn't stop crying. Their mercurial temperaments used to have the effect of bomb explosions and tsunamis in my imaginary peaceful world.

Like a seer, Di could prophesy an imminent quarrel between our old folks. I guessed this for she would find means to distract me. Either she'd play with me or if it was close to bedtime, she'd tell me story after story with sweet patience till I fell asleep. At desperate times, she would block my ears or close my eyes with her soft hands so I neither heard their heated disputes nor saw their vulgar actions. Despite all her efforts, I used to know that things were not right. "But what if I see bad dreams, Di?" I'd say. "I'll be right next to you, so all you have to do is hug me tight." Like a torch, Di's words and presence shone through half the way to the unlit tunnel of my childhood days.

We stayed in Shamshed Dada's place when we first came to Hayapur, Bangladesh. This Dada was a few years older than Abba but in relation he was our paternal grandfather's cousin. He was a lawyer. He had four daughters, two servants, and a big house. We called his wife Dida. She was much younger than Amma and very sweet-tempered. We stayed for almost a month and I loved it there. Their kids were closer in age to me so we played, ate, slept, and even bathed together. Sometimes we danced in the rain and almost every late afternoon, we would shake the sweet smelling *Shefali* tree in their modest garden so the small white flowers would drop like an avalanche. We used to thread these exotic, white blooms into garlands, necklaces, and wrist corsages. The lingering scent of these flowers used to pervade the air and upholsteries even inside the house.

Abba was busy looking for a suitable flat for us since he decided to base a private surgery in Kakongonj, which was about a four hours' journey by train from Hayapur. I asked him why he didn't stay with us here so he said that Kakongonj was our main homeland and people were more in need of a doctor there than the people here.

We moved to our new flat the day the TV was plastered with the news of Bosnia Herzegovina. There was only one channel and this news shrouded the television screen at every interval. There was corporeal terror in people's faces and eyes.

The flat was spacious with three en-suite bedrooms, a kitchen, a dining room and a reception room. It took us some time to adapt to the people, shops, roads, and the education system but I perked up when a neighbour volunteered to run the errand for Amma to buy our school books. I loved studying ever since I was taught the art of reading. I was a somewhat little-miss-goody-two-shoes. So, the fact that I'd get to see my books this evening excited me beyond words and I was getting impatient. I tried to imagine the smell of the new books. When the books arrived, Di allowed me to check them out briefly but warned me to be diligent when turning any page. She then covered the front and back of all my paperback books neatly with sheets from old calendars that had either a floral, sunset, or waterfall motif. This wrapping up of books was part of the ethos of Asian schools. It was to protect books from premature tear and wear.

I was elated. 'I can't wait to go school tomorrow and show my books to all my new classmates and teachers!'

'Make sure you write down your homework or any tests that you may have in this diary,' Di instructed in her usual mother/teacher like manner.

'I will,' I promised.

But I was unable to keep that promise for the first whole week of school. Amma and Abba had had another argument. Amma was saying that she had to give the neighbour extra money for buying the books, which Abba denied. She was trying to get reimbursement and as Abba refused, the fight took place.

'What are you two staring at? Look down or I'll fork your eyes out!' Amma shouted at us. Right at that moment, I believed her.

Abba looked at us coldly. 'None of you are going to school.' I never quite understood why we had to pay the price for whatever else ticked them off. In fact, most of the time I never knew what the argument was all about. All I knew was that I was utterly dismayed. I spent that week of detention by admiring the book covers that Di had done for me and it never ceased to amuse me. I read and re-read most of the books too. But I also wished that Di spent time with me. I didn't realise back then that a seventeen-year-old had different preferences from that of a nine-year-old.

From time to time, I'd pop into our room where Di would either chat to our cousin Hena, who often came around, or read the "book in a book". This was basically a small romantic storybook that they read in secret by placing it in the middle of a larger, decent book, to fool others.

'Ranya, why don't you run along and play or watch cartoon or something?' Hena said.

'There's nothing on telly and this place is not like the compound where we stayed in Dubai. And we're not allowed to go out because it's not safe.'

'She meant *in* the house.' I could sense agitation in Di's tone. 'Go from here now!' Di and Hena never allowed me to take part in their conversations. Either they stopped talking when I came in or they would tell me to get out as soon as possible. Sometimes I wish Di knew just how awful I felt when she behaved like this.

***

I used to walk around the flat, talking to myself more than usual. What recently began to bug me here were the bugs. There were mosquitoes, flies of all sorts, cockroaches, spiders and geckos. They roamed around like security guards. The grotesque geckos shed their tails and lay their eggs anywhere. The increase in their number was in correlation with the increase in temperature; and it was already a lot warmer. Aromatic mango and lychee blossoms, the harbingers of spring, would've permeated the environment had pollution, the vanguard, allowed it.

Although I was privileged to eat these organic and redolent fruits, I couldn't remember the last time I ate chicken, meat, and desserts. I craved them badly. Amma said that we had a tight budget now and wouldn't be able to afford the luxury we had before. I wondered about the money she'd made in Dubai but dared not to ask. Amma also said that rich foods were not available in Bangladesh. This didn't make sense since my friends in school ate the kind we ate in Dubai as their school packed lunch. When I said this to Amma she told me to shut my big mouth. We ate vegetables and pulses all the time and only once a month, when Abba came for visits, did animal proteins get cooked. Even a better quality of rice used to be boiled when Abba was around.

Often Amma went shopping and bought herself a variety of sarees and salwar kameez. On Eid days, I used to be embarrassed to wear the cheap dresses Amma used to buy me from the markets in the streets. Di used to be even more upset since she used to be given half an outfit, like only a top or a skirt. Once she was given a bottle green shirt with a black waistcoat. To her horror, it turned out that it was from the boys' section. Di commented on this and the result was the confiscation of the top. It piqued us when the landlord's daughter wore a magnificent, white, Indian lehenga suit as just her "number one" outfit for the day.

'Why don't we get to wear beautiful clothes like her, Di?'

''Cos there's too many of us,' Di said. Her voice was low but the tone was sharper than a razor. Amma and Abba didn't spare our landlord and his wife too. Once they witnessed our parents' vociferous fights and came to our flat upon Amma's shameless invitation to intervene. From Abba's stinginess to his infidelity – Amma complained about it all in front of me. The whole time the landlady stared at me with a look of tacit sympathy.

Seeing this, Amma said to her, 'Don't worry, she doesn't understand anything.'

The landlady looked at me again and gave an empathetic smile. I looked down and sighed in response. One of the times Abba came around to visit us was as memorable as a scar. It was some time after breakfast. Amma was in the kitchen preparing lunch while Abba, Di, and I were in the living room watching a horticulture programme on TV. We had no *VCR* here like we did in Dubai. Abba said it was to prevent us from watching inappropriate things but I felt it was to save money.

Di was massaging Abba's head and I was massaging Abba's feet. His arthritis was bothering him and he was having to take expensive medication for that. Di's eyes watered at this. She could not take it when Abba was in pain. She and Abba had a special bond. Just like Bhaiyya and Amma shared one. For Di, Abba could lay a hand on Amma and to impress Abba Di could hide her true feelings. She proved that when Abba said, 'We need to revise our budget. I had to spend a lot of money when I set up my surgery in Kakongonj. School, housing, food and all that are very expensive nowadays. So how about we all make a list about how to cut down on things?'

I was agitated hearing this. 'We have no *VCR*, no jam and butter, no tuna, hardly any chicken and meat. What more should we cut down on?'

'Your sister takes after her Amma, doesn't she, Megha?'

Di nodded her head in agreement. I felt like kicking her. She was egging Abba in his unreasonable decision.

'How about we cut down on shampoo, conditioner, and *Lux* soap? Instead of those, we should use *wheel* detergent soap for all purposes,' Abba suggested.

'No way,' I said. I wished I didn't sound as pernickety.

'Ah, you know how Ranya is. She likes to pretend that she is one of the actresses who advertise those beauty bar soaps.' Di demonstrated this piece of false information by acting it out while I landed a flying kick into Di's face in my mind. I was livid. I felt like crying. Were we that poor all of a sudden? Amma came in and I told her what Abba said. She bellowed and called Abba all sorts of names. Abba laughed a fake laughter and casually told me to go and study. I didn't get up immediately so he held my hand to hurry me up. His other hand cupped my upper arm. He didn't sound angry at all yet I felt the riveting grip stinging the skin off my arm.

'Ouch. You're hurting me.' I looked at him. He said sorry but he didn't look at me.

***

I underestimated our financial situation. Di's and my school fees were not paid on time. As a result, they didn't allow us to sit for that entire term and the half yearly exam. We were disappointed but nothing could be done. We studied at home for four long months. From time to time, our neighbour, Hena, kept Di company in the guise of doing her homework with her. I had no one to do my studies with. I was shoved out of their room like a housefly and was ordered to study all the time. Besides communing with myself, I doodled when Di didn't check on me. My maths book made out of recycled papers came in small, black ink writing. It was one of the most child-*un*friendly books I had ever come across.

I loved my English and Bengali books though. They too were black and white but they had pictorial pages and an inviting feel to them. But sooner or later I'd have to revert to my daunting maths book. One morning, after a breakfast of dry toast and tea, I sat down to memorise times tables when I felt my knickers quite wet. We had no toilet paper as part of the budget scheme so often my undergarment being damp was a consequence. I went to the bathroom and to my horror, the orange knickers I wore had an obvious red stain on them. I put them back on instantly and knew what it was, just as quickly.

I recalled how in Dubai, Amma and Di told me that they used special nappies which I'd need when I'd be about twelve. But I was just over ten so I was shocked and terrified. Also, I had no idea what to do about it presently. As part of the budget scheme, these special nappies were also cut out. I noticed though that Di and Amma used several rectangular pieces of cotton fabric sometimes and assumed that they were those special nappy substitutes. My first thought was to tell Amma but I quickly dropped the idea.

What if she blamed me for starting my own period?

My second idea was to confide in Di. But recently she was getting distant from me in a way I couldn't quite grasp so I rejected that thought too. I went to our room and got two knickers out from my drawer. I was glad for the first time that Hena and Di ignored me. In the bathroom, I wore one of them, folded the other one and placed it inside the one I wore. I washed the bloodstained underwear properly and hung it out on the washing line in the veranda. An hour later I found that the stains of blood had permeated the underwear I was wearing. I was getting well scared now. I stuffed a few more knickers and repeated this process for four days. I improvised by choosing to wear only the red dresses I had. Several times I tried to confess to Di but she was always immersed in a storybook. I wished she'd just look at me and read my thoughts.

But on the fifth day, I was caught red-handed. Or maybe I should say, *red-bummed.* Amma called me and I knew that she'd figured it out. I felt like a criminal whose game was over. Amma turned me around and checked me.

She smiled and said, 'Congratulations, you're a woman now.' Di put her hand out to shake mine, to congratulate me. Stupidly, I shook it. Amma instructed Di to teach me what to do. She cut out four rectangular pieces of cloths from an old cotton saree of Amma's.

She demonstrated how to hold one of the corners and fold them diagonally before placing them inside the knickers. She then warned that it was every girl's duty to wash her own "period cloth" and dry it in secret as it was a shameful thing. But on the bright side, girls were exempted from prayers and excused from fasting when menstruating.

Often, I couldn't clean them properly so Di would wash them for me. A few times I had to come back from school early due to leakages. Amma would scold me for my lack of shame. I never knew how it happened. Then one day came which was ten times more embarrassing than this. And the repercussion that entailed the incident made me wish that I had leaked again instead.

A particular man whom we called Uncle Rocky began to visit us frequently. He was a couple of years younger than Amma. He was tall and had a beard like Abba. He'd come for lunch or dinner every now and then and Amma would tell Lulubu and Samia to prepare fancy dishes. She would serve him first and give him the best piece of chicken. It somewhat vexed me but I couldn't do anything about it. Amma used to constantly attend to his needs. I remembered times when she used to do stuff like this for Abba.

One day as Di and I were studying, Di told me to go to the living room and lower the volume of the TV. I told her to do it herself to which she was not very pleased so I had to get up and do as I was told. How I wished that Di had gone and done it. As *salt and pepper,* I found myself once again in a situation where I couldn't quite comprehend nor deny the travesty of the incident I witnessed. I found the door of the living room ajar. I found it strange since this door was *always* wide open. I opened it without knocking thinking the door must've closed by the wind. But then I shut the door abruptly as soon as I opened it. It was a reflex – I didn't have time to think anything else. Uncle Rocky was sitting on the larger sofa and Amma was on top of him with one of her hands on the wall. Her face was an inch or so away from his. Her entire poise was not *decent.* I ran back to our room, straight into the bathroom, and locked the door. Di asked me what was wrong; I refused to answer. What was I supposed to say?

I stayed in there for a whole hour. Our bathroom had a perennial sewage smell since we had moved in. Today seemed to be the worst but I couldn't care less. I didn't want to face Amma. I was worried that by shutting the door like that, I indicated to her that I saw something I shouldn't have seen and I was now dying slowly just pondering on the consequence. I knew it was futile but I couldn't help thinking the possibility of going back in time to avert my decision to lower the volume of the TV. I concluded by blaming Di for sending me in the first place.

Presently, I heard Amma's footsteps. They seemed hurried, like she had to sort this out before it was too late. She called out my name; her tone seemed deliberately calm. I didn't answer her.

She was in our room now. I could hear her explaining to Di that I misinterpreted the scene in the living groom. There was a long hiatus and I couldn't tell if Amma had left or not. Di asked me again as to why I wasn't coming out. She started to sing silly songs about me in love with smelly places. It was annoying but the foreboding contained my anger. Amma sweetly asked me to come out as no one was angry with me. I was sceptical but I had to come out.

Very slowly, I opened the door with my gaze on the floor. I glanced at Amma; she was standing, looking a bit nervous. She laughed a fake laugh and said, 'Didn't you see my hand on the wall? I was trying to get a spider that was just behind Rocky. He's scared of spiders so I tried to swat it.'

'There you go, Ranya. You were distraught over nothing after all,' Di said. Then looking at Amma she asked, 'Why was the door ajar?'

'Because of the sound of the TV. I didn't want to disturb you lot.'

I clearly remembered what I saw. Amma's knee was on top of Rocky's thigh. If that was me, I would've gone on the side and then tried to swat the spider. But I was *salt and pepper* and sometimes it was best to drop a dispute, which would attract only distress.

RANYA

Days in Dubai were blissful. I could go out in the doctors' campus area whenever I wanted, as it was safe. Vast swathes were everywhere to be seen with plenty of olive trees. I used to meet up with my Indian friends and together we used to spend all day long as explorers. I missed them and the open space a lot after we came Bangladesh.

School here was a torture too as we used to be laden with a colossal amount of homework.

I used to play with Samia when Di used to ignore me. Lulubu was raised up in my maternal grandparents' home when she was a toddler. When Amma got married to Abba, two maids were sent with her to help her with the household chores. One of them was Lulubu and she was more like a family member. She did all the cooking and cleaning for us. Her cooking, however, wasn't the greatest but we appreciated her contribution since our mother was useless. Once she made noodles for me as my school lunch. When it was break time, I took it out and was disgusted and shocked that the oil from the noodles, about a half a cup, had leaked from the container onto all my books and spread out in the thin linen school bag.

Every morning, after sorting out our breakfast and lunch bags, Lulubu would hand us our clean uniforms which she used to wash by hand and iron every day after we'd return from school (we only had one set each of our uniform which used to get very sweaty and dirty in the humid climate). Then she'd go out and call a "baby taxi", climb up to the sixth floor and tell us that she managed to haggle the price down. Amma would scold her that she could've bartered more. It used to take about half an hour to reach our school, provided there was no traffic. On the way, I used to pray that we reached there on time. Seven forty-five was the latest to reach school and I used to wish that I'd arrive at quarter past seven. There were sixty-three students in my class and by the time I was dropped off, all the seats from the front half row used to be taken. If anyone was late more than three times in the week, the teacher would make them stand outside the class. They never consulted the parents. Some of us used to cry and tell them that it wasn't our fault but they used to say that *we* ought to tell our parents about this rule.

I was desperate for the front row because Dina used to always come early and sit in the front row, right in front of the teacher. She was a teacher's pet, pretty, and brainy. We had three teachers: one for Bengali, one for religious studies and another main teacher for the rest of the subjects such as English, maths, geography, history and science. The teachers would have to control all the sixty-three students on their own. Often, they'd ignore pupils after the first three rows. But all of the teachers had a motto for us; to be like Dina and to make her our role model.

Dina was an only child. Her parents were well off, very generous, and loving towards her. Unlike my boy cut hair, she had long, silky hair, which her mum styled in different plaits and braids every day. Her lunchbox and water bottle were the prettiest ones I'd ever seen. And every time the food in that lunchbox was a gourmet meal. Amma rationed my food, toys, and clothes too. I had only one pencil in my pencil case and had to make it last for at least two months. It was a cheap pencil and its point kept breaking every time I sharpened it. On the other hand, Dina's parents filled her pencil case with eight, fine quality HB pencils, all sharpened.

I didn't want to be like Dina like the rest of them. I wanted to *be* Dina.

***

Along with the proteins, Amma cut down jam and even my favourite jar of marmalade. Then she stopped buying butter so we'd have plain bread or puffed rice with tea. Then fresh milk powder tins were rationed to just one small tin a month. Amma gave strict orders that only one flat teaspoon should be used for tea and I shouldn't be having more than one cup of milk in the week. I was over ten and I heard Lulubu telling Amma that growing children needed milk. Amma told her to shut her big mouth and stay in her disposition of a servant.

We stayed in Hayapur for three years and Amma was getting more volatile in her temperament and attitude. She'd hit Di and me more often than she took showers, and she'd hit Lulubu and Samia for matters that didn't bother her as much before. We couldn't predict Amma's mood at all so we always tried to compliment her in hope that she'd feel cheery.

One day, Di was ironing in our room. I was doing my homework, Amma was lying down on our double bed while Samia massaged her legs.

By now this massaging was equivalent to an addiction to smoking or drinking.

'Guess what, Amma?' Di said as she turned her blouse over for ironing. 'That day when I was waiting for Lulubu to pick me up from my English coaching class, I heard a few people nearby talking about you.'

'What were they saying?' Amma asked.

'They were praising you. They were talking about the song you sang last week on TV.'

Amma was sitting in a half nelson position now. 'What else did they say?'

'That was it.'

'Didn't you tell them that you were the daughter of the singer they were praising?' Amma had a frown on her face.

'N... no. I didn't know who those men were. You told us not to talk to strangers.' Di and I both wished that she hadn't mentioned this in the first place.

Amma got up now and was in front of Di. She looked calculative: like a predator, waiting for the right moment to pounce on its prey.

'Why wouldn't you use that brain of yours to say that to them? Are you jealous of me? Huh?' She knocked on Di's head with her knuckle.

'What's there to be jealous, I... I just... Di couldn't finish her sentence. Amma got hold of the hot iron and threatened to burn her face. Di was moving back to protect herself. I was scared but didn't know what to do. I ran and fetched Lulubu who tried to remove the iron, but Amma was so mad that she branded Lulubu's hand with it. Samia called her a monster so Amma branded one side of her mouth. Amma told Di to get lost so she went to the kitchen. We could hear some clatter of utensils and this provoked Amma to follow her into the kitchen.

'Are you giving me an attitude? To me, the greatest and most beautiful singer?'

'No, I'm not.'

'I'm going to skin you alive. You're just jealous of me. I've been watching you. Every time your Abba's here, I've noticed how you frolic about with him. I'm going to cut your tits out and stuff them in your shithole, you whore.'

Saying this, Amma got a kitchen knife out, pointing it at Di – I shrieked. It was pure reflex. That cry I had let out was so chilling that I believe that in some deep valley in my head, the last echo of that shriek is still reverberating. A couple of minutes later, the landlady rang our doorbell, which Amma refused to answer. But the landlady threatened to call the police so Amma opened it. Prior to that, she warned us that we shouldn't reveal the truth if we wished to live.

A few days later, we woke up one morning to find Lulubu and Samia missing. We came to the conclusion that they had run away. Amma's first worry was her wardrobe. She quickly went there and screamed. Di and I went to her room and found her opening a box that had bundles and bundles of five hundred taka notes. She wailed that one bundle had two thousand takas missing.

Di and I went back to our room. I had lots of questions and she gave me straight answers this time. Abba usually gave Amma twenty thousand taka on the first of every month. Amma was miserly so after the cost of the rent and school fees, she spent just a thousand taka for us while saving the rest for herself. She didn't inform the police as she knew that she could be jailed for physically harming the maids.

'Little would she be thankful that out of loyalty to our grandmother and us, Lulubu will not complain against Amma or Abba to the cops,' Di said. I reminded her that Abba had nothing to do with this. Di just smirked.

'How can you be so sure that they won't complain?' I asked.

'I helped them to escape,' she replied.

RANYA

Losing Lulubu was one of our greatest losses. For no one else was as trustworthy, hardworking, and well-wishing as she was. Amma warned Di and me that we should always be very careful because none of us was safe.

Di was applying a soothing medical cream on her arm from a blow she received from Amma following the recent incident. I asked Di what Amma meant.

''Cos Amma's a bitch and Abba's a son of a bitch,' Di said. Tears ran down her cheeks as she said that. It was all very strange. Di seemed to have a polarised personality towards Abba. I didn't understand why but felt that I shouldn't question her. So, I did what I was best at doing – studying, as long as hunger, slumber and the call of nature didn't take over. At times, I used to fall asleep on the desk in our room.

One fine day, Abba came to visit us from Kakongonj. He told us that he was planning to bring back Bhaiyya for good. Amma, Di, and I were delighted beyond verbal explanation. When the glorious day finally came, I felt awkward. I didn't spring up to Bhaiyya like I'd done before in Dubai. I hoped that he'd have a better stay this time here, than Dubai. As I looked at him from time to time, I discovered that Bhaiyya had changed a lot from before. He was no longer into acid rock music and fashion. He seemed to have become spiritually radicalised.

Abba stayed with us for about ten days after Bhaiyya came, before leaving for Kakongonj. It was then, over lunch, that Bhaiyya confessed to Amma that he didn't want to stay in Bangladesh. Abba may have brought him out of London but he wouldn't be able to take London out of him. Since his arrival, our parents had upgraded our eating standards. We were spreading butter, after years, on our toast. Marmalade was back in the larder and so was milk, besides poultry, fish and meat. I was never happier but Bhaiyya was crying. Amma always had a predilection for sons. She told me once that when she was pregnant with me, she thought I was going to be a boy. A week before I was due, she fell off the bed. An emergency C-section had to be done and the doctors feared the baby to be stillborn. But miraculously, I survived. When Amma discovered my sex, she declared that she wished I had died as they had predicted.

Amma couldn't bear to see her one and only son, at the ripe age of twenty-two, cry and neither could Di. They both promised him that they'd endeavour to gather all the money that was needed to send him back.

'What about Abba?' Bhaiyya asked.

'Who cares about that old man? Don't you worry about him, I'll sort him out.' Amma spoke in her usual brash way. 'In fact, I have a better idea. Once you go back, sponsor us so we three can join you there.'

'What do you mean? Couldn't Abba do that for you all?' Bhaiyya didn't look comfortable at this extended version of Amma's cooperation.

'I want to leave him. I've had enough of him.' Amma hugged Bhaiyya. 'But don't trouble yourself with all that now. We need to make preparations to send you back to London.' I noticed that he didn't look convinced but I was too busy finishing off Bhaiyya's untouched chicken drumstick. Amma always gave him the drumstick. Usually, all I had to do was tell Bhaiyya that what he was eating was really nice and the next thing I'd know, he'd give it to me, happily. However, years later this would become the cause for a great deal of friction.

Amma didn't turn out to be treacherous. She spoke to Abba over the telephone, but he said that it wasn't a good idea to send him back to London since Bhaiyya wasn't interested in studying medicine. Amma argued with Abba that he couldn't force Bhaiyya to do as he pleased. Abba said that if she thought that Bhaiyya was better off in London then she should arrange the money to send him over. Amma tried her utmost to get some money off him but Abba refused. So Amma opened her wardrobe and got the bundles of cash out. The money that was usurped from us was donated all to Bhaiyya, just like that.

KOLSUM (BIBHA)

I am utterly thankful to God for bestowing upon me the parents I have. I am the first one in our family who has managed to convince my dad to be allowed to go to university. I still can't believe that Abba allowed it! Being a widow with a child hadn't been easy for my mother. Amma had to endure a lot of harsh treatment from her new in-laws who were against her marriage to my stepfather. But Abba, my stepfather, has been just as nice to me as my own Abba would perhaps have been. My biological father passed away while my mother was still expecting me. My stepfather had always liked my mother who was his paternal cousin. He married my mum and accepted me as his very own. I don't remember a single time that he told me off; rather my half-brothers would get told off if they ever annoyed me. I am indebted to my Abba. I don't like introducing Abba as my stepfather because of the connotations that entail step-parents. Fathers like him break all those misconceptions. I was two when my mother bore him twin boys. Then Amma gave birth to Kimi, my baby sister when I was almost sixteen years old. Blimey, was I embarrassed or what.

Now that I've graduated and passed my driving test (first attempt) I couldn't wait to tell my best friends – Zeenat, Hawa, Ferdousi, and Arifa at Vicky Park tomorrow that I was getting married to the person I like, as Abba had agreed to that too!

Getting Abba's approval for this marriage was not difficult – it was *impossible*. But my lovely, adorable Amma helped me to convince Abba; of course, I had to convince Amma first. My good friend Samira had brought the proposal.

'Here's the brother's CV,' Samira said, handing me a paper wallet. The name *Yasin Kuraishi* stood out in handwritten black ink. Access to a computer was still a privilege back in the mid-nineties.

His personal statement read like this:

I am twenty-two years old, working part-time and studying part-time too. I am a practising Muslim and would therefore want to adhere to the Sunnah by getting married and fulfil my desire in an acceptable manner, that is, avoid free-mixing. My ideal wife should be a good Muslim woman who follows the Quran and Sunnah and is obedient to her husband.

'He seems quite straightforward. But I need more information, like how old is he exactly? Did he turn twenty-two already or will he be twenty-three this year? Either way, he's younger than me.'

'Does that bother you?'

'No. But it depends on the brother.'

'I can speak to my husband and they can arrange a day for him to come around your place so you two can talk and stuff.'

The following week, brother Yasin and Samira's husband came to our house. My four best friends and I saw them entering the reception room from above the stairs where we hunkered. This ideally blocked the guests' view but not ours. First Samira's husband entered, then a young boy followed with a third and a fourth man behind him. This confused us as we weren't sure which one was Yasin.

It turned out that the "young boy" who looked no more than fifteen happened to be Yasin. I straightened my light blue hijab and black abaya which I had especially got made for this day. I was sitting on my bed. Yasin sat on the armchair which was next to (and part of) my dressing/study table. He was very eloquent and I really wanted to marry him – firstly because he was very cute and secondly because I felt very sorry for him. His predicament made me appreciate my privileges. I told him that I'd like to do my PGCE and then become a teacher (my grades were good but not good enough to study medicine).

I told him that I'd like to work after marriage. He didn't say yes, but neither did he protest. I regretted saying that afterwards. What if he decided not to marry me because of that silly demand? Deep down I knew that had he a better position, he probably wouldn't have considered me.

But when Samira informed me the following morning that Yasin was more than happy to go ahead with this marriage, I knew that his disposition outdid his circumstance.

'You can't marry Yasin,' Abba said. Amma looked helpless. From her eyes, I could tell that she tried her best to convince him. No one, and that included my Amma, has ever dared to dispute Abba's decision. This was the second time I dared to refute his choice. I respected my father, all right. But I had to speak here despite the fear.

I took a deep breath. 'But why, Abba?'

'He has no job, no education, no parents.' I reminded Abba that this was disclosed at the very beginning.

'That's not the point.' Abba sounded decisive. 'The point is his parents are not involved. He isn't a British citizen yet so he's probably marrying you only for that.' Abba always crossed his arms when he was serious. 'Supposedly his mother is a TV artiste. Just because he seems religious now, it doesn't mean that he will not deviate later.'

'He is a good, practising Muslim brother who is only following the *sunnah*. He is all by himself with all the freedom a young man could possibly want. He could've been into drugs, women, and other heinous things but he chose to be on a righteous path. He also overlooked the fact that I am four years older than him. Is it fair that we disregard a person's abilities and potential merely because we believe that the fruit doesn't fall far from the tree?' I was shaking with fear for no one in our family ever spoke like this to Abba.

But he didn't interrupt me. So, that encouraged me that he didn't think my words were an asinine justification.

'Usually husbands are meant to be older than their wives,' Abba said quietly.

'That's right, and usually a single, young man wouldn't have married a widow who already had a child.' I left the room having said that. I didn't know what Abba would say after this.

Abba came to my room later in the night and asked me if I really wanted to marry Yasin. I felt very shy all of a sudden. I couldn't believe that I had spoken earlier that day to my dad defending a total stranger so I remained silent.

'I hope you two will be happy together.' Abba kissed my forehead; I cried joyously.

RANYA

Eleven months had gone by since Bhaiyya left Bangladesh. Amma didn't try to hide her indignation for she was angry with Bhaiyya, big time.

Amma went to Kakongonj after she sent Bhaiyya to London. She came back a week later, all shattered. She said that Abba didn't want her any more as he'd married some nineteen-year-old girl. Amma wrote a letter to Bhaiyya asking to take all three of us to London. He replied that Abba had stopped funding him a while back and he was now in abject poverty. Abba also challenged Bhaiyya to prove himself a man and earn a living without Abba's help.

Seeing that Bhaiyya was in more need than her, Amma contacted the police and all her brothers and sisters to resolve the nuptial irreverence that had taken place. We had to endure warlike days and nights. The ultimatum was that for the sake of the children, Abba and Amma should stay together. So, the nineteen-year-old girl was out of the house and we were back in. Six months later, we all left Hayapur and moved to Kakongonj for good as Amma felt this was the best way to keep a short lead on Abba.

A year later, Bhaiyya wrote a letter which Abba read to us a week later.

Bhaiyya outsmarted Abba and got his citizenship, by getting married.

There was a brief pause before Amma giggled. This developed into a laughter, and finally she cried till she went berserk.

'How could Yasin do this? How could my one and only son do this to me?' She felt betrayed and had become vindictive ever since this news.

Usually, the husband is taller and older than the wife. Bhaiyya was taller but younger than his wife. This highly infuriated our traditional-according-to-the-circumstance of a mother. She didn't understand why someone would allow their twenty-six-year-old daughter who had a degree, a job and of course a UK citizenship to marry a twenty-two-year-old laddish man who didn't have any of that. Abba and Amma were against the marriage but they were helpless. Deep down we all knew that the predicament they had put Bhaiyya in nullified all their objections. I kind of felt sorry for Amma since her lunacy had subsided while Bhaiyya was around. It hurt me to see that she favoured Bhaiyya over us but at least the little light of goodness Amma had in her, emitted because of him. And its effect, though passive, gave us some respite. But as *salt and pepper*, I also felt that Amma was expiating now for this predilection.

KOLSUM (BIBHA)

My Mehndi day was a total BLAST! All my friends and family, even distant relatives whom I never saw before came around. I couldn't be happier. My friends helped out as though I were their very own sister. I felt so blessed. Yasin's photo which came with his CV became the object of a "pass the parcel" game.

'Good catch,' someone said.

'You're lucky to get such young and good-looking boy,' a fifty-something-year-old lady remarked. I felt piqued but played it down by agreeing with her.

My mum and aunts cooked their hearts out. I wanted to help out but whoever does that at their mum's? All the girls were playing on the drum and singing silly songs about Yasin and me. By now both my hands were decorated with henna up to my elbows. Hawa did an amazing job. I persuaded her that she should take this skill seriously and the others urged as well.

In the meantime, Zeenat fed me a samosa and then whispered, 'Guess what? That lady sitting on that sofa next to the telly was asking me in the kitchen before if you and Yasin knew each other from college. I told her no. She looked sceptical anyway.'

Discreetly, I checked out the direction where that lady was sitting. It was that same fifty-something-year-old lady. I couldn't help grimacing.

'Imagine having an obnoxious mother-in-law like her,' Hawa joked. We all prayed aloud that none of us did.

'Actually, I'm pretty lucky since Yasin's parents are back home. I mean even if I did have a monster for a mother-in-law, at least we are two countries apart.'

'Hmm, I wonder if this was all planned after all?' said Arifa. We all gave her a perplexed look. 'Hey, only kidding.' The exuberance of the occasion got more contagious.

***

Yasin poured his heart out to me a few days after our wedding. He had been rejected by all the fathers of the possible brides he could've had. Everyone stepped back the minute they heard that his parents were not involved in the marriage. I felt bad for him for he had all the ostensible features of an ideal husband. I just couldn't understand why his educated and high-profile parents would literally abandon him in London while they basked in their wealth and power back home.

'But you are their one and only son; surely there has been some misunderstanding?'

'My dad was disheartened as I didn't follow into his footsteps of being a doctor. My good friend and teacher, Brother Ahmed, explained to my dad that I wanted to stay here as I have adapted to the lifestyle here, but my mum is a very modern and non-practising Muslim woman. She would never accept this side of me.'

'What about your uncle with whom they left you?' I asked.

'I had to leave them because I constantly had to run errands for them. Fupu would tell me to clean the house if her son would soil the carpet. Once I was dying to speak to my mum. They weren't home so I thought I'd use the house phone – only to find a lock on it. I was so angry that I broke it. Eventually I moved to my maternal aunt's house and things got sour there too. Then I moved into my friend's home. His folks were nice but like a foster child, I felt awkward at times. I couldn't just open the cupboard and help myself to cookies or stuff, you know? So, I began to share a flat with some of my mates.' Yasin raked his fingers through his hair. 'Thing is, no one is your own and I just long to belong to a loving family.'

'Oh well, now you're here in my parents' home. You will get all the love and care you never got. I'll make sure of it,' I said. And I meant it. I had my heart broken once and never thought I'd fall in love again. But I have and I was glad that it happened in a *halal* way, after marriage with my own husband.

A few months later, I fell pregnant. I was so happy and so was Yasin, but I couldn't do my PGCE. Yasin said that it wouldn't be right for my health if I travelled to uni now so despite all my requests, he refused.

'But I've got my final exam and I got a grant for it too. I won't get another one again,' I implored.

'Are you disputing my decision?' Yasin questioned. His tone was icy.

'No, I'm just saying…'

'You are now my wife and you will soon become a mother. Your priorities are very different now. Once I get a stable job, you should quit your job too.'

The good news was, I was granted a one-bedroom council flat. Amma kept nagging me that she should be thanked entirely since she was the one who insisted that I applied for one.

We moved to the flat during my second trimester but we stayed the last month at my parents' place so that I could use the perks of my mum's delicious food and my dad's and siblings' perpetual offers to be of any service. After all, everyone was expecting their first grandchild, and nephew or niece.

RANYA

It was a hot and humid winter in Kakongonj. Amma and I were waiting for Abba to come home from the airport with Bhaiyya, his wife called Kolsum, and their one-year-old daughter. I didn't even know her name yet.

I was thirteen and my friends and I were going through the phase of dressing all in black. I experienced anxiety, fear and frustration- all at the same time. Amma did cook *Kacchi Biryani* and some other dishes. But her escalating anger, which was to some extent understandable, was giving me a panic attack.

'Hello, Ranya,' a familiar male voice said. I felt tears forming in my eyes. I was about to turn around and see my brother after six years.

'H… hello.' I could hardly hear myself.

'Give her a hug then. It's your sister,' a lady in a black burka and hijab said.

'Yeah, c'mon. Give your one and only handsome Bhaiyya a big bear hug.'

'Now that's more like it,' the lady said. I looked at Bhaiyya to introduce me to her.

'Oh, Ranya, meet Kolsum, your Bhabi.'

She came over and hugged me straightaway. A bit too quickly but I found it very genuine. And I liked her.

'I'll call you Bibha,' I said. She smiled and seemed very bubbly. I wondered how long she would be able to maintain this side of her in this dysfunctional house.

After dinner, Amma told me to go my room and study for my exam which was on the following day. I said I'd help with clearing the table and washing up of the dishes as our servant lady only worked during the day time. In fact, Amma always ordered me to do that every evening. But for some reason, which I couldn't figure out, she urged me to go and study. I dared not refute her for Amma was the type who didn't care; if needed, she'd hit me and humiliate me in front of anyone.

The next morning, I got up at my usual time to get ready for school. Amma always woke around midday, so I was surprised to find her awake at half seven in the morning.

'What's the queen doing, still sleeping? Go tell Yasin's wife to wake up and clean the house and make breakfast,' Amma roared.

'I can't do that,' I said. She pulled my ponytail so hard that I had no choice but to execute her order. I knocked gently a few times.

'Knock harder!' Amma barked.

Before I could knock again, Bibha opened the door. She smiled at me with sleepy eyes. I felt very sorry for her. And I worried how Amma would treat her after I went to school. At least if I was around, I could stop Mum. I already felt terrible for last night's incident. I heard Abba sounding his horn so I grabbed my bag and left .

I couldn't wait to cuddle baby Amanah, my niece. But when I came back from school around four o'clock. The house was unusually quiet. I found Amma sitting in front of the telly. I asked her about Bhaiyya, Bibha, and Amanah.

'The witch is gone and she has taken my son along too. She cast a spell on my one and only beloved son!' Amma wailed. I didn't see or hear from them any more for the next three years.

KOLSUM (BIBHA)

It was hard motivating Yasin to stay on his university course but I kept encouraging him. Sometimes it was hard for me because I too wanted to pursue further education but he didn't want me to. Yasin was a really nice person but he was quite strict too. I enjoyed my job at *Woolies* but I had to quit that. As soon as he got a job, he didn't want me to work anymore. I hoped that he'd give me a choice: either to work or to carry on with my education. I said this to him one day; it was a wrong move.

Rumaisa, who was Yasin's teacher-turned-friend, brother Ahmed's wife, came around this afternoon for tea and to see our three-month-old-daughter, Amanah. I have known Rumaisa since college days. She was funny and a bit cocky. But I was nonetheless wittier. I put makeup on and hoped that she wouldn't notice my puffy eyes. She came with her eighteen-month-old son and was already expecting her second child.

'I'm really glad that I'm expecting again. I hope it's a girl. Do you have any preferences this time?'

'I'm happy with whatever Allah blesses us with. Although I wish I had taken a few years' gap between the two pregnancies.'

'Just get it over and done with,' Rumaisa said. I looked down at my tea which was cold by now. 'Wassup, Kolsum?'

Rumaisa knew me too well. She knew that I always finished my tea while it was still piping hot.

'Yasin is planning to go Bangladesh with us for the Christmas holiday. He's already booked the tickets.'

'That's a good thing, innit?'

'His parents were against this marriage. Especially his mum. So, yeah, I am just a bit tense.'

'Oh, I'm sure it'll be fine. I'm glad I've got white in-laws.'

I gave a deliberate, fake grin. Rumaisa got up and gave me a hug.

'Yasin's mum hasn't accepted me yet. Rumour has it s that she is quite mouthy.'

'They should be grateful to you. You practically gave their son an identity. C'mon chin up.'

***

I was four months pregnant in December but morning sickness was still draining my soul out of me. I was worried about the journey on the plane. As the plane took off, I told Yasin that I felt nauseous. He tried to help me but I could tell that his mind was somewhere else.

I was glad that I didn't actually have any vomiting episodes. In fact, Amanah and I slept most of the time. I only woke when Amanah needed a feed. I checked the map on the screen and it said that we had roughly an hour left before we landed. Yasin was not in his seat. Scanning around quickly, I assumed that he was in the toilet. He was taking a long time for I had given Amanah a feed, changed her nappy and clothes too.

Yasin came sometime later and sat next to me. I glanced at him and smiled. Then I took a double look at him and my jaws dropped. He'd shaved his beard off.

'I don't want my mum to take me to the barbers like she did last time. You don't know her. I don't want to be embarrassed in front of you and Amanah.' I was shocked but I couldn't help giggling either. Had I known any better, I would've looked grave instead.

We arrived at Hayapur airport around midday. The scorching heat and putrid smell enveloped me the minute we came out of the plane. We were very tired and so was Amanah, but she didn't trouble me. People kept staring at me and kept whispering with no effort to be discreet. My hijab seemed to bother them just as much as the weather was annoying me.

I expected to see all the members of Yasin's family but only his dad was waiting for us. He looked like a decent man. As he walked towards us he handed us two bottles of Cola drinks. There was another bag in his hand which seemed to have other snacks in them. The drinks were ice cold and just what we needed. We exchanged salutations but he told us to hurry since the driver for the car had been waiting long enough. It took us about three and a half hours to reach Kakongonj. I felt really scared as the driver drove quite fast amongst the bumpy roads with open drains on either side. There seemed to be zilch rules to the road.

We got out of the car in front of a grey building, split into two flats, in a cul de sac. I was gestured to go to the left flat. The right one happened to be my father-in-law's private surgery.

I felt nervous. A tall lady in a saree greeted me, introducing herself as Shamshed Dadi (paternal grandmother). I was impressed that unlike my mother-in-law, she was soft spoken. She asked me my name and I felt a bit at ease. My heart skipped a beat when I heard some footsteps approaching.

'That's your mother-in-law,' she said gently, 'go and give her Salam.'

I knew that she meant to touch her feet. Muslims are not supposed to do this but I didn't want to create animosity at our first meeting so I touched my mother-in-law's feet.

'You are very short,' my mother-in-law commented in a condescending tone. Standing at five feet, I knew I was short but that was a bit uncalled for since she herself was at least two inches shorter than me. I smiled and ignored the remark. But then she asked the tall lady if she agreed or not. The lady smiled and looked embarrassed.

'You and I can't do anything about it, I'm afraid.' I laughed.

Amma, as I heard Yasin referring to her, gave me a contemptuous look. 'Are you pregnant again?'

She has a sharp eye, I thought to myself. 'Yes.'

She looked at Dadi and said, 'She's going to turn my young son into an oldie like her.'

Dadi blushed. 'Bou (which meant *bride)* must be hungry. Let us all eat.'

I was hungry but found it very difficult to eat. I felt like going in some corner and crying. Amanah started to cry so that gave me the excuse to leave.

I came back to find the table empty. I offered to help with the dishes but before I could utter that Amma ordered me to wash the pile of dishes in the sink. I felt repulsed to see the state of the dirty plates. I was then told to brush the floor and mop it too. Yasin was probably in Abba's surgery next door. I was very tired but didn't dare to complain since I wanted to glean my mother-in-law's approval while I stayed here – at any cost.

KOLSUM (BIBHA)

It was coming up to one a.m. yet Amma kept talking away. I was struggling to keep my eyes open but had to keep a straight face. Amma talked about some family in the neighbourhood whose son was supposedly ensnared into marriage by a low-class girl in London. Seeing no reaction from me whatsoever, she began to speak about herself. She was furious that she had to become a mother-in-law and grandmother so soon. She claimed that she was thirty-nine years old but who knows if that was fabricated like all her other anecdotes? People back home remained the same age for almost ten years straight. I tried my best to keep my self-composure. Yasin tried to talk to her but she just wasn't listening.

Eventually, I had to nudge Yasin's elbow. 'I'm really tired.'

Abba, Yasin's dad, got up and called it a night. I was glad he was there. He defended me every time Amma threw a sarcastic comment at me.

I was completely gone when my head hit the pillow. Amanah slept through the night too. I couldn't even tell when Yasin came into the room. All I remembered was that he was trying to tell me something. And before I knew it, I was dreaming. It was a nice dream. I saw my Amma and Abba. How they nurtured me when I was a child. How they never hurt my feelings. My Abba. Oh, my sweet, loving Abba. He always let me get away with anything, yet he didn't allow me to become spoilt.

And my Amma. I knew she loved her older son a teeny bit more but she was still just in her love with all her other three children. In my dream, Amma was frying chicken samosas while the three of us cavorted around Abba who kept warning us of the hot tea on the coffee table. I was old enough to be responsible but I was quite boisterous. My brother, who was a year younger than me, was the calm one. I spilled the tea on the carpet, knew it was my fault, and that Amma would not spare me. But Abba saved me. He would never let me get told off. I guess I was a little spoilt after all. Amma never spoke back to Abba. But she was mad that she didn't get to chastise me. So, to dissipate her anger, she went to the kitchen. I could hear unnecessary clatter of the utensils. Usually Amma did that but it was only for a few minutes. But today it seemed longer than usual. And the sound was deafening; so much as so that I had to see what the matter was. And that's when I opened my eyes.

The noise was coming from the door. Knocking, no, *banging.* Amanah was still asleep. I turned to my left and saw that Yasin was not there. I somehow recalled his words last night, '...*with Abba first thing in the morning.'*

I could hear Bengali swear words now so I hurried to open the door. I didn't want Amanah to wake up. It was Ranya. I smiled even though she looked serious. She reported that Amma wanted me to get up. I felt sorry for her. I could tell that Amma just pulled her hair out of place. She said that she was leaving for school.

And then the ordeal commenced. I wore my headscarf for I heard the presence of someone else in the house and I wasn't sure if it were a man.

To this simple action, my mother-in-law said, 'Do you wear that headscarf to hide your *bodsuroth,* ugliness?' There was another a lady besides Amma. From the way she was dressed, it appeared that she was a servant lady. She stared at me as though she too couldn't believe what was just said regarding my head cover.

'You are so much older than my son. I found out your real age. You are seven years older than him. And you look even older than your actual years. I am embarrassed to call you my daughter-in-law. How could you think of marrying my son? If you were so desperate, why didn't you just become a *magi,* hooker?'

Tears streamed down my whole face. I felt so embarrassed. I wanted to run away from here. I went back in the room and sat in an armchair next to our suitcases. I saw the extra suitcase my parents bought and had paid for as extra baggage allowance. My parents had been to Green Street and had bought a beige, cashmere cardigan, two shirts and a scarf from Marks and Sparks for my father-in-law. A designer saree was conscientiously chosen for my mother-in-law, worth three hundred pounds, a dress and a cardigan for Ranya from Debenhams, and a twenty-two-carat gold ring with a navy stone for Megha. As Yasin had the car, I had gone late in the evening with Amanah in a pushchair to buy four by three stacks of tuna cans, eight boxes of Fox's biscuits, half a dozen shower gels, two bottles of Givenchy and Gucci perfumes, and moisturisers for my mother-in-law. And I still felt like I hadn't got enough gifts for them.

'You and your notorious, low-class parents deliberately trapped my son. He is so young and innocent. What did he know? How could he agree to marry an old hag with a horse's face like you?' my mother-in-law spat at me. Yes, she literally did. I had never heard such harrowing speech being directed towards me even from a racist in London.

Next, she dragged my arm and swung me to the floor and attempted to hit me. I covered my face to which she said, 'What? Are you scared that your face will be ruined? Tell me, what is there to get ruined? You listen to me, *bitch,* I am going to get my son married *again.* And did you see that servant in our house? You will take her place then. I've been waiting for your arrival.

'I will get my son a proper bride and you will be their maid. Is this how your parents raised you up? To be a paedophile? Did your mum do the same thing to your dad? Like mother like daughter, eh?'

'Please don't talk like this about my parents. Do be civilised,' I said through sobs. Having said this, she left and slammed the door. I heard a click. I ran up to the door to find it locked from the outside. I banged on it frantically.

'Open the door, please. Please give me some food. I am pregnant. Please for God's sake don't do this.'

'I want you to rot in there. I curse you that you never bear a son. You will only have daughters who will only bring shame to you,' Yasin's mum shouted. I could hear the servant lady requesting if she could open the door but it seemed that she must've been slapped for asking that.

There was no clock in the room and neither did I have a watch. It felt like a lifetime.

I changed Amanah's nappy and nursed her. As I did that, I began to feel lightheaded.

After placing my baby on the bed, I took the Farley's rusks from my handbag and her milk bottle. I mixed formula milk with some purified water that I had in a flask, mixed it and had that out of hunger and desperation. And I couldn't stop crying. How I wish I could turn back time.

I must've fallen asleep or fainted for I found myself opening my eyes on the bed when I could clearly recall sitting in the armchair before. I could hear voices arguing. Amanah was not in the room so I got up and opened the door a little, which to my surprise was open now. Yasin saw me. He was carrying Amanah.

'Kolsum, you need to rest. I have called your uncle and aunt in your village home. They are sending someone to pick us up. They should be here any minute. Get everything ready. We are leaving.'

'You are my son. You will go nowhere. Send that whore away to the village where she comes from. I want you to divorce this slut, whose mother's a slut too,' Yasin's mum said.

'Please mind your language.' Yasin was struggling to keep his cool. 'You need to give me a good reason for divorcing her.'

'She is too old for you.'

'She is the same age as me.'

She guffawed. 'I got certain people to verify this for me. She is a lot older than you. You will never be happy with her.'

'I don't care how old she is. She is a good woman of good character and that's why I married her. You are a lot younger than Abba. But all I remember is you two arguing and fighting like animals.'

'I would've accepted that she is older than you but she is not even pretty enough for you.' She turned towards me and I could see her from the bedroom. 'My son is so tall and handsome but look at you! He is way out of your league. Just because you're fair doesn't mean you're pretty.' She paced about the room with her arms akimbo. 'Didn't anyone ever tell you the difference between moonlight and a firefly? Well, let me explain. Both emit light. But while the moon shines out of beauty the other gives off light from its backside. *You* are the firefly. And that's why you are incompatible with my son.'

'Enough, Amma.' Yasin raised his voice this time. 'Abba stopped the funding for me when I was in London. When I used to be here, you were too busy running after your career. The two of you were always fighting. Megha and I only got married because we weren't being looked after. You are insulting Kolsum and her parents without realising that they are the ones who took pity on me. You lot just boast about your family title yet you do nothing to keep up with its reputation.'

Yasin's mum looked savage. 'I see. So now it's all about Kolsum? Is she the one who also carried you for nine months and then nursed you that you seem so obliged to be loyal to her?'

Yasin winced. 'Amma, please. You are my mother and no one can take that place but please try to understand. Kolsum was not in need of me. I needed her.' A car sounded its horn loudly. I assumed it was our taxi. We left without saying anything else. I didn't take the extra suitcase since it was meant for them anyway. After forty minutes or so, we reached my village place. But when Yasin tried to pay the driver, he discovered that his wallet was empty. He just couldn't figure out where all his money had disappeared. My uncle paid the driver and we were grateful.

'The maid probably robbed me,' Yasin said. 'But the maid came after I had left the house in the morning. Beats me.'

I didn't say anything. I didn't want to embarrass Yasin. As I'd cried out of hunger, I must have blacked out. But I regained consciousness when Yasin's mum came in the room thinking if I'd died or something. I pretended to be unconscious because I didn't want to hear any more of her unspeakable words. That's when I noticed Amma checking our bags. She took the money Yasin kept in his rucksack. She then opened our suitcase and took out my brand-new shoes, toiletries, and some clothes. She looked back to see if I was looking at her or not. Relieved that I wasn't, she stealthily left with the little booty she had found.

But I told Yasin later in the evening about our missing items and how I was locked in the room. He was flabbergasted and enraged; I was vengeful. Yasin kept apologising on his mum's behalf. I accepted under one condition. That he never ever allowed any of his family members to ever harm me in any way – physically, verbally, or emotionally. He agreed and I made him take an oath.

I just couldn't be more relieved that I was away from that hell of a place. I didn't tell my aunt the reason behind our sudden departure from my in-laws' house. But my swollen eyes cried out the gist of my stay there.

After ten days of a warm and cordial holiday, we bid everyone farewell at my uncle's place. My dad was waiting for us at the airport and drove us all to their home for lunch. My mum cooked all my favourite dishes including Yasin's favourite ones too. But when it came to serving the food, my mum was too busy ensuring Yasin got the best chicken piece, the best meat pieces, and the best fish cutlets. She topped up his plate till he begged that he couldn't possibly eat any more. I admired them, watching this.

And I also noticed how this hospitality was in stark contrast to the hostility I was made to face with my mother-in-law.

We stayed the night at my mum's. I booked a hospital appointment the following morning. Briefly I explained my reason for a scan. I was told to come in the following day. I put the phone down and found my mum standing at the door. She looked scared.

'What happened to you back home?'

'Nothing, Amma. The heat got me and I fainted. That's all. I just saw some spotting. So, I was thinking if that had something to do with it,' I lied.

***

I was fine and so was the baby who was a week late. It was a beautiful, healthy *boy*. I was thankful. Yasin called up back home and gave them the good news. How I wished that I could've seen my mother's-in-law face when she heard the news.

RANYA

Whoever cakes their face with layers of makeup is either someone who can't embrace their natural look or someone who's trying to hide the effects of domestic violence. Amma kept taunting me that now that I was eleven, she was hoping that I'd evolve into a swan.

It made me sad that I was not pretty enough for Amma. For if I were, then perhaps she would've loved me as much as she loved Di. She didn't actually love Di that much but at least Di could get away with almost anything. We used to have this uncle called Naim, who used to visit us quite often. Amma would boast that he came around all the time because she still looked young and hot. Amma also said that she wasn't having an affair and that she was just teasing Abba.

But it all came as a shock when one night Di woke me up from deep sleep in the middle of the night. 'Ranya, I've got to tell you a very big and important secret!'

I was expecting the worst. Like she found out that Amma was going to elope with Uncle Naim. 'Okay?' I prompted her to carry on. Di had a twinkle in her eye and I felt uneasy.

'I'll tell but you have to take oath that you will *never* tell anyone about it.'

'I can't make a promise if I don't know what it is.' I was dying to know. The fact that Di wanted to share her secret with me and solely me made me feel worth it. But I knew the importance of making a promise – you'd have to keep it no matter what. So, I wanted to make sure that I knew what I was taking the oath for. I still couldn't believe that Di chose me to have the privilege of knowing *her* secret!

'Fine! I won't tell you then,' Di said.

'All right, all right! I promise.'

***

Three days later, at breakfast, Amma gave me her signature dirty look and said, 'You horrible little *lesbian.*' I looked shocked but not for the right reason. I looked at Di who laughed her head off. I ran to my room as fast as my legs could carry me and rummaged the bookcase for the *Oxford Dictionary*. I opened the part that had words beginning with L till I came down to the word *lesbian*. We were in the mid-nineties, in a very small and conservative town, where English was as quaint as caviar. I had heard that word before but I had to ensure the meaning myself.

Although religiously acknowledged, culturally homosexuality wasn't a familiar term back then in Kakongonj. This place was commercially, pedagogically, and fashionably ten years behind Hayapur city.

Too many things were going on in my head. I was feeling giddy so I had to speak to someone. I went next door and asked to speak to our cousin, Hena. They moved to Kakongonj too when we did.

At once, she exclaimed, 'What? And here I freaked out when you gave me that gift thinking you were, you know, had a *thing* for me.'

'Ugh! You too think like this?' I felt the bile rise up to my mouth.

'Excuse me! I'm the one who should feel disgusted.' It took me a couple of seconds to figure out what she just said. She was right after all. I sat down and gestured Hena to do the same. After taking a deep breath, I confided everything in her.

'I did *not* give Di the hickey. Uncle Naim did that to her and she told me that if anyone asked then I should say that I did it. I had absolutely no idea what it all meant.'

'Didn't you find it all uncanny? I mean, why on earth would you take the blame?' Hena asked.

I was quiet. I couldn't explain to her what Di meant to me. She had no idea how I yearned Di's attention and friendship. I generally took promises seriously but I wasn't worried any more that I had just broken one. Why should I be? I was still a minor. I was fooled and ensnared. No wonder Di made me promise before she disclosed the secret.

Amma was banging on the door. I'd locked it for this tête-à-tête. When I opened it, she looked even stonier than before. To see the woman, who swore enough to raise the dead, at a loss for words, indeed called for the seriousness of the matter. I looked at Hena. She made a gesture with her eyes that she would clarify the misconception.

The repercussion of this matter turned out to be more exaggerated than I had thought. Di was in an uproar that night. Her eyes were bloodshot and looked like they would pop out of their sockets. 'You betrayed me! You went back on your oath! You had promised! You liar! You'll burn in hell!' Di wailed like a banshee. I couldn't tell if she was doing all that for real or not. She looked like a spitting image of Amma.

I was mortified as my guilty conscience flared up. I felt I was cruel. The promise was baseless but how couldn't have I thought about Di's feelings? Or the trouble I'd now had gotten her into? Abba must be enraged by now and probably he'd kill Di. I felt like killing myself for hurting my mother-like sister this bad.

A whole week went by. I was convinced that Abba knew nothing about this affair. A part of me was waiting for some catastrophe but it never happened. Amma said nothing to Di. *Nothing at all!* Either Di's melodrama convinced Amma that her insolent act had made her insane with shame or she was going to use this incident to blackmail her. Two days later, I overheard Amma saying to Di, 'Make sure your Abba doesn't get to know about this.' But Abba must've sensed something. Di was being quite rebellious with Abba these days and Abba was swearing at her whenever she made a mistake. Abba loved Di more than me. Once Amma slapped Di. Abba warned her not to but she slapped her again to wind him up. So, Abba squeezed her neck between his thumb and fingers. Amma looked terrified. I was even more frightened for Di. For when Abba would be at work, Amma would take it out on Di. And she did.

Di had the tolerance of an inanimate object. Once in Dubai, we were out for dinner in a restaurant when Di remembered that she forgot to turn the gas off the cooker. We had to hurry home and call the fire brigade. There was no fire but the gas had engulfed most of the flat. Abba slapped Di very hard that day. The following day he bought her a new dress and chocolates and told her that he was sorry.

I hoped he got me a little something too. But the bags he carried had nothing else in them. I felt hurt but didn't express that. A month later or so, Abba slapped me for making too much noise when he was taking his afternoon nap. Boy was I happy. I was confident that I would get a new dress and chocolates the following day.

But I never did; and he didn't say sorry either. But this time was not the same as then. Di was going to get married soon. I would've thought that Abba would be nicer to her as she would be leaving us. But that wasn't the case.

He came out of the shower one day and hollered, 'Who was the last one to have had a shower?' I was about to speak when Di signalled me to remain silent.

'Me,' Di said. Amma was next to Di. She too was shocked to see the anger in Abba. He was a calm person generally. I was motionless out of fear. I didn't dare speak a word.

Abba went to the kitchen and got a very thin wooden stick. This was kept especially, to discipline us as a last resort. With that he hit Di ruthlessly. I closed my ears and eyes.

'Make sure you replace shampoo bottles if you are the last one to empty it. You wanton. Sleeping around with any men you see, eh?'

Di had very fair, blemish-free skin with chiselled features. Her clear forehead now had a one-and-a-half-inch long bruise with a lesion. It was purple and mottled with specks of blood through it. Throughout the beating, which took place for what felt like an age, Di was mute, physically as well as verbally. She didn't even shed a tear.

Abba and Amma didn't know but Di must've known that it was *I* who was the last one to have had a shower. *I* emptied out the shampoo bottle. And it was *I* who forgot to replace it. *As salt and pepper, I assumed that that was a token of Di's apology.*

RANYA

As we shifted from city to city, so did my weight. Nothing changed for the better between my old folks but as for me, I was now over thirteen, with fat and spots in the wrong places. There were exactly seven spots just within the perimeter of my forehead but it felt like a hundred and seven.

My friends suggested getting a haircut with a fringe to hide them but that would make me look even younger than people usually thought I was. Besides, Amma would never spend money to get me a decent haircut. She would do a DIY on me and that would make me look worse than the fringe. Only last year, Amma cut my hair in the one and only hairstyle she knew, a boy-cut. When she cut my hair, she wouldn't tell me to move my head; instead she would jerk my head to the side she needed me to face. Once she used the end part of the shears and cut my temple. I had two neat parallel cuts on it. It was bleeding and I was crying, silently. So, she picked up some of the hair that was on the floor and stuck it on the cut to stop the blood. Haircuts from my mum were one of my many living nightmares.

I stepped outside in the early morning where a drizzle from a nimbus cloud promised an imminent heavy shower. I was attending my sixth school now. Abba was already in the car, fiddling with the demister. Innumerable water droplets spritzed on the earth creating the sound anklets make when the tiny little bells in them shake with vigour. People generally complained when it rained but I absolutely loved it. It seemed to cleanse the scum from the world.

It happened to be that time when most girls my age were hitting puberty. As I walked through the hallway, this girl called Fiza tapped me on the shoulder. Fiza was a petite, cute girl with big doll-like black eyes and a mass of jet-black hair. Something I wished I had too instead of my sunburnt and flyaway hair. She looked at me curiously and whispered something.

'Huh?' I looked on naively. Her voice was inaudible. Personally, I hated sibilant whispers.

'You know...' and then she mouthed the word *period*.

'Oh that! Yeah, I have.'

Fiza put a finger on her lips and ordered me to talk quietly as there were boys about. The coiled snake ring on her forefinger emphasised the importance of the secrecy. I looked over my shoulders and didn't see a single boy around us. Not even in the vicinity to hear us speaking.

Fiza's mum was one of Amma's childhood friends. Like us, they too used to live abroad before they settled in Bangladesh. Recently I'd been feeling some kind of tension between our mums. Fiza's mum noticed that my mum flirted with Fiza's dad, for I noticed a stony aura around Fiza's mum the last couple of times we went around. Fiza had been also acting weird with me since then. She hardly spoke to me whenever she visited me and every time I suggested that we did something together, like a group-study or watch a film, Fiza made some kind of an excuse, which was very unlike her.

So today when she just came up to me to ask that stupid question, I decided to get to the bottom of this. I asked her during recess what really was the reason behind this polarised behaviour.

'You aren't the way you used to be,' Fiza said as she smoothened her crisp white uniform without looking at me.

'What do you mean?'

It came out more as a scoff. I couldn't help it since she should've known for sure that it was the other way around. 'You hardly ever speak to me when we go around your place and, to avoid talking to me, you tell me to either watch the telly or help you with homework and stuff!' Fiza blurted out which baffled me even more. But then I thought for a bit. I was lucky to be saved from the embarrassment of Fiza accusing my mum of being facetious. I knew I didn't avoid her when she came around but pleading guilty for the latter was better than acknowledging the former.

'Probably you're right. I suppose I have been a bit aloof. I'm sorry... I really am.' Fiza didn't say anything and neither did she look like she had accepted the apology. 'Erm... do you think we can be friends again?' I abhorred arguments so wanted to close the matter quickly.

Fiza replied after a short pause. 'I guess... oh! what the heck!' She hugged me as she said that. Hugs were also on the list of things I didn't like. For some reason, I never liked any sort of physical contact with anyone. By the time recess was over, we both sat together, for the rest of the lessons, like two best friends. But somewhere deep down, I felt awkward with her sudden over-friendliness.

It was raining still by the time school finished, but not as heavily. I was soaking wet as I waited for Abba. I was sneezing all the way and by evening I got a temperature. I was absent from school for three days. Whenever I fell ill, Amma always left the house and returned, only when I got better. 'Why do you do that?' I asked in a croaky voice – the result of a sore throat and subdued tears.

'I'm too sensitive. I can't risk catching any bug off you! I have a huge phobia of diseases anyway.' An angry tear escaped from my eyes. I moved my face away from her for I didn't want her to find me pathetic.

Women like her should not be burdened with children, especially ill children.

'Your Abba can look after you. Besides, I have an audition coming up and I also have to go out now. Don't forget to boil some rice for tonight,' Amma ordered as she powdered her face. I went to the kitchen to check if Amma had cooked anything. There was a bit of a leftover chicken curry and some fish curry she had cooked two days ago.

As I placed rice on the hob, I remembered the time when I was about four. Amma, Bhaiyya, Di and I were in another place in Kakongonj, while Abba was sorting out the paperwork for Dubai.

I was playing in the neighbourhood with three other girls when I stepped on a frog and all of them gasped. 'Oh no, I hurt the poor frog!'

'Who cares about that!' and then, in a more sombre tone they said, 'You should rather worry about what happens tonight when you sleep.'

'What do you mean?' I didn't expect to hear what they said and neither did I believe them. But I also couldn't help thinking about what they said.

What if it happens after all? But that's not possible. What's the connection between stepping on a frog and bedwetting?

'Get out of my bed!' Amma shouted a lot more after that but I couldn't figure out the meanings as I was stupefied from the dream I had. Just as those girls had predicted, I did wet the bed after all in the middle of the night. Amma sent me in the servant quarters that night to sleep with our maid, Lulubu.

She looked after me the whole night as for some reason I had developed a temperature. She told Amma about it, but she refused to have me back in her bed.

I cried the whole night despite Lulubu's effort to comfort me. Eventually I gave in and fell asleep.

The boiling water from the rice spat on to the hob and that brought me back to reality. It reminded me how much I loathed living in the moment. School and daydreaming were the only ways I could escape reality. I felt more depressed now as I wouldn't get to say goodbye to Fiza who was leaving Bangladesh with her parents to settle in America. Amma told me so before she left. I tried to call her on their landline number but her mum said she was busy. It was rather odd since I thought I heard Fiza's voice in the background when her mum was talking to me.

I called her two to three times each day for the next three days but Fiza's mum always made an excuse for her not being available. I surmised that they were just busy packing all their stuff and hoped that she'd call before she left. I was glad that we made up and put all those hard feelings behind us. Besides,

I was now well enough to go back to school and chill out with my other friends. I took a quick shower in the morning. I was hungry but at the same time desperate to lose weight so I skipped breakfast. Amma wasn't the kind to ever wake up in the morning to make breakfast for anyone and with Di gone, and Bhaiyya *long* gone, I had no one to worry that I didn't have breakfast. Abba got me late for school again but I didn't have the courage to tell him that. I sulked instead. For five minutes, I sat in the car while he drove, without any of us uttering a word. 'How's school?' Abba asked. I didn't like speaking to my parents but tried to answer his questions without sounding disgruntled.

'It's all right.'

'How's your best friend... what's her name again?'

'I have three best friends, actually.' I didn't feel like telling their names to him.

'Let me guess... Yaara, Amina, and Jariyah? Or is it Jakiyah?'

'Zakiyya,' I say flatly.

'You all are quite close, aren't you?'

'Hmm.' There was an awkward silence till we reached my school. He pulled up at the road in the corner and I tried to get out quickly.

'Erm, listen.'

'Yeah?' I said without looking. I felt bad that I was being rude but I had no explanation for the way I behaved with Abba, at times. He was nothing like Amma. Rather he'd be kind and gentle towards me. Yet, I didn't know why a force within drove me to be cold towards him.

'Don't talk about everything to your friends, okay?'

I stopped midway. 'What do you mean?'

'You know, like our household problems.'

Your and Amma's household problems you mean?

'Okay,' I said. Once Abba left, I muttered, 'My pathetic life's so much better at school.'

Amidst the flock of students and chaos I managed to enter the classroom in one piece. But as soon as I did that, Amina whispered to me, 'You won't believe this!' To this Yaara, Zakiyya, and some other girls nodded too.

I was able to guess that this surprise was not going to be a pleasant one. As we briskly walked, my friend informed me that they'd fill me in at recess.

I tried very hard to concentrate but my mind was too busy trying to figure out what my friends were going to tell me. From the corner of my eye, I noticed a couple of boys trying to look at me discreetly, but it was an epic fail.

'They know about it too,' Zakiyya whispered to my ear. *About what?* I wondered. By now I was frantic. The bell went off. Now was the time to discover *the* news.

***

I didn't know how I came home from school that day. I couldn't be bothered to freshen up which I religiously did once I came back from school. I found cleaning my hands always therapeutic. I wished that the state of my mind would kill my appetite, but that was a case beyond impossibility; my appetite was undefeatable, no matter how upset or angry I was. So, for comfort, I consoled myself that it was all baby fat that would be shed one day.

I was munching on whatever edible I could find and while I indulged in gluttony, my mind constantly played and re-played the "big news" my friends told me at recess.

'Fiza said that your parents are always arguing like cats and dogs,' Yaara spoke to the point.

'And that your mum hits you with anything and everything like hangers and iron rods, and she also makes you do all the household chores,' filled in Zakiyya.

Amina added, 'That's the reason why sometimes you're unmindful and teary-eyed.'

While another girl pointed out, 'Fiza also said that your elder sister Megha Di supposedly eloped with her boyfriend before they got married.'

This hit a very sensitive spot. I was enraged. How dare she say that about my sister? But most importantly, how did she even know about it? Was it uttered in anger from her part? Revenge? Fiza's or her mum's?

I thought my brain would explode with all these questions. It was futile thinking about it but I couldn't help it nor could I talk about it to anyone other than my friends, from whom I'd rather not show my face any more. Fiza even mentioned some other details such as, I am the oldest in the class, since I started my period before everyone in our year and that once I had even leaked.

'She told all this to us the way our English teacher reads out our lesson to us,' Yaara said. I tried to figure out what made people sadder. When rumours were told or when true, embarrassing gossip were spread about them. I reckoned that it was the latter, for at least with the former, there was a chance for the truth to prevail, but with the latter, you'd just have to live with it.

Once our maths teacher, Mr Bakar, caught me red-handed for bunking my lesson.

'Why didn't you turn up for the lesson?' he said.

'Because… I didn't do my homework.'

'But I never gave any homework,' Mr Bakar said. He looked confused.

'Uh… oh, yeah…' I was well embarrassed by then.

Mr Bakar looked me straight in the eye. There was a twinkle that I couldn't miss. 'Ranya, don't lie because you're a bad liar. If you don't want to tell the truth then just remain silent and when you bunk, try hiding in a more inconspicuous place so you don't get caught,' he advised.

Surprisingly, I found it much easier to implement the advice, often though with unpleasant consequences. So, the following day at school when my friends enquired if what Fiza had said was true, I didn't lie and neither did I ascertain its truth. To my amazement, I found my friends to be very supportive.

'Everyone has family problems!' Yaara said.

'Yeah man!' the rest agreed.

I deeply appreciated that my friends understood and didn't mock me. 'Thanks, guys.' I excused myself shortly.

I went into the girls' restroom and sat on the toilet seat in one of the cubicles for privacy and cried my heart and eyes out in utter silence. About five or ten minutes later, I washed and dried my face. I checked my face in the mirror to make sure I looked as fresh as a daisy – I didn't.

When school finished, I came home by myself. Abba usually picked me up but today he was almost two and a half hours late. The head teacher allowed me to go by myself since I couldn't reach Abba through the phone.

The rain stopped and a shark-grey hue stretched the entire horizon; lightning and distant thunder signalled that the macabre shroud above would soon bring about the flood of 1998. A sinister sense suddenly engulfed me but I brushed the thought away. So long as I had my friends' moral support, I had nothing to worry about. I scampered into an alleyway and managed to reach the doorstep of our, what I forcefully had to call *home*, before I got drenched in the rain. It was pouring in buckets now. As I opened the door, all I could think of was having some hot food. The house was unusually dark when I stepped in and as I groped for the switch, something smashed under my shoe. When the light came on, I let out a gasp. The entire living room was snowed in confetti – only these confetti were made from shards of broken glass.

MEGHA (DI)

It happened again. It was hard during my O Levels. I managed to pass with one A, three Bs and two Cs. Abba and I stayed in a hotel in Hayapur for my exams. I just couldn't concentrate on my studies. I told him that I wanted a separate room but he said it was too expensive. The son of a stingy bitch. I knew he did this to me so that I wouldn't do good in my studies. So that he could blame *me* for not doing well in my exams. He knew very well that shyness would prevent me from telling everyone what he did to me.

But now I had my A Levels to worry about. I was studying when Abba called me to the living room. He was sitting down with his legs crossed. He was smoking and the room had become foggy-just like my future.

'*Ji*, Abba?' I said.

'Sit down. You didn't do too well in your O Levels even though I paid for your coaching classes.' He paused here a bit. I didn't say anything and he continued, 'I don't think there is any point in you doing any more classes. It is very expensive.'

'What do you mean?' I had to cough out the sarcasm in my throat. 'A level is tougher than O Level.'

'You will not be able to study medicine with those grades. I studied a lot harder and got better results without any extra classes,' Abba said. He mentioned this information as frequently as the common cold. I reiterated that he should stop comparing his times to ours. To this he said, 'What if I were to die now? Who will pay for your A Levels?'

'But you're not dead,' I said, deadpan.

'Imagine I am.'

'I can't imagine something that hasn't happened. You shouldn't be talking like this. As my father, it is your duty to provide me an education,' I said.

'Fuck your education.'

I wished Ranya wasn't around. Abba had changed since he came to know that I know about his character. The only way I could palliate this psychological trauma was by free-mixing even in this ultra conservative society of Kakongonj. But if my own father didn't give a crap then, why should I? I didn't feel guilty. I didn't feel anything for this family any more. I just wanted to find Mr Right and, in that quest, I socialised. I didn't want my life to turn out like Amma's. She too has to survive and maybe that's why she dissipates her distress by lashing out on us. I felt sorry for her deep down. Amma felt bad for hitting me again so she told me to find someone as soon as possible, get married, and leave here.

This led me to find my Prince Charming – Jahid, my Mr Right. He'd been around all the time yet I never acknowledged him and neither realised that he'd been in love with me for ages. I told him everything about my life and he still loved me. I hoped that Ranya would find someone like that too. But I worried that she was still in the dark about our father.

***

Amma and Abba had been fighting like crazy in the last few days that I remembered. Amma would take it out on me by hitting me with whatever she could find but I happily took the shit because I knew that it wouldn't be for too long. I was just waiting for the day I would stick my middle finger at them all and leave.

Quite frankly, I couldn't believe my luck since things were going just the way I wanted them to. Jahid and I would be getting married and his whole family were coming tomorrow evening. I had cleaned the house inside out and had also cut up all the onions, ginger and garlic, washed and cut up all the meat, chicken, and fish. Even my twelve-year-old little Ranya helped out so much. I owed her for being a scapegoat every time Jahid and I feared that Abba might find out that we'd been making out.

There was a power cut and the household chores made me all sweaty but I felt chuffed knowing that it would help me shed a few pounds. I sorted the house out from morning till dusk. My body ached and my fingers were deprived of serious *tlc*. I felt exhausted and I had to lumber myself to the bathroom to take a shower. I scrubbed the bathroom for half an hour before I actually took the shower. When I came out, my sister looked dismayed.

'What's the matter, Ranya?'

'Amma and Abba just had another argument. Amma's saying that she won't do any cooking for tomorrow.'

'Where's she?'

'Sleeping.'

Our engagement was to take place the next day. I went to the room where Amma was sleeping and called her softly. She was sleeping with her back to me, and she moved ever so slightly. I volunteered to massage her legs. Yes, *that's* how desperate I was.

Once the wedding took place, I'd be a free bird. I'd been giving charity to the beggars that came around in return for their prayers for my wedding to go smoothly. Amma let me massage her legs and that was a good sign. She was supposed to cook in the evening as they were coming over the next day.

'It's almost nine p.m. Do you need me to help you with the cooking?' I asked tentatively.

'I won't be doing any cooking,' Amma said.

'Why not?'

'Don't question me.'

I gritted my teeth. Tears rolled down my rigid face. Without saying a word, I left the room. Ranya was already asleep. I didn't have dinner and was getting cramps but the pangs of betrayal pricked me more.

I had no idea what time it was. All I remembered was that I woke up with a throbbing pain in one of the sides of my head. It wasn't a headache.

It was Amma.

She was knocking that side of my head with her knuckles and then she pulled my ponytail and dragged me off the pillow.

'You whore. Are you dying to sleep with him? That's why you're trying to be all buddy-buddy with me, isn't it? Do you think I'm that stupid? I was testing you all this time. You were only using me for my money. As if I would finance your wedding. Humph! You will not be marrying Jahid. We have cancelled it. Go ask your Abba yourself. Besides, who will marry a slut like you?'

I ran to Abba's surgery, which was next door. I told him what Amma had said.

He indirectly confirmed it. He added that. Jahid's parents refused to register one of the flats in their apartment building in my name and that Jahid didn't have a job.

'So how will a jobless person support a wife? Besides, I still think you should reconsider the alliance I brought for you. My friend's son's a doctor. He's not bad-looking.'

I'd had enough. I couldn't play along any more.

When Abba went out, I called Jahid. I had to first pick the lock Abba put on the telephone. I told him the latest update.

We decided that in a week I was to leave here.

I knew that people would call this eloping and that our reputations would be stained. That it could possibly ruin Ranya's future when it would be her turn to get married. But that wasn't my problem anymore.

RANYA

At first, I thought some burglary had taken place but then logic hit me. My parents had had another fight. I didn't bother to check if there was any food or not. I straightaway got a broom from the kitchen and began to sweep. I still had my school uniform on and couldn't be bothered to change. Half an hour later, I heard someone opening the front door. I had finished brushing so I quickly put the broom away to see who had come in, but before I could do that, Abba walked in with some cops, telling them to take a look at the state of the house.

He gave a double look and then stopped talking at mid-sentence, as the house showed no proof to what he was saying.

They started talking again and I gathered from the conversation that Amma supposedly smashed the chandelier with a chair whilst in an argument with Abba. He got the cops to see the evidence, which in turn would vouch for the fact that Amma was mentally unstable.

'You shouldn't have cleaned this up, I looked like a fool in front of them,' Abba muttered after the cops left.

'I'm sorry. If I knew, I wouldn't have taken the trouble to clean up.' I half expected to be thanked. 'There's no food cooked by the way.' I helped dad make some fried eggs and toast which we ate in silence.

I wasn't sure if that was because we were both hungry or because of the situation we were in. I was gradually becoming desensitised, so didn't bother asking anything about the civil war in the house. Besides, I was just fed up of their fights and could live without having to listen to the malarkey. When Amma would arrive (from wherever she had gone to) she would go on and on, about the matter anyway; literally, day and night, for as long as two weeks in a row, until they somehow made up.

'I was hoping you would ask me about what has happened,' Abba's voice suddenly interrupted.

I almost forgot that he was even there.

'I kind of figured out what happened.' After a short pause, I asked, 'Where's Amma?'

'I don't care,' he snapped. Then a couple of seconds later, as though he realised he was rather curt, he added, 'She's gone to one of her auditions.'

I was somewhat relieved to know that Amma was away somewhere for some time. At least that would save me from hearing an earful. She didn't quite talk to me. She sort of talked to herself, aloud. At least I talked quietly to myself, in my own mind. I knew how to empathise but Amma would start off with what Abba said or did and then she would somehow end up blaming and hitting me. It just wasn't fair but then a lot of things in life weren't. The flood had made countless people homeless, jobless, ill, bereaved, and even dead. At least I had a roof over my head.

***

The only entertainments in Kakongonj were the cool January breeze and our stereo cassette player. It had been just a month and a bit since Bhaiyya got married. No one agreed yet it was a fact that had to be accepted. Abba was getting more aloof while Amma ranted more than usual. Di was happy, relieved more like it. She too was going to be free from here very soon. But one cold night, I found Di crying. Our parents had agreed to get her married off to the person she loved, so I wasn't sure why she was crying like this.

'I feel very bad to leave you,' Di sobbed.

I wish I read between those lines. When I woke up the next morning, Di was not on or anywhere near her single bed where she'd normally be asleep at that hour. Her bed was unmade too and that didn't look right.

Whenever she woke up, the first thing she'd do was make her bed. At once I jumped off my bed and searched for her in the bathroom, which was next to our room. It was empty.

I went to the kitchen and there was no sign of anyone having been there since the night before. I then went back to our room to check if any of Di's belongings were missing. I opened her side of the wardrobe. Everything was intact but I had a gut feeling that something was out of place. My attention was then drawn to the door of our room. Her favourite satchel, which I gave her on her nineteenth birthday, last year, was not hanging on her peg.

I had to sit down as I felt lightheaded. I rewound the latest incidents in my head and recalled a certain uncanny detail. She was not wearing her PJs that time in the middle of the night when she was crying; she still had her day clothes on.

By now my stomach was churning. This only meant one thing – Di had run away.

It was all planned and perhaps this abrupt decision to run away was why she was crying. *I feel very bad to leave you.*

I wasn't sure whether I should wake Amma and Abba up and break the news, wait for them to wake up and then tell them about it, or just let them figure it out themselves and pretend to be all shocked along with them. Either of these ways, I would get beaten up, since Amma would have to dissipate her anger some way or the other.

I chose to wait.

Whack. I got a slap from Amma, all right. It was straight after I disclosed that Di was missing. Amma wailed and blamed anyone and everyone. Then she shrieked that Di might have committed suicide. Abba disagreed. I disagreed too but didn't say anything in case I got slapped again.

Whenever Amma was angry, she didn't need a reason to hit. For almost the whole day, which seemed like a year, we didn't know of Di's whereabouts, until a maternal relative informed us in the evening that Di was safe and sound. Jahid Bhai and Di got married straightaway before leaving Kakongonj for Hayapur.

Since then, for almost a year, I hadn't seen Di. Amma and I never mentioned her name in front of Abba. We wrote letters to each other in secret, which I usually got our school security guard to post for me. Our landline was restricted from making calls outside Kakongonj so I couldn't speak to Di unless she called. Whenever she rang, I would pretend it was a friend. I felt lifeless after Di left but I was always proud to claim (to myself) that I hadn't shed a single tear for her. This was because the love for her in my heart dissolved into acrimony. Di just left and now she was living happily while I was still

115

stuck in that dungeon of a house. At least Di had me while she was here. Our sorrows and fears were all shared out. But now I was all alone. With no one to talk to. A rescue boat came to save her and she boarded it, leaving me in the ocean. A voice in me cajoled that I may not understand but needed to accept the fact that she had to leave. It was my *salt and pepper* intuition again that advised me to let go; the resentment I harboured against her had to sail off even if it meant that I needed to drown in the sea of tears and turn pain into a panacea.

MEGHA (DI)

It had been a year since Jahid and I got married. Amma told me that Abba had disowned me. I felt that in a way Abba got what he wanted; he didn't want to spend anything on my wedding and apart from his blackened reputation, his pockets were as exultant as he was.

I told Jahid about Shamshed Dada and Dida and we arranged to visit them on the coming Friday. Dida cried when she realized who I was and hugged me for a long time.

'You have become so beautiful,' Dida said as she pulled herself away. I smiled. 'I mean it. You are absolutely gorgeous, and you're married now! Oh, you are so young. How old are you?'

'I'll be twenty soon.'

Dida called out to her maids and told them to give us tea and snacks. Within half an hour, the dining table was full with samosas, shingaras, pasties, and five different kinds of *pithas-choi pitha, bhapa pitha, puli pitha, mal poa and nun gora*. Dida also began to make preparations for dinner. I insisted that we wouldn't stay that long but she chided me.

'We can't not feed you and our *nati-jamai!*' We are from the Kuraishi family. We have to keep up with our traditions and customs.'

I was flabbergasted. Dida was a distant paternal relative yet she was more hospitable than my own mother.

She was stirring a pot of meat biryani while I sat on a stool sipping cardamom and ginger tea. I wore a magenta-coloured saree and smiled from time to time despite feeling uncomfortable in both my saree but more so in the situation.

'Your Abba must've thrown a lavish wedding party for you, isn't that right? We weren't told anything about your marriage so we couldn't come.' A thorny silence engulfed the air. 'Oh, you must've looked like a princess,' Dida said.

I smiled and said nothing. I prayed that she didn't ask anything that would make me feel uneasy. It wasn't her fault but my situation was the kind that cultivated secrets. She then said something that startled me. She was talking about the wedding of one of my cousins, presuming I knew about it already.

'Who's wedding?' I asked.

'Your Chacha's, paternal uncle's daughter. She got married six months ago. Your Abba is very generous. He funded her entire wedding. Ah, the wedding gold was exquisite.' Dida shook her head in bewilderment. 'If he could spend so much for his brother's daughter, one can only wonder how much he must've spent on his own daughter's wedding.'

RANYA

These days my fourteen-year-old friends were interested in three main topics only – fashion, makeup, and *boys*. During recess, we would be busy trying out affordable makeup without caring how loud it looked, while chatting about which guy we thought was cute, which one looked geeky, or which one might have a crush on someone. Usually after school, we'd all meet up in one of our friends' houses to chill in the name of group-study. The best part was listening to tracks from *The Backstreet Boys* or *Britney Spears,* and looking through teen and fashion magazines.

'Oh, come on! You're not that innocent, Ranya!' challenged Yaara. She was tall, skinny with an olive tone and came across very confident.

'Oooh, Ranya is feeling very shy,' teased Zakiyya. She was petite with light brown eyes, which complimented her caramel complexion.

'I know, Ranya has a crush on a girl!' Amina snorted. She was the shortest amongst us with boyish looks. 'Let's tickle till she admits, eh?' Having said that Amina started tickling me straightaway, and the others joined in too. I hated to be tickled and that was number three in my list of most hated things.

'Okay, okay, stop, please!' I said as I hugged my tummy in protection. 'Fine! I do like someone but that someone is *not* a girl! In fact, I *love* him!' I emphasised by pointing my forefinger. I didn't want to sound homophobic but such a false notion had ostracised me in the past so I had to defend myself.

'Don't tell me it's Kartik! None of you are allowed to have a crush on him 'cos he's mine!' Yaara commanded.

Kartik was a year older than us. Despite being Bangladeshi, he too like us was born and brought up abroad. According to Yaara, he was a walking creature of cuteness. I thought he just looked like a white kid.

'Erm... you don't really know if he likes you too, you know,' Amina pointed out.

'So, what? I like him so that's it! None of you should even think of liking him!'

'Yes, Ma'am!' we all chorused except Yaara, who gave a triumphant smile.

'But I thought you fancied Abram,' Amina said.

'Aby Baby likes me. I'm just going with the flow and hopefully that should get Kartik's attention, you know what I mean,' Yaara reasoned.

'Go on, who is it, Ranya?' reminded Zakiyya. I was busy thinking of a name all this time.

'Kevin. He's so mysteriously handsome!' I said dreamily.

'Kevin who?'

'From *the Backstreet Boys*.'

'*Puhleeeze*! Not a celebrity! We mean a real person!' Zakiyya sighed irritably.

Thinking hard and quick, I found a name that I believed none of my friends had a crush on. 'Himel,' I said. I didn't really have a crush on him but I convinced myself that I did.

Everyone my age seemed to have a crush on someone. For now, I either fancied an actor or some guy from a boy band. I knew it was weird that I didn't like someone. Especially since I knew that I wasn't gay and neither was I religious. For some reason, I just cringed at the thought of romance.

My friends didn't feel like that. So why did I?

My popularity was at stake. I hated to pretend but the peer pressure was too much. So, I thought about Himel. I tried to picture what he looked like. He was tall and a bit on the big side, but cute.

'Oooohhhh,' they all cooed.

Bingo. Popularity restored. My mind drifted off while they chattered frivolously. I was around four years old when we moved to Dubai. I loved it there. By six, I had already made future plans: my wedding. I was going to marry Dr Khaliq, Abba's colleague. He was a junior doctor, supervised by Abba who was in a senior position by then. He was half Lebanese and half Emirati. He had black wavy hair and a goatee. Whenever I saw him, I used to hear imaginary violins playing around me and see cupids and hearts flying by.

One wintry evening, we all got ready to go to a party. It was being held in one of the flats within the vast doctors' campus where we stayed. It was some couple celebrating their wedding anniversary.

I wore my best red dress and red pumps. Di had chosen them for me. The couple who were celebrating were both doctors, very rich, and therefore must've been happily married. I didn't know why but I thought that when I saw his smiling wife, her eyes looked puffy and red. Their children, with whom I used to play whenever we met, were rather quiet that day too. I somewhat figured out what may have happened.

Yes. I'm not the only one with crazy parents. However, the joy of this revelation was short-lived. A certain ringing of feminine laughter, from my right, drew my attention. I saw a sight that tore the strings of the imaginary violins, resulting in cacophonous tunes. The hearts popped like burst balloons, perhaps by the illusive Cupid's bow and arrow.

Our hosts' spacious living room was furnished with modern furniture. On that modern furniture sat Dr Khaliq. And on his lap sat the woman who had laughed. She was his Lebanese girlfriend. She was dressed in an oversize mustard-coloured jumper over a black mini skirt. Black stockings and stiletto heels adorned her endless legs and loose, dark brown curls fell just under her shoulders. Her red lips had a tinge of orange in them which parted in a smile to reveal perfect white teeth. Her green eyes with thick lashes sparkled against symmetrical cheekbones. She was gorgeous.

'Ranya. Come here,' Dr Khaliq called me in his accented voice. 'Meet Huda.' I asked him who she was. He said something which I didn't understand. And I was too shy to ask the meaning of *"fiancée"*.

Whenever Dr Khaliq saw me, he would carry me and swing me in the air. He didn't do that today.

'Are you also a doctor?' I asked Huda. I knew that she would say no. Amma said that very pretty girls were generally dumb.

'Yes.'

'Oh. I thought you were beautiful so…' my *salt and pepper* eponym suddenly warned me to not finish the sentence.

122

Huda laughed that laughter again. 'You're so cute. Thank you.'

'I told you she was,' her "fiancé" said.

No, I'm not. I'm heartbroken. I said to myself. Dinner was over and some couples either danced or drank. My parents abstained from drinking. Di said that this was so that they could practise what they preached to us. Abba was taking photographs with his camera. I looked at Amma. She was posing *more* than cutting the cake. She tried to make it look like she was unaware that photos of her were being snapped. She looked beautiful in her teal, white and pink paisley printed saree. She got our Indian neighbour to buy it for her when they went for a holiday to India. I wished she had got Di and I something too.

Amma's makeup of blue eye shadow, kohl rimmed eyes and pink lipstick was immaculate. She chopped her knee length hair to an urchin haircut back in London. Ever since then she maintained this look. Di said that it proved one's posh personality and status. Abba was not pleased but Amma never cared what Abba thought.

Dr Khaliq and Abba were arm wrestling now. He asked Abba to quit for he claimed that he might dislocate Abba's wrist.

An hour later we left. As predicted, Abba's wrist got sprained. I was enraged, but I couldn't do anything about it. Abba had to wear a wristband for a week. I told everyone that I hated Dr Khaliq for what he did to Abba. But I knew that that was just a pretext. Abba hugged and kissed me on the forehead and told me not to worry. I asked him when the reels of photos would be developed. He told me to get the envelope from the pocket of his coat hanging on the coat stand. I rushed to get it. Di got up from the beanbag and sat on the sofa where Abba and Amma were sitting. The photos were all colourful and luckily none of them were blurred. When no one looked, I took a photo and hid it in the pocket of my burgundy corduroy trousers. Casually I made an excuse to go to the bathroom, closed the door behind me and took the photograph out. It was the photo of a grinning Dr Khaliq and a laughing Dr Huda sitting on his lap.

'Do you think he likes you too?' Yaara asked.

'Huh?'

'Himel. Do you think he fancies you too?'

I shrugged.

'Hey, why don't we all tell Himel that Ranya likes him?' Zakiyya suggested which perturbed me. I didn't want this story to materialize.

'N... n... no, don't do that!'

But the girls had already started plotting and I couldn't think of any way to stop it!

***

The weekend, which felt like two weeks, was over. Everyone moaned to be at school yet I loved it. I loved to be anywhere else other than home. After all, school and friends were my means to escape from my dysfunctional life at home. I mulled over whether my friends too, had to portray double personalities like me. At school I was one of the popular and happy-go-lucky girls, but at home, I desperately endeavoured to be noticed, to be heard, to be saved.

'Psssst,' whispered Yaara, as she handed me a scrap of paper. When the teacher wasn't looking, I took the opportunity to read it. I couldn't help but giggle at the seriousness of my friends' mission to tell Himel that I liked him and I laughed at it secretly because I too, had a plan of my own.

'You're OK with the plan, right?' asked my friends.

'Yeah, sure, why not?' I said confidently.

This was going just the way I wanted it to go. In my mind, I pictured the domino-effect of my scheme; the girls were going to tell Himel that I liked him; he'd say that he didn't like me or that he liked someone else. Then I would pretend to be all heartbroken with the denouement resulting in me telling my friends to never hook me up with anyone for I wouldn't have my heart crushed again. I felt pretty amused with my novel idea.

The girls should leave me alone after that.

The bell rang for our recess. Yaara, Amina, and Zakiyya dashed for the basketball court where Kartik, Himel, Abram, and other boys were playing.

'Hey guys, wassup?' the girls asked.

'You all right, Kartik?' asked Yaara trying not to sound shy. They were all playing basketball now.

'Where's that other girl who usually hangs about with you lot?' Kartik asked.

'She's tied up with homework and stuff. Why do you ask, anyway?' Yaara said with a bit more promptness than necessary. Amina and Zakiyya gave each other a quick knowing look.

I was in the girls' common room and indeed busy with my homework – but the one that was due for the following week.

As I looked up, I saw my three friends approaching me looking rather serious.

This is too good to be true, I thought, but this was what I said, 'Oh I know, he likes someone else, doesn't he?' I tried to sound hurt.

'Not really,' Amina mumbled. Then she and Zakiyya looked at Yaara for a cue. For the next couple of minutes, all three of them just looked at each other, stupidly, asking one another "you say it", "no, you say it!"

'What? Why are you guys giving me that look?'

Tell her!' Yaara said, sounding well annoyed.

'Erm…' started off Amina.

'Uhh…' Zakiyya began.

'Uh-huh, whenever you guys are ready,' I said, totally oblivious to what I was about to hear.

'Oh, for crying out loud!' Yaara exclaimed, 'Himel and Kartik – they both fancy you.'

I did not, at all, expect to hear this. Even Kartik? And since when did Himel like me? I didn't particularly find any of them attractive. I always used to tease Yaara for her poor taste in guys.

One thing was for sure, that my plan had flopped, big time, and now there was even a bigger problem. If Kartik did like me then that would cause some friction between Yaara and me, despite the fact that I didn't like him.

That week had been the longest week ever for I didn't know how to come across to my friend. Yaara didn't say much and I didn't feel like talking about all this malarkey. By Friday, Amina decided that we should all have a meet up. This sure cheered me up, but again, I wasn't sure how to behave with

Yaara. We both tried to act normally while the others tried to play along.

When it was time to leave, I tried to speak to Yaara in person. 'Listen, Yaara, I'm not…' I had just mustered enough guts to speak when Yaara gave me a big bear hug.

I couldn't finish for she interrupted, 'Hey, I'm cool! I was never serious about Kartik! Yeah, he's cute but I'm not crazy about him. You know me, one day this guy is cute; tomorrow that guy is. I'm fine, really.' She sipped her can of coke as she spoke but I knew Yaara too well. The other girls all walked in but we didn't fill them in about what we had just talked about; but they must've guessed though.

'Shall we start on that geometry homework unless anyone wants to start with literature?' Amina asked. We all agreed on the latter. There was an awkward moment of silence before any of us said anything. Suddenly Zakiyya mimicked our English teacher, Mr Alim, who was known for his highfalutin jargons. There was a tacit acknowledgement that everyone was putting in an effort for *the talk,* except Yaara and myself. But I'd had enough and had to share my true feelings with my friends.

Yaara must've sensed what was going on in my head so she got there first. 'They want to know whom you will choose,' Yaara said as she handed round the worksheets. Without further ado, I confessed. I had played a trick by lying and it got back to me as usual.

'All right, guys.' I harrumphed to buy time. 'It's time I confessed. I don't really like any of them. I was merely pretending all along the way just to stop you guys from nagging me.' But my friends were being adamant and completely missing the point.

'You've got to choose one of them!' said Amina and Zakiyya nodded in agreement.

'If you don't choose, then I'll take it that you are trying to rub it on me by being all great and sympathetic,' stated Yaara.

'Besides, you don't really have to like any of them, just have fun while you can,' put in Amina. I rolled my eyes.

'Yeah, imagine, you could tell your children in future, "I was sought after by many a handsome fellow".' Zakiyya imitated Mr Alim's voice again and we all were in stitches.

'You've got to choose!' All three of them started to chant till I closed my ears with my palms and said, 'OK, fine, I'll take Himel. I thought he was sweet after all.'

Damn this peer pressure!

The next day at school, I was informed that Himel had pulled out because he felt his friend liked me more than he did. Once again, my friends tried to convince me that I too fancied Kartik.

'I *don't like* him!' I shouted to deaf ears.

A while later, Amina came in and announced, 'Kartik wants to go out with you, Ranya.'

'Man, I so don't want to be part of this mess!' I said, as I raked all ten fingers through my hair in frustration. I glanced at Amina and noticed the troubled look on her face. 'What is it?' I asked.

'I kind of heard something.'

'Heard what?' I questioned.

Before she could answer, Yaara and Zakiyya walked in. 'Oh, my God! You won't believe this!' whispered Zakiyya.

'Well, what is it?' I asked.

'They're saying that, if you like Kartik then you have to make out with him too, or else he's gonna dump you,' finished Yaara.

'Make out as in…?'

'As in sleep with him.'

RANYA

'Happy fifteenth birthday, Ranya,' Abba sang in the typical traditional tune.

I opened the door for him, smiling. 'You're a young woman now. I hope you like this.'

'Aww, thanks.' It was a small box of sponge cake from God knows where.

'One of the patients brought that as a token.' A part of me wished he hadn't mentioned that. The tenth of October was an inevitable date. I always tried hard to forget my birthday, but I always remembered it.

My friends had already wished me a happy birthday and had given me presents. Amma never said anything on this day, so I assumed that she never really remembered and I preferred it that way too. Abba and I had tea and the "cake" in silence.

Shortly, I excused myself and went upstairs to my room. I looked at all my presents. Mo, the only boy who was practically one of the girls, gave me a box of chocolates and Asif gave me a CD – *the Backstreet Boys' Millennium* album. Yaara, Amina, and Zakiyya had been saving up money for the past month so that they could buy me a decent makeup box. I was very touched by all the presents I was given. I waited till my parents were out of the house, to try the makeup out, because they didn't usually allow me to do so.

They were going to some relative's house when my friends came in. For the next two hours, we played loud music, put makeup on, did some dress rehearsals, ate lots of crisps, pizza, and chocolates, (my friends' parents had sent those with them) watched a few episodes of *Friends*, and finally talked.

'You OK, Ranya?' Amina asked. It had been two weeks since I had confronted Kartik straight after the bizarre demand he had made. *'Did you actually say what we think you said?'*

'Yep! That's just how we are and that's why we're popular and cool,' Kartik had stated boisterously. Himel, who stood next to him, had nodded in agreement.

Whenever my anger heightened regarding something, I found it pointless to talk about it at that time. But this was also subject to the idiocy of the person concerned. In the case of Kartik and Himel, I disregarded them as two village imbeciles. But what bothered me was that everyone seemed to pity *me* for being "dumped". Frankly, I was annoyed at myself for I shouldn't have pretended to like anyone. I should've just told my friends that I wasn't into guys because I hadn't found the right one yet; that I doubted the existence of a decent guy, all together. I simply had no attraction to the opposite sex, for the time being.

'I'm fine guys,' I said to my friends. 'Listen, I need to clarify something with you all,' I began. 'I'm the kind of person who believes that there is someone out there for you, and you need to keep yourself intact for that person. I want that person who has been "made for me" to not only love me, but to also respect me for who I am. Love and respect goes hand in hand and it also has to be mutual. And I definitely know that that person whom I shall love with my heart and soul, is at least not in this school.' They were all quiet so I carried on, 'I was worried that you guys would think that I'm a weirdo for not liking anyone yet. So, I pretended that I liked Himel. I'm sorry, guys.' There was a moment of silence.

'I knew you didn't like him,' said Zakiyya who was sitting in a bean-bag.

'Me too,' joined in Amina who was having a third can of coke.

'Yeah, I could tell you were pretending.' Yaara laughed, then added, 'Did anyone ever tell you that you're a lousy liar?'

I scoffed at first but then grinned and nodded my head at the same time.

***

The summer holiday had started. The humid air clung onto my skin and so did the cotton, cobalt blue maxi dress. But I didn't mind at all as it was a size ten. I went down an entire dress size. I was in the garden watering Abba's *Kodu gourd* plants when Amma called me to get the phone.

'Hello?' I asked.

'Ranya?' asked a polite, boyish voice that had recently broken.

'Erm… yeah… who is this?' I asked.

'Do you recognise me?'

'No.'

'Well, why don't you take a guess?' asked the voice.

'I'm not really good at guessing,' I answered, getting a bit frustrated by now. I tried to hide that by asking, 'Why don't you give me a clue?'

'OK, let's see, but will you promise not to hang up on me if you figure out who I am?' he asked.

'I'll try.'

There was pause, which followed a sigh. 'I… erm… I…' I said nothing, just waited. 'I hurt your feelings against my wish.'

'Kartik?' I asked.

'Yeah, it's me.'

'You OK?' I asked, as I couldn't think of anything else to say.

'Yeah. *You* okay?'

'Yeah,' I replied and once again I couldn't think of anything else to say or ask.

'Listen, Ranya, I need to explain myself to you, if you'll allow me.' Kartik sounded sheepish.

'Go on.'

'I never wanted to say that hideous thing to you, you know what I mean?' I didn't say anything so he carried on. 'It's just that Himel is my best friend and he liked you too and that's what got it complicated. When he pulled out, I was relieved, but then he called me a traitor for not doing the same for him and that caused a row between us. Then I thought about it and decided that I couldn't let a girl come into our friendship just like that. So, I said something stupid like what I said to you to restore my friendship with my best friend,' Kartik explained.

Had I taken a liking to Kartik, then conventionally I would've had to show some degree of resentment as that would be a proof of love in disguise. I was annoyed by his abrupt behaviour but it had no connection with romance. His predicament was understandable but unacceptable. He, along with his friends, violated my self-respect in front of everyone. 'OK. So, what am I supposed to do now?'

'I wanted to ask you something. Please be as honest as possible, OK?'

'Yeah sure.'

'Did you really like Himel?' Kartik sounded tentative.

'Well, frankly, I haven't been a very good person myself either.' I paused for a couple of seconds to see if Kartik asked anything. Taking a silent cue to go ahead, I continued, 'My friends were simply trying very hard to hook me up with someone, and in an effort to stop them from pestering me, I had to choose someone on whom none of the girls had a crush. And so, I thought of Himel.

'So, you don't fancy Himel.' It sounded more like a statement than a question. I was able to feel a faint sense of elation from the other end.

'No, I don't,' I confirmed.

'So...'

'So...?' I mimicked.

'Do you like... *me*?' Kartik asked.

I thought for a moment then replied, 'You see, Kartik, when you said that time that you guys were cool, you were right. But I guess,' here I paused a bit, sighing pretentiously, 'you guys just ain't "cool" enough for me. Hope you have better luck next time. Bye.'

I felt good; so good that I felt like celebrating. But that night, I found myself crying for no reason at all. I used the elimination method. Did I feel bad that I taught Kartik a lesson? I thought for a moment. I had positively no feelings for him, not even an ounce.

My parents hadn't had any arguments recently either.

It was such a weird feeling and I felt like having a bath to clean it off myself. I decided to take a shower. As I entered the bathroom I made sure that I didn't look into the mirror. I never ever looked at myself without any clothes on. I felt embarrassed. I wasn't appallingly big. I just felt disgusted at the idea of my own naked body.

I reasoned that the fact that Himel and Kartik liked me, was why I felt like this. It made me sick. *They* seemed sick. A part of me wanted to see them die slowly, in pain.

Why am I thinking like this? What's wrong with me?

I cried like this pretty often these days. Sometimes I felt like skinning myself alive or do something that would rid me of this feeling. This feeling akin to being... *raped.*

I resolved to harm myself by making several slashes to my arm with a razor.

Blood diffused on the wet, white sink. Surprisingly I didn't feel squeamish this time. Rather the sight had a calming effect on me. I felt as though I was flying – either that or things around me were. This uneasy feeling always came when any guy told me that he liked me. I always found it repulsive as it always led me to think that the guy intended to get physical with me.

My insides convulsed.

RANYA

A week went by and things were still peaceful between my parents. We went around relatives' houses, and even invited guests around. The rain and flood had subsided and Amma even cooked regularly now without getting her dander up over the task of preparing meals. I found it quite uncomfortable when matters ran this smooth as they seemed to be portents of an even bigger crisis.

This morning I woke up hearing some noise coming from the kitchen. I half sat up rubbing my eyes and checked the time. There were still fifteen minutes left before my alarm went off. I began to feel nervous so got up and walked towards the kitchen. Usually at this hour, the house remained very quiet as Amma would stay asleep. Even Abba sometimes skipped his breakfast in case he made too much noise and disturbed her. As I entered the dining room, I found Amma talking on the phone. What petrified me next was that which lay on the dining table. I was alert, yet I felt as though I was in a daze.

How can this be possible? This is way too bizarre!

Before my eyes was the dining table, spread with a variety of breakfast items: toast, boiled eggs, paneer, parathas, semolina halwa, hot tea and a couple of cereal boxes with milk in a jug. I tried to recall the last time Amma had prepared something like that and failed to remember such a scenario. I always wished, though, that like my friends' mothers, my mum too would make me breakfast, lunch, and dinner. It was usually a privilege if Amma ever cooked at all.

Back in Dubai when I was much younger, Di told Amma that I needed a new lunchbox. But she never seemed to ever remember to buy me one. Like her friends, Di was on a diet so she never took any lunch with her to school. But she had to sort out my lunchbox and this was frustrating her. For a month, all I had for lunch was a slice of processed cheese. I used to try hard to not look at my friends' food during lunchtime. But once from a distance I observed an Indian girl, whose doctor parents used to live in the flat below us in the same compound. She was a year older than me and had a beautiful *Hello Kitty* lunchbox and water bottle. Her lunch looked scrumptious. She and her friends were sharing their food with merriment. A Korean boy on my right was eating a chocolate wafer bar, completely ignoring his club sandwich. I wondered what the filling was.

I made a proper decision that day when I went home.

I will make my own lunchbox. I looked around the house thoroughly for anything that could be a suitable lunchbox. At length, I found a massive tub of *Nivea* cream in the bin in Amma's room. I opened it and found the last remains of the cream smeared around.

Bingo. Amma was sitting in the living room watching an Indian film on the *VCR*. Some of Abba's friends used to lend us current or old Indian and Bengali films. This was an old one and was being watched for the fourth time now. I asked her a few times if I could use the *Nivea* pot and finally she nodded without looking at me. I went to the kitchen and got the stepping stool. I squirted some washing up liquid on the sponge and cleaned the pot and lid, properly. I dried it and took it to Di in our room. She was lying down on her bed, reading one of her teen storybooks while some English music was playing on the stereo.

Holding out my new lunchbox, I told her that she could give me my school lunch in that from now on. Di looked at it and remained silent for a couple seconds before laughing her head off. I didn't care for I quite liked it. Usually I paid one hundred and ten per cent attention when our teacher taught us. But today I couldn't wait till it was break time. I happily opened my backpack and took my new lunchbox out. I opened it and found a fried egg, sunny side up and six carrot sticks. Unfortunately, the yellow gooey liquid from the yoke was smeared all over the carrot sticks.

I tried to pick a carrot stick with my thumb and forefinger. The carrot didn't taste like carrot. I couldn't taste the egg either for my humble meal was redolent with the aromatic *Nivea*.

I argued with Di and even pushed her, in front of her friends. I reproached her for giving me such a ridiculous combination of food for lunch. She took me aside and told me that there was no bread and she had to give me something. Though furious, deep down I knew that it wasn't Di's fault but she was my only punchbag. I hated it too when she didn't retaliate because, after all, she did all the things that Amma was supposed to do.

'Good morning, Ranya dear. Here's your sandwich,' Amma greeted, pointing at a plate. I was finally awake.

'G... good morning... Amma,' I stammered. I didn't know what to say. I thought of not stating the obvious and so complimented the breakfast instead. 'The omelette... is really interesting,' I said with some difficulty as I swallowed the bite I had just taken from the egg sandwich.

When Amma wasn't looking, I quickly peeked to see what was inside the sandwich, besides the egg. There was no butter on either side of the slices of bread. But that didn't bother me. I was just amazed that my mum, who never made her own breakfast, rather ordered others to make hers, had made breakfast for *me* for the first time ever. As I ate, I realised that it wasn't just the lack of butter that caused me the difficulty in swallowing. For there seemed to be an odd lump in my throat causing the friction. All this had delayed me and I gathered that I wouldn't have the time to make myself a packed lunch. Abba sometimes gave me money to buy snacks so I thought that'd do for today but just as I was about to leave Amma called out my name. 'Take your lunch.' Saying that Amma handed out a lunchbox. I took it somewhat dumbfounded. This was getting too weird. She never ever made breakfast for me let alone lunch for school!

At break time, I opened my lunchbox and found a couple of the same sandwiches I'd had in the morning. But I didn't complain nor kiss my teeth, which I would've typically done.

I was overwhelmed and by now the effect of the lump in my throat seemed like tonsillitis. I'd discovered over the years that when I tried very hard not to cry, a lump like this formed in my throat. I didn't eat and simply stared at the sandwiches.

'Erm... are you going to have those sandwiches?' asked Mo. I didn't reply. 'Ranya?'

Mo nudged me this time. I couldn't respond so Mo took a bite off my sandwich.

'Ew! There's no butter in this. How can...' Mo started to complain when he noticed tears running down my cheeks. 'You're not crying because I took your sandwiches, eh?' asked Mo, rather concerned.

I shook my head. 'I'm crying because I had the same thing for breakfast,' I joked.

'I guess I would've cried too if my mum was making things like this for me,' Mo guffawed.

That evening I went to Amma in her room and said, 'Can I ask you something, if you don't mind?' She was sitting up in her bed resting her back on the cushioned headboard.

'Sure, what is it?' she said without looking up. Amma usually wore D-shaped glasses when she read the newspaper.

'I really appreciate what you did for me today but please don't make me breakfast or lunch for school.' I paused a bit here. 'I'm just not used to you doing things like that for me.'

'But why?'

I was worried that Amma would shout at me due to my docile manner, but she didn't. 'Just don't, please.' I turned around and walked away. I didn't want Amma to see me crying. I didn't like anyone seeing me crying. The fourth thing I hated.

Later during the night, I heard Amma and Abba having another heated argument. I could hear Amma uttering the foulest and filthiest words. I quickly shut the door of my room and put the earphones of my walkman on full blast volume. But even that couldn't mask the bangs and crashes next door so I went to the bathroom. I paced about nervously before turning the taps on. Suddenly, the sound of the water aided my distraction. I started to wash my hands. I rubbed a soap bar onto my palms and then scrubbed slowly till my hands were gloved in white. Then I washed my hands clean; then repeated the steps three times. I repeated this in another three sets of three but a sudden loud cry disturbed this pattern midway. I started all over again, hoping that I'd finish without any interruption, but fearing too that I might be unable to do so. Soon it began to feel therapeutic; a tranquil fortress seemed to materialise around me. I was able to filter out all the unwanted noise that was taking place. My sight was affixed at the mirror, but my vision was lost in a world of total blankness.

RANYA

Bhaiyya's existence was intangible and I was now used to Di not being around anymore; in fact, I didn't want Di to be around anymore. Amma constantly compared me to her and so did our relatives.

They would compare and contrast our complexion, beauty, and height and didn't care to be discreet in exchanging these views. Whenever I was at home, I tried to kill time by reading newspapers, books borrowed from friends or the school library, or cleaning the house. After years of procrastination, due to fear and repulsion, I decided to spring-clean our kitchen. It was the weekend but as the time relativity was the span of two weeks, I figured that I could sort out the rather big kitchen just by myself. We didn't have the luxury of maids any more so I couldn't depend on anyone else.

A large dark wood and glass cabinet was on the left side. This was bought the first time we came to Bangladesh. It was the same cabinet whose glass doors were smashed by Abba once when Amma was calling his dead mother an incestuous whore. Amma somehow gleaned money from him and got it mended a week later. It was filled with the tableware and showpieces from the countries my parents visited over the years.

At the bottom, there were three deep drawers full of cutlery, batteries, bulbs, candles, matches and other things, whose purpose were unknown but not considered worthless enough to throw away. First, I cleaned the top part of the cabinet which had four doors on it. For almost three hours, I washed, dried and placed each item neatly before embarking on the drawers. I paused to have a glass of water and gathered the three large cans of insect killing spray that I had asked Abba to buy the day before. The dining table matched the show cabinet and it came with eight chairs. I moved them out of the way when I had to take the drawers out.

Hesitantly, I removed them one by one till a massive black space gaped at me. I sighed a sigh of relief. I couldn't see anything from a standing position so went a bit further back and kneeled down. My head was sideways, almost touching the kitchen floor. I rummaged for the torch in one of the drawers and shone it inside.

A morbid sight expanded before my eyes; the entire back of the show cabinet was infested with cockroach eggs while about two-inch-long, big, flying cockroaches were embossed in a quasi-hexagonal pattern. I gasped silently in case I got attacked. I wrapped a shawl around my head, mouth, and nose for a thick fog of insect killing spray blocked my vision. I had to spray all three cans till they all finished.

Cockroaches flew left, right and centre, filling the room with a cacophony of swatting sounds. The poisonous gas floundered the trajectory of the vermin, resulting in the swarm of pests knocking themselves out. There was a time when a few cockroaches nearly sucked the life out of me when they landed on me. I was in a battlefield with at least a thousand of them. Some landed on my face, on the walls, the table but eventually they all dropped dead. When the fog subsided, I counted each one of them; 243 adult cockroaches, and 567 cockroach eggs.

And I annihilated them all.

There were shelves all around the kitchen wall with pots and pans stacked on them along with years of accumulated dust. One by one, I got them all down. I scrubbed them with lemon and sand once the dishwashing bar of soap ran out. One pot was so big that I had to get inside it to clean its sides. Amma hardly cooked, let alone on a large scale so I had no idea why these were bought in the first place. I checked my fingernails at one point; they were all black to the quick.

Around two o'clock, Amma and Abba called me to eat with them but I said I was too grubby to eat.

By half four I was mopping the kitchen floor for the third time. Not once did Amma come to check on me. I went upstairs, had a shower and decided to dust and tidy the bookcases for the following day. The kitchen looked somewhat renovated. I felt like patting myself on the back.

An audible grumble indicated that I was starving. I opened the lids of the pots and found catfish with red spinach and a chicken curry. The weather was hot and humid, so the curries were still warm. Amma and Abba were on good terms at the moment or else she wouldn't have cooked.

The curries tasted awesome and I ate voraciously. Amma was a very good cook. In fact, I never ate anyone else's biryani other than hers for no one else's biryani looked or tasted as good as hers. Sometimes she would make parathas and *kalo jams* and they would taste heavenly. She always had a rustic style of slapping a bit of this and a bit of that in a mixing bowl before she produced those black dumplings of delight. But these things happened rarely. I sat on the sofa afterwards to watch TV. After two long years, we got a cable line known as "dish antenna line". Until then, I was malnourished of TV nutrients. This satellite cable provided about twenty different channels, mainly Indian ones. We had access to some western channels but all the rude bits were censored before transmission to Kakongonj. Sometimes kissing scenes were shown accidentally. We still had no VCP, VCR or VCD system so I never got to watch any current films. I knew of them, however, through my friends in school. I was glad that we had this line for it was my best friend. I could watch TV all day and all night long. It made me happy and nostalgic for all the right reasons.

Amma and Abba would threaten me at times that they'd stop this line if I carried on like this. That used to bring me back to reality. But when I didn't watch TV, I thought about it. Today Abba and Amma didn't say anything to me. They told me that the kitchen looked very clean so I guessed that I earned some legit TV time. I felt exhausted and almost dozed off when I smelt a strong whiff of a *Chanel* perfume. It was coming from Amma obviously. I looked at her and saw that both she and Abba were ready to go out.

'Where are you two going?'

'We're going to the Pride Club.' Pride Club was for senior doctors and their wives. Abba looked handsome and even taller in his charcoal grey suit and navy tie. Amma looked gorgeous in her coffee-coloured saree, filigreed with golden borders. She was at least five inches shorter than me. Yet she carried herself tall with her vibrant persona while I shrank everyday with humiliation over Amma's comments on my plain looks.

'When will you return?' I didn't care when they returned. I loved to be alone with my best friend, the TV.

'We'll be home by eight or nine.'

It was just over midnight and there was still no sign of my parents. It was still a mobile-free epoch; I didn't know of any landline number that I could call on and neither did they try to call me. There was a power cut from seven p.m. to ten p.m. and the electricity people decided to do their load shedding again at midnight. There was only a small candle left from before and it wasn't long before the light diminished in a pool of melted wax. I had the torch but that too became dim. Unfortunately, the batteries that I arranged in the drawers were all used up ones. I was in utter darkness, in a three-storey house, almost in the middle of nowhere. It was unbelievably hot and clammy. My cotton salwar kameez was stuck to my skin. Sweat dripped down my temples every three minutes or so and I stank. I couldn't wait for the electricity to be back so that I could have another shower. If it wasn't for the humming of the mosquitoes that kept piercing my skin and sucking my blood, I would've thought that I was dead.

I spent most of my childhood days alone; Amma would take me places where she had fun, talking away but where there were no children of my age. At weddings, she wouldn't allow me to play with the other children. I had to sit put next to her on a chair and not complain. Other mothers often remarked at how good my mother was at disciplining us since their children never listened to them. *'Yes, I'm blessed,'* she'd gloat. All she had to do was give me her signature deathly look

– tighten her lips and widen her eyes so much that her pupils wouldn't touch both her waterlines. That look was enough to congeal the running blood in my body.

To kill time, I began to escape into an imaginary world where things went on how I wanted them to be. I always translated the settings, characters and themes from the soaps I watched on TV or the books I read into my imagination. Time was fluid when I did that. It was a sort of self-hypnosis technique.

Amma never got along with the neighbours so no one ever checked on us. But I was glad that no one checked on us. Who knew? Maybe while checking on us they'd notice my plain looks and leave an insensitive comment.

The electricity came back about twenty minutes before my parents did. I quickly showered then in case the current went again. I was downstairs when I heard them talking in the porch. They came into the living room and were still talking about the fun they had.

'You looked rather beautiful today. You looked as though you were still eighteen,' Abba complimented.

'Aww, thank you,' Amma blushed. 'You know what, you didn't look too bad yourself either. You looked as if you were still in your mid-twenties,' Amma complimented back.

They must've realised my presence all of a sudden for they became really quiet. My back was facing them as I watched TV.

'Erm... you're rather quiet, Ranya,' Abba said.

I sighed. 'Oh well, you're in your mid-twenties and Amma isn't twenty yet; in that case, I haven't been born yet to say anything.'

They laughed heartily at this. They didn't ask me how I was, nor explain their delay, and I too remained nonchalant. Being *salt and pepper* taught me to hide feelings that were unfathomable by others.

RANYA

The inevitable domestic feuds took place eventually, all right; but this time between Amma and me. Even though I was sixteen, it was still *she* who decided what I wore. I wouldn't have objected, but to be dressed like a twelve-year-old, all in the effort to make my mum appear younger, simply infuriated me. I wondered if she had the faculty to think of anyone else other than herself. 'I can't believe that you spent all the money that Abba gave for the two of us, almost entirely on yourself.'

Amma heard but ignored me. She usually did that to think of something plausible to answer anyone. Abba was at work. Amma's bad and fickle mien prevented even the temporary maids from working for us. Amma constantly suspected them of flirting with Abba, which bothered me. Because first of all she shouldn't be suspecting Abba. And secondly, *I'd* have to do most of the household work if the maids refused to come. As I got older, I often had to cook too, after school.

It seemed like Amma was going out somewhere. Normally she put her blouse and petticoat on while she did her makeup and hair, and she only ever did that when she went out. At home, she usually wore a maxi with no makeup on. In fact, the two looks were so stark in difference that once when she opened the door to some workers, they assumed her to be the maid. Later when she dressed up, they asked her where the maid was as they needed some water.

'You always think about yourself. Whether it's food, clothes, my grades – everything. Everything has to have an impact on *your* image. Here you are showing off to me eight expensive sarees you got for yourself when you told me that Abba gave just about enough money to buy only two outfits – one for each of us.' I couldn't hide the reproach, even though a voice in my head was warning me about the outcome of such defiance.

'That's true; I bought the other seven outfits with my money.' Amma continued to apply her makeup.

'You don't earn that much to afford such luxury,' I said under my breath.

'What did you say?' Amma had stopped brushing her hair by now and looked at my reflection on the mirror. I was silent and a chill ran down my spine. I knew I was in trouble now. *Big trouble.* My insides were churning and sinking at the same time. Amma was facing me now, asked me the same question, and I repeated my assertion. No sooner had I finished the sentence than I felt a massive blow to my face, which sent me flying onto the floor. Amma disappeared for a few seconds and this in no way was a good sign. I could suddenly hear the TV getting louder. It quickly dawned on me as to what would follow now. A part of me felt like standing up for myself. Another part was in contradiction since it was my mother. Amma came back with an iron rod with which she began to hit me on my elbows and knees for what seemed to be forever.

I screamed and pleaded, 'Amma, please, please, don't hit me, I'm so sorry. I'll never say that again.' But she showed no sign to stop or forgive. At one point, she threatened to hit my face. I never saw Satan but if someone told me to describe him then after that day I'd describe the demon I saw in Amma. She ordered me to remain silent, while still hitting me at almost every joint. She also had a habit of pulling my ear all the time, especially the left one. Recently I noticed that the flap of my left ear stood out a bit.

Fear engulfed me so much that I disconnected my body from my mind. I obeyed her by taking every single hit in utter silence. I wasn't thinking anything anymore and so I couldn't feel anything anymore too. Hitting me and hitting a vegetable was the same now – for neither of us showed pain.

At this point, I felt really sorry for myself. So, tears streaked down my mottled face out of self-pity. I guess it was the same mind that got detached and became another person within me.

Amma dropped the rod and shook me by my arms. My eyes had an empty look in them like I had become a cabbage. A while later the door slammed shut and so did my eyes.

***

Dripping sweat woke me up from my slumber. There was a power cut so the fan stopped rotating above the ceiling. It took me sometime to recall the last event. I tried to hear if Amma was back and she was as the TV sound indicated the dramas she watched. I went to the bathroom and had a quick shower. My body ached a lot but I tried to ignore the cuts and bruises. I went downstairs and checked the time.

Abba should be back from work any time soon so I went to the kitchen only to find that nothing had been cooked. I put the rice on and quickly made an omelette with onions, coriander, and green chilies.

Abba will be happy to see that at least I prepared some food for him. 'An omelette. Is that it?'

'There wasn't much time so an omelette was the quickest thing I could make.'

'You could've made an egg curry instead.'

I looked at Abba but he was too busy eating.

I didn't say anything and neither could I eat any more. I got up and opened the cabinet where all the utensils were kept. I found a paring knife that looked sharp enough to cut easily. Abba didn't seem to notice that I had left the kitchen. I didn't try to hide the knife. Amma saw me walking upstairs and asked me what I was doing with the knife but I blanked her. A couple of minutes later I saw Amma standing in front of me so I smiled at her to which she screeched. Terrified, she fled from my room like the devil would've, had it been shown the cross or something. She kept shouting for Abba. 'Where are you? Come here at once. Ranya has slashed her arm. She's bleeding a lot!'

This all followed a commotion and a blame game, which I laughed at like a psycho. This petrified them even more. I lived and, why wouldn't I? I had no intention to kill myself. No one was informed of this lest relatives presumed that I was having a love affair and that either due to pregnancy or my parents' discovery of the affair, I had decided to end my life.

Suicide often traversed my vulnerable mind but the thought was a lot weaker than me. I just made a sundry of shallow cuts above my elbow and then sucked the blood to spit it out in the sink. I had read a homeopathic journal recently that mentioned about cupping being a Chinese remedy. The place where I applied the technique was known to release endorphins, which in turn produced a feeling of euphoria. In retrospect, this event turned out to be in my favour, because for long periods of time, Amma and Abba treated me just like a daughter.

RANYA

The day started off normally. The birds were chirping. Monsoon clouds gathered after months of scorching heat, and Amma and Abba had an immense fight; only this time Abba did what he did about six or seven years ago – he deserted us. He was furtive both of the times too. We were in Hayapur when he did this the first time. He was away for three months. Amma must've been stressed out at my never-ending query of where Abba was and when he was coming back. So, one day she had enough, slapped me and said, 'Your Abba's dead.'

I was too naïve to realise that she said it out of exasperation. This was also before I acknowledged that Amma's words always required verification. I was too mournful to repeat this "fact" to Di, Lulubu, or Samia. I just assumed that they knew too and were coping in their own ways. It seemed like they were doing better than me.

Two days later, I developed a high temperature so Amma spoke to the landlord who knew of a doctor. The doctor came and diagnosed me with chicken pox and prescribed massive pellets of painkillers and antihistamines. I almost choked once. Lulubu used to crush them in warm orange juice for me, which was a bitter-sweet gesture. While Lulubu washed my head to lower my temperature, Amma prattled to the landlady about her marital problems. I was devastated; Abba was dead, how could she talk like that still? Lulubu consoled me by saying that Abba would be back very soon. I shouted at her when she said that. I blamed her for soothing me with lies. She just looked down and stayed quiet.

'He's not coming back, ever,' I sobbed.

'No, he will.'

I told her to buzz off and she did. I was getting better but then the following week, around one a.m. in the morning I woke Di up. I had no idea what I said. Lulubu later on told me that I had collapsed as my temperature had risen. Di looked after me the whole night and, though she wasn't the type who prayed, she did so that dawn. She was shaking as she cried in her prostration, for my good health. She didn't sleep at all and yet had to go to school. She had an exam too which she couldn't do well at.

Then one glorious day, Abba came back, unannounced. He told us that he had gone India and Egypt to buy medical equipment, which wasn't available in Bangladesh. He didn't bring us any presents, though, but I was springing with happiness that he was back.

This time he deserted only Amma and me. It was a couple of years after Di got married. One day, at dawn, Amma kept telling me to check what Abba was doing. He was up earlier than usual and was at his surgery next door but I was too sleepy. It was the weekend and I didn't want to wake up for some dumb reason. Amma had been suspicious for some time that Abba was up to something and, unluckily for me, her hunch proved true. I woke up around eleven a.m. and noticed a thick envelope on the floor in front of the main door. It wasn't sealed, so I opened it. It was from Abba. It was a very long letter and I could sense what it signified – Abba's second, successful abscondence. I was scared about what awaited me now. I woke up Amma and since then she had hit me and blamed me at regular intervals, until Abba came back, four months later.

With Amma against me like this, I couldn't even muster up the courage to tell her that a particular young male teacher at school had been perving on me for some time. I was terrified. He was tall and fairly good-looking, and all the female teachers used to flirt with him. So, I found it very strange as to why *I* was of any interest to him; I even had braces. Some of my friends approached me one day and told me that that teacher told them that I had something which they didn't have. One of the girls whispered to me that he was talking about my boobs and then all the girls giggled.

Then one day, he stalked me when I was returning home from school. I wished Abba was here so I could've confided in him. I had to do the something as things were going too far. I told Amma, hoping she'd give at least a morsel of support, if any at all. When I finished telling everything, she stared at me in disbelief.

'That teacher is my friend's son and he's very good-looking.' Then looking me up and down, she said, 'What on earth would *he* see in *you?* It'd make more sense had you said that he was interested in *me.'* She laughed. 'You're such a Plain-Jane! You're definitely mistaken. Actually no. You're getting overconfident with your simple looks.'

I had nothing to say. I never saw Amma come across more contemptuous and haughty, than that day. The temerity with which she spoke and scoffed, put me in an invidious position both towards her and myself; I should've known that a snake would never protect me.

Abba returned the following month. This time he called and informed us the day and time he would arrive; Amma was super excited but I was indifferent. He could've flown in with a cape on and an underwear on top of his clothes for all I cared.

As we sat around the dining table, he showed me the new watch he bought. As usual, he didn't get anything for us but it didn't matter since I was inured to my parents' egotism. After dinner, I casually asked him to transfer me to a different school.

'I thought you didn't like changing schools,' Abba said.

'Yeah, but I just don't think the school I'm going to is good enough, academically.' The latter worked like a charm and, within a couple of weeks, my wish was granted. I was truthful about what I said; however, the new school I was going to now had just inaugurated their first batch preparing for their O Levels. They were hiring novices and everyone doubted the school's prosperity. But I had no choice; I just couldn't stand that perv of a teacher.

I spent six months in that school. I was over sixteen but appeared like a twelve-year-old. The girls in my class were much taller than me and I felt like a midget amongst them. I had lost all the vigour and studiousness I used to possess before. I just didn't feel like studying as my unblessed looks kept getting in the way. I wanted to get out of here – not just the school but the entire country. I needed a break; a change in scenery would definitely motivate me. With this in mind for a whole two weeks, I approached Amma and Abba one afternoon, in a sycophantic manner with tea and noodles, to put forward a proposition about my future.

I asked them if it'd be possible for me to go London and stay with Bhaiyya to pursue further education.

'You two want me to study medicine, right?' They nodded. 'I can't see how that'll be possible here. Even Di says that it'll be impossible to achieve good results in Kakongonj. And she knows what she's saying as she's a senior teacher in one of the best English medium schools in Hayapur.' A voice in me said that they'd come around to agree with me more for they accepted Bhaiyya's and Di's unconventional life decisions whereas I was making a more acceptable one.

Amma and Abba were quiet for a long time. I was getting excited for I felt that they agreed with my points. They said that they'd have to think about it.

A week or so later, Amma announced that they had thought about what I had said and they too felt that I should go abroad. In the meantime, they had spoken to Bhaiyya and apparently he agreed for me to stay with him and his family in London for my O Levels. I was bubbling with joy but didn't want to express it. Abba began to sort out my passport as it hadn't been renewed since I was eight. For some reason, Amma and Abba had to go India to renew it although there was a British Embassy in Bangladesh.

They had to be away for ten days so I was sent over to Di's place in Hayapur.

Di seemed happy but her smile lacked vivacity. Jahid Bhai in a lot of ways reminded me of Bhaiyya, especially the times he pestered me. Their daughter, Neha, was almost two now. I looked at Di while she put her to sleep, and noticed, in awe, that she was indeed drop-dead gorgeous. I acknowledged then that Amma had been right all along about my looks; I was nothing compared to Di.

Often before Eid, Amma would gather some of her old sarees and give them to the tailor to transform them into salwar kameez (we weren't always privileged to have new clothes). Then she'd give them to Di. I used to loiter around in the hope that she'd give me one too. I wasn't scared to ask but rather scared of the answer I'd receive: *"You don't need any salwar kameez. In a few years, they'll fit you anyway."* The coarseness of reality taught me to contain my curiosity.

We went back to Kakongonj a couple of days after my parents came back. Abba said that I should leave as soon as possible. I was elated. Things were going so smoothly that it was scaring me again. I turned the TV on and there was a breaking news about the dengue fever. It was reported that this strain was lethal and had reached epidemic proportions. This didn't frighten me for I had a very strong immune system; there was probably ninety-nine-point nine percent chance that I would *not* be affected by the infection. I asked Abba how soon we'd leave for London. He said the travel agents would let him know in three days' time.

'Ouch!' I screamed. An impregnated mosquito scattered blood on my arm when I swatted it.

***

It started off with a mild temperature and by the end of the week I was bedridden. I had all the symptoms of the lethal dengue fever disease. I was still in the primary stage and a part of me wished that I'd be able to conquer this turn in fate.

But fatigue was engulfing me and, as usual, Amma left the house for some respite. I begged Abba to admit me to the clinic but he stressed that the clinics all over the country were full with patients and that sanitary levels were not meeting the usual standards. I was therefore better off at home as he arranged for all the medications and emergency precautions.

'I'll look after you, don't worry. I will not desert you like your Amma in your time of need,' Abba assured me. 'I looked after your Di too once when she was ill and bedridden like you are now.'

RANYA

I prayed like crazy even though I was ill. I wanted to get better and leave the country and be far away from my parents. I felt treacherous for I was using them for this mission, but both Bhaiyya and Di had sorted their lives out and it was high time that I did something about my life too. But marriage wasn't the route I was taking like my siblings did.

I was in better health now but Abba and Amma were upset about something. Abba said that he felt that Bhaiyya was not keen on me staying with him. He had a family to look after so money would be an issue. Abba told him that he'd be giving money for me so he needn't worry about that but then one day he called and spoke to Amma expressing his concern.

'I'm scared that Abba will stop giving money at some point like he did with me.'

'Is it your or your wife's concern?' Amma said.

They belaboured this topic for over two hours. Abba called Bhaiyya later in the evening and they further bickered about the past till Abba stated that I wouldn't be staying with Bhaiyya. Amma told me later that I wouldn't be going London after all.

At this point, I realised that I was running towards a mirage the whole time. But what was more harrowing, was that I had already told my friends at school that I wouldn't be coming back after the holidays as I'd be in London by then. So, for them to see me again would be mortifying. For days, no one spoke about this matter and I was getting anxious. Amma and Abba pretended that nothing was wrong. One evening, at the end of the week, I went to Abba's room. I sat next to him on the bed, and just cried. After some time, I left.

A couple of days later, Amma told me that Abba had spoken to Fupu and Fupa about the argument with Bhaiyya and they had suggested that we all came to their place as they'd sort out something, eventually. The strings of my hope got elevated again but I pulled them down. *Finally, I'm going to be free. No more hitting and having a daily helping of foul language.*

It felt more believable this time as Amma was taking me around to our relatives' houses to bid farewell. I was still dubious about my departure since anything was possible, like tickets being cancelled even in the last minute.

As I sat on the plane, I still couldn't believe how I had managed to get past all the hurdles that kept coming my way. At Zia airport, we bumped into some of Amma's relatives, a man and two of his sisters. All three looked much younger than Amma and their appearance seemed over the top for a twelve-hour long journey. The ladies were very friendly and were drawn into Amma's posh ambience.

They were flying back to London after a holiday. We had a transit flight to Hayapur from Kakongonj and the flight to London wasn't a direct flight either; we'd have to stop at Dubai at some point.

On that plane, Amma ordered me to swap seats with one of the sisters so that she could sit with Amma and her other sister in the middle aisle. I didn't mind that but what followed for the next twelve hours or so made me recoil in extreme shame. in her mid-forties, Amma was behaving like a teenybopper. From the very start she began to bully and pull pranks on the stewardesses. She kept calling them names like *whores, sluts, slappers, and tarts* in the *Sylhety* dialect and that sounded highly uncivilized and audible. The stewardesses kept giving her dirty looks so Amma returned those back with even dirtier ones.

At one point, I made eye contact with the sisters who looked very uncomfortable. I acknowledged their predicament by rolling my eyes and sighing. When we stopped at Dubai for an hour, the sisters rushed out and Amma got up too, to join them. Politely, they suggested that I went with them instead as I might have felt left out. Amma protested that I was a bookworm and that I'd need to look after the hand luggage anyway. They looked at me showing feelings that suggested sympathy and helplessness. I rolled my eyes and carried on reading my book, feeling sorry for the sisters. I peeked around after they left. Abba had been sitting away from us with the brother of the sisters. I couldn't see them and assumed that they went out in the airport too. I wished I could've gone but tried to feel glad about being released from my eccentric parents in the long run.

I resumed listening to the track *Show Me the Meaning of Being Lonely* by the *BSB* on my half-broken walkman. Di and Jahid Bhai had given it to me as a farewell gift. One day, I didn't respond to Amma when she called me as I was listening to some Indian songs on full volume. Amma came into my room, walloped the walkman on the concrete floor, and slapped me on both of my ears. She slapped so hard that I couldn't hear properly for a few days.

'Excuse me, are you that lady's daughter?' I turned around and saw that the man sitting behind me had asked that question. By that lady, he meant Amma.

'Erm, yes.'

He introduced himself as a distant relative from Amma's side. He seemed like a man in his late thirties. He kept reiterating that he had heard of *my* mother's mouthiness but he didn't think it was as bad as to what he witnessed on this plane. The more he backbit, the more I felt insulted. He kept asking if Amma had seen a shrink or not for she appeared to have become a lunatic. I wanted to protest but I couldn't find even a passable morsel of goodness to defend her with. With nothing better to defend myself with, I said, 'And yet there's a fine line between people like you and people like my mother.'

'I don't know what you mean,' he said. 'Of course, it's your mum after all. I... I didn't mean to turn you against your mother or anything.'

'I think my mum's back,' I said. I didn't hear from the man again.

***

We landed early in the morning at Heathrow airport. Abba went to collect our suitcases while we sat on one of the benches. When the time was right, I told Amma off for her misconduct on the plane. She glowered at me but I carried on ranting. Then her eyes welled up and she turned her face away from me. At first, I felt good for I felt my words had an effect on her but then guilt overtook me.

I heard a familiar voice and turned around. Fupa was walking towards us and Bhaiyya followed him closely. I was seeing Bhaiyya after a good few years. Resentment soon masked the happiness I felt to see him.

Abba came with the luggage and Bhaiyya went to hug him. Abba looked reluctant to hug him back and he didn't ask Bhaiyya how he was after Bhaiyya inquired about his well-being. As Abba gave Fupa the suitcases, he said to Bhaiyya, 'You shouldn't have bothered to come.'

Abba sounded formidable.

We all went to Fupu's place. It was a spacious, three-bedroom council flat. They had three children and Fupu was expecting her fourth. Abba and Amma sat in the living room and looked stony the whole time. Bhaiyya tried to speak to them but they refused to respond. Fupa liaised, coaxed, and even chastised Bhaiyya for being impudent towards his parents. His misdemeanours were listed in front of everyone, while all of Fupu's three sons aged ten, nine, and eight, took turns to record the whole scene on their new camcorder. They didn't realise the magnitude of the action with regards to the solemnity of the situation and their parents didn't seem to notice either. Fupu served us with all kinds of food while all this happened. The grave atmosphere was reduced to a humourless farce.

The following day Bhaiyya came around again, this time with Bibha and their daughter, Amanah, and son, Zain. Eventually it was decided that I'd be staying with him. I wasn't sure how I felt. I missed Bhaiyya dearly but he seemed a bit aloof. Bibha just seemed like a very nice person who had been mistreated by my mum. I vowed that I'd make up for that by being at her beck and call for everything when I was living at their place. Any place away from my parents would be a blissful haven. After all, Bibha was doing me a great favour by allowing me to stay at her place when she had been kicked out of my parents' house.

RANYA

There comes a time in your life when you realise that things were not how they had seemed. And such a thing happened the day my parents left. Amma was crying saying that she'd miss me. I hugged her but it wasn't out of love. It felt as necessary as a prescribed medicine. I felt sad too but this was the moment I had been praying for. I had finally broken free from my dysfunctional family.

On the way back from the airport, Bhaiyya decided to get takeaway from Kebabish. The days were much shorter now so it was already dark outside. Amanah wanted to sit at the front so Bibha moved back. I was seated between her and Zain. As we waited, we struck up a conversation about miscellaneous stuff: from food to fashion, from celebrities to ordinary people including ourselves.

'I'm glad I don't have sideburns like you.' Bibha laughed.

'I'm glad I don't have a moustache like you,' I guffawed.

'I'm not hairy. My skin is a bit sensitive that's why…'

'You shouldn't've taken it off in the first place.' Had I known Bibha better, I would've never spoken like this for besides sensitiveness, her skin also wasn't thick. 'Some things should just be left alone and not be meddled with,' I finished.

'Yeah, like your nose.' Having said that she grabbed my nose between her thumb and forefinger and squeezed it worse than a pimple. And she wouldn't let go. I yelled and, even then, she didn't stop. Eventually she did. I had tears running down my eyes already. Not the crying type. The type you get when an extremely cold gust of wind blows into your face. 'Bibha, what did you do that for?' I said.

'Aw c'mon, Ranya. Who's being a spoilsport now? Surely you know that we were both joking with one another. Come here, you.' She grabbed me again but this time she gave me a bearhug. I was still in excruciating pain.

Bhaiyya came back and for some reason Bibha sounded very cheery, almost a tad bit flippant. We arrived home and soon after we all gathered around the table to eat.

'I'll just go wash my hands,' I said. Bhaiyya was too busy eating and Bibha was dishing out the food to her children.

As I washed my hands I tried to calculate the whole incident in my head. I knew the gesture was malicious. If she admitted it then it meant that I couldn't live in her flat where Bhaiyya was staying. We both were at her disposal. And if I told my parents, then this would mean only one thing – that I went back to my dysfunctional parents. At length, I decided that there was no point creating a hoo-ha about such a petty issue. Some things should just be overlooked. Perhaps she was just being funny like she said.

I glanced at the mirror as I shook excess water from my hands in the sink. And this made me take a double look. The tip of my nose had a stark reddish-purple mark. It was a bruise.

RANYA

Di was like a mum to me all right, but she wasn't quite a friend. We had a subtle communication gap, which was bridged by Bhaiyya, both Di's and my elder brother. He was my first babysitter and I knew this since he had told me so himself. When we were in London, (I was the only one who was born there) Amma and Abba used to sometimes leave me with Bhaiyya. I was nearly two, Bhaiyya was almost fourteen, and Di was just over nine. It was quite risky and worrying since our parents were quite immature and reckless back then. Often, they would end up drinking in the parties, argue like mad, and then drive back.

Whenever my parents spoke loudly, Bhaiyya would assure me that they were only shouting in a whisper. He had the answers to all my questions. All of them. He never got irritated. No matter how many questions I asked, how stupid the questions were or how often I repeated them, and no matter what time of the day or night it was. Bhaiyya would always respond back amiably.

There was, however, one thing that I didn't like about him. And that was his perpetual attempts to convince me that I was a boy. He was desperate to have a little brother and I was the next best thing he had to make do with. And because of my resemblance to him more than Di (who was very pretty even at a young age) and the boyish hairstyle Amma forced me to

169

wear, people often mistook me for a boy. It was a salient humiliation that followed me like a shadow for a long time.

But apart from that, I loved my Bhaiyya. He used to adulate me for almost everything while annoy Di for nothing. Di fancied a friend's brother, which Bhaiyya got to know about somehow. Since that insight, he pestered her relentlessly, about her weight. Sometimes their brawls used to end up with Bhaiyya slapping Di. This used to amplify the intensity of their squabble. So, one day Amma had experienced enough. She opened the front door and told Bhaiyya to get out. And he did. I was aghast. In fact, I was certain that I noticed an imperceptible look of shock in Amma at Bhaiyya's sudden, obsequious attitude. Half an hour or so later, Amma began to look for him. At first, she was enraged that he left. But then she was overcome with anxiety. Di and I searched for him everywhere and we also rang everyone's doorbell in the apartment, to enquire about him.

On an impulse, I made a quick trip home to get a few things. I had a gut feeling that Bhaiyya was hiding in one of those colossal, silver-coloured metal boxes that were on the roof. Although they were filled with builders' detritus, like sand and gravel, it was his and my secret sanctuary. I climbed up the ladder and peered inside. Bhaiyya was crouched in one of the corners. He gave an unsure smile when he saw me. He helped me to get inside and once we sat down, I proffered a couple of slices of fruit loaf, two slivers of cheese in a plastic film, and a strawberry milk carton from under my jumper. The jumper was too big for me and a hand-me-down from Bhaiyya. He thanked me as he ate. I told him how Amma was worried to which he chuckled.

Then, upon noticing my subtle quietness he asked, 'Wassup?'

I let out a long sigh. 'I feel left out all the time. Di doesn't play with me. I want to play with girls, not with boys. She says I'm too young and blah, blah, blah.' I wiped a tear.

'Who wants to play and chat rubbish with that silly girl, anyway? Bhaiyya said. 'You are my very important little broth... I mean, friend. And did you know that my friends and I will be going to a safari park where we'll see lots of amazing animals?'

I shook my head.

'Stupid girls like Megha are not allowed. But you can come with me,' Bhaiyya said as he tousled my hair. Whenever he did that, it assured me further to believe whatever he was saying. I was thrilled for the entire week. And sure enough, I did go. But to my chagrin, I was disguised and introduced as a little boy throughout the trip.

I was very cross with Bhaiyya. He tried every possible way to mollify me. He even tried to propitiate me by letting me play with his Gameboy, the gadget which neither Di nor I was allowed to touch.

But I didn't budge. Then one evening, Amma and Abba discussed something of great importance with all of us at the dinner table. Well, not exactly me. I was salt and pepper.

'We will be going to Switzerland, London, and Paris this summer holiday,' Amma said. We were all excited. Di and I screamed out of joy.

'We will be leaving Yasin in London with your Fupu's family.' Fupu was Abba's sister. I couldn't remember ever seeing her before. 'We want him to study medicine and

London is the best place to study.' Then pointing at Bhaiyya and Di, Amma continued, 'Besides, you two are always squabbling and it'll be better for you to have some distance between each other. I'll get some peace of mind too.'

'Why can't I go instead?' Di said.

'You're too young. And Yasin is our only boy so he should be the doctor.' I was shocked at this morsel of news. I was too *salt and pepper* to react to the sexist part of the remark. What concerned me instead was, *who'd play with me if Bhaiyya left? Who'd I commune with when my head would pop with asinine queries? And who'd feed me, for God's sake?*

I wasn't angry with Bhaiyya any more. Usually I sat next to him but for the past few days I didn't. I sat opposite to him. I looked at Bhaiyya expecting him to reciprocate the same concerns. But I was dismayed not to hear or see those same worries reflected back. Effulgence filled his adolescent looks so much as so that had there been a power cut, his visage alone could've lit the whole dining room. He was euphoric.

'Ranya, remember how you used to get angry every time I used to tell you that you were a boy and dress you up as my brother?' Bhaiyya asked. I nodded. 'Well, consider that insufferable phase to be gone forever.'

For the first time, I wanted to take that phase back. I was upset with Bhaiyya. I was very upset about this entire decision. But as I was *salt and pepper*, I wouldn't understand anything properly, my opinions wouldn't be heard, let alone matter.

Things followed very quickly thereafter, and once we travelled, I felt better; till the day we had to leave Bhaiyya in Fupu's house. Bhaiyya was smiling from ear to ear. He didn't cry nor show the least bit of emotion to see us leave. Perhaps that was his way of coping with the despondency I was feeling.

For days, I didn't eat properly. Amma didn't have the patience to deal with me so Di did most of the things for me.

A year later, Abba and Amma told us that Bhaiyya would be visiting us in the summer. We had moved to a new house now so we got busy fixing a room for him. I was sprinting with joy. *My* Bhaiyya was coming back.

After four days, Abba returned with Bhaiyya because first he had to go Belgium to sort out Bhaiyya's visa for the following year.

Bhaiyya looked like the same loving brother I knew, only taller. I hugged him and didn't want to let go. I told him all about my school and the trophies I won for sports. He told me to get them to show him and afterwards, I went to put the trophies back on the desk in Di's room. We shared the study corner and the wardrobe in there but I always slept next to Amma in her room. I had to go past the kitchen and the guest room (which was actually Abba's bedroom) to go to Di's room, when I heard a brief conversation between my parents.

'Why don't you just sort out his passport for good? It's ridiculous to go Belgium every ten months to renew his visa,' Amma said.

'I'm going through this extra mile for everyone's good. If I get him a British passport, then chances are that he won't come back. I know my son.' Abba was sitting in one of the chairs at the dining table while Amma was washing some dishes in the sink. She clattered the utensils out of frustration. Abba shifted his position each time a plate or saucer clanked. As he dipped a biscuit in his tea, he carried on, 'And this way, he will have no choice but to return once he finishes his studies.'

I went to see Bhaiyya after this and found him somewhat eavesdropping on our parents' conversation. After lunch, we spent some time looking at the gifts Bhaiyya brought back for us. For Amma he got a crystal vase and for Abba, a woollen scarf.

He gave Di a book on art and for me he got beads and strings in a colourful box. He even spent time making a few bracelets with me.

I was at peace. I went around the neighbourhood the following few days boasting to all my friends about having my big brother back.

'And should any of you bully me, then he'll sort you out,' I bragged.

He was, after all, an expert in Taekwondo.

At dinner time, Abba seemed agitated. He wasn't happy with Bhaiyya's progress at school. He rebuked him saying that Bhaiyya's teacher, a revert white brother called Ahmed, informed him that the only thing Bhaiyya was keen on was Taekwondo.

Amma got very mad at Abba. She accosted him for harassing Bhaiyya in front of everyone especially since he was around for only six weeks. Abba remained silent and clenched his jaws.

We all ate in silence, and I couldn't eat to my fill as the atmosphere was saturated with tension. Bhaiyya, Di, and Amma spent almost the whole night talking. I was with them too, but as *salt and pepper*. We had been doing that almost every night. Bhaiyya shared stories of the hard time he was having at Fupu's place.

'Fupu is potty-training her son and for some reason he keeps having his accidents in my room. The first few times Fupu cleaned up. But afterwards she would tell me to clean it up. Why does she tell me to do it?' Bhaiyya said. Amma went ballistic when she heard this. She said that she'd make a phone call to Fupu for this outrageous behaviour.

A couple of days later Abba and Amma had a fight over this phone call. Amma swore at Abba since she couldn't carry on doing that over the phone with Fupu.

'How dare your sister mistreat *my* son like this? Who the hell is she to treat *my* son as her servant? You were accusing my son for not progressing enough in his studies, right? Well, now you have the reason. His precious time has been wasted on scrubbing faeces and urine off the carpets in their house.'

Abba reiterated what Fupu said, that it was just that one time since Fupu, pregnant for the third time, was busy cooking and looking after her second, two-month-old son who had a high temperature. But Amma didn't buy that. Amma spoke over the phone to her sister who also lived in London and asked her to let Bhaiyya stay at her place once he went back. Her sister agreed at once.

Everything was going okay again. Bhaiyya was back to feeding me the way he used to before as I wouldn't eat unless he was around. I even slept in a sleeping bag on the floor in his room. I followed him everywhere like a puppy. One night he was out with his old friends to a birthday party. He was dropped off by his friend's dad at ten o'clock. I quickly went to Bhaiyya and told him that I hadn't eaten as I was waiting for him to feed me.

He didn't even get changed; he washed his hands and got a plate out for me with some food on it. The uncle who dropped him off was amazed to see that at seventeen and as a brother, Bhaiyya was so sensitive and kind towards his five-year-old sister. Bhaiyya used to feed me just the way he used to eat himself. He would put lots of *jhol*, curry sauce, in the rice when he fed me. Years later I noticed that he didn't eat like that any more. But I still did.

The last month of Bhaiyya's stay was detrimental to him and to all of us too. Amma began to play mind games. She would use Bhaiyya as a pawn to stir things up. I sensed it but couldn't put it into words then. It was a *salt and pepper* thing, I guess. Bhaiyya couldn't figure it out though. Amma would speak against Abba to him. True facts. But facts she could've chosen not to tell. This in turn vexed Bhaiyya and he began to loath Abba. The Bhaiyya who used to stand before his father with acquiescence started to talk back to him, refuse his orders, and scoff at his back.

Then came one dark night; the night the earth stood still. *My* earth stood still. Amma and Abba had been giving the cold shoulder to one another for the past week. Amma cooked just enough food for her children so Abba would often come home and make himself a sandwich. One evening, a couple of Abba's friends came and rang the doorbell. Di was in her room reading a book and listening to music quietly. Bhaiyya and I were in his room and so was Amma, who was crying and mumbling about problems she'd had in the past with Abba.

Bhaiyya was sitting on an armchair opposite to his single bed, fuming. His hands were in fists. I was sitting on the floor at the headboard end of the bed, playing with the beads. No one could actually see me there.

We heard Abba ordering Bhaiyya from the living room to answer the door. Amma was sitting right next to Bhaiyya on a footstool. 'Don't bother. Let him answer it,' she whispered.

Bhaiyya kissed his teeth before saying, 'I can't. I'm busy.' How I wished that Bhaiyya hadn't said that for sometimes one could stop an imminent war from taking place by simply keeping their mouth shut.

I remembered some time back when Abba had bought me a baby blue bouncy ball. Even after I came home I didn't let go of it. I loved it so much. I asked Di to give me a pen and with that pen I stippled my name all over the ball. This infuriated Di for some reason. She was in the middle of a geometry homework when she got up and chastised me for ruining the new toy like this.

She was still holding her compass and with that she pointed on the ball saying, 'Go on, write it here too, like an idiot. And here, and here, and…'

whoooossshhh.

I looked at her with big eyes. This followed an anguished cry. I knew it was unintentional but I couldn't help it. My parents hardly ever bought me toys. So, this ball had been too precious to lose at once.

Di apologised straightaway. 'I didn't mean to puncture it Ranya. It… it was an accident, I swear.'

Amma came in the room and knew what had happened. She dragged Di by her ponytail all the way to the bathroom. Di's hair was her prized possession and she used to spend hours on it: oiling, shampooing, detangling, and brushing it. There used to be a look in Amma's eyes that told me that she was envious of that thick, dark brown cascade of flowing hair. I was scared that she'd punish Di more than she deserved. I heard Di begging a heart-wrenching 'Nooo!'

I ran to the bathroom but it was too late. Amma had already got the shears and chopped Di's waist-length hair up to her ears. Just like that.

By dawn, Di's profuse crying had ebbed to sobs and, in the morning, I found strands of her hair everywhere. I found her sitting on her bed with her back facing me. She didn't brush her hair nor speak to anyone for days. Her ponytail looked puny and embarrassingly uneven. How I had wished that I could turn back time and stop myself from crying out.

Now there was a choking silence for some time. Like the calm before a storm, it was a sign that an incipient anger was spuming in Abba. I saw a cheeky smile on Amma's face. She was rejoicing for she knew that Bhaiyya was on her side. We heard a little murmur and assumed that it was Abba opening the door.

Shortly, we heard quick footsteps. My heart skipped a beat when I heard his voice; Abba entered the room we were in and questioned Bhaiyya at once. Like a despot, he was incisive and demanded to know what important work Bhaiyya had been doing that made him disobey his father. I could tell from Abba's tone that he was feral enough to tear the flesh out of a living being. I wished that I was in Di's room but it was too late now so I hid under the bed. Amma intervened and at this point I heard a ferocious slap, like the kind where you find the perfect time to find a housefly on a window and swat it dead.

Amma screamed and Di came running. Abba ordered her to take Amma away to which Di was obedient. Abba went to the door, locked it, and without further ado he began to scourge the life out of Bhaiyya. I had seen Abba mad before but this was an implacable wrath. Bhaiyya was flung from one side of the room to another. He was whacked, punched, and hit; it was no less than an exorcism. Abba swore to purge the rebel out of him. It seemed to last forever. Abba stopped after some time before spitting and leaving the room. A bit later, we heard a loud slam of the front door. The jangling of keys confirmed his departure so Amma and Di ran into the room.

Amma wailed, 'My Yasin, my Yasin.'

Through sobs Di said, *'You* are responsible for all this Amma. *You've* been instigating Bhaiyya's actions against Abba. You know he's hot-tempered and loves you a lot and you took advantage of that.' This made Amma turn vicious towards her but Di was so furious that she couldn't care less. From their argument, it was clarified that Amma wasn't the one who received the very first slap I heard. Amma explained that Abba was jealous that Bhaiyya was on Amma's side.

So, he deliberately avoided hitting Amma by hitting Bhaiyya in front of her.

I slithered out from under the bed and was back, by the headboard. Like a spy, I glanced at Bhaiyya and saw a swollen, florid, tear-streaked face. I held my breath as I felt like exploding in tears. Amma and Di were bickering still. Bhaiyya got up and went to the bathroom.

179

I never asked him about this incident and just pretended it never happened. I made him believe that I bought his lame explanation about the bruises on his arms and shoulders resulting from Taekwondo. With a *salt and pepper* amount of understanding, one wouldn't apprehend everything anyway, right?

KOLSUM (BIBHA)

Our one-bedroom flat was getting congested as there were now five of us living here. I still had two children, Amanah and Zain and the fifth member was my sister-in-law, Ranya.

For about three months, Yasin had been spending a lot of the time speaking over the phone with his dad. His parents were planning to send over their youngest daughter, Ranya, to ours so that she could do her secondary and higher education. When my parents heard this, they were more than ready and happy to offer a bedroom, as their house was much bigger than our small flat.

Yasin refused as this was his duty and so with us she stayed. I wasn't too sure at the beginning. 'What if your mum instigates problems through Ranya?' I said.

'Ranya is only sixteen. She wouldn't do you any harm, and I'm here so don't worry. Besides, she can help you with the babysitting, cooking, and cleaning,' he said.

When they came, Yasin's parents and sister stayed at Yasin's Fupu's aunt's, house – the one where he stayed when he first came here. My parents, as usual, went overboard to cater for my in-laws in any way possible. My mum cooked about ten different dishes and made her famous curd and pumpkin jelly. My mum's sister, Khala, who was more like an elder sister to me, helped out a lot too.

I could see my mother-in-law, all dolled up, piling up her plate and eating with a voracious appetite. And all the while she kept praising me as to how wonderful a wife I was to her son.

'My son has put on weight and that's how I know that you are a good wife. It means that you cook good food for him.' The words gurgled out of her mouth.

Really? In that case, you probably do the opposite since my father-in-law looks emaciated.

Later on, Yasin's parents and Ranya moved to our flat as within a week his parents were to leave for Bangladesh. That week yielded no physical torture from my mother-in-law but I had to endure emotional abuse from both her and Yasin.

It started when we went Kent. It was the day before my parents-in-law went back home. We went to visit my father-in-law's friend, Abdul Ghafur, and his family; Yasin had also stayed in their house at some point during his late teens.

Abdul Ghafur was a very tall man. He had a son and two daughters. They had a spacious house with a good size garden both at the front and back. I remembered Yasin telling me that the son was a couple of years older than him, the eldest girl was similar age to Yasin, and the second girl was Ranya's age.

I felt uneasy and upon my perusal, I felt that this visit would take a wrong turn.

Thank God they followed Islamic segregation so the men sat in the reception room while the women were in the open plan kitchen-cum-dining room. My mother-in-law started the conversation with a brazen air.

'I'm so glad you have a big house. I feel so claustrophobic in tight spaces.' She paused to laugh. 'I'm just too used to big mansions.' Abdul Ghafur's taciturn wife smiled an antipathetic smile. Yasin's mum continued, 'Ah I just adore your eldest daughter. I liked her back in the late eighties when we came here to visit you.'

I knew what their eldest daughter, called Parvin, looked like but after hearing this, I took a good look at her. She sat in front of me on a single black leather sofa. She looked uncomfortable. She looked barely five feet and her features didn't stand out. My mother-in-law declared that I was not pretty but from an objective point of view anyone would agree that I was lesser of the two uglies! Knowing my mother-in-law's aesthetic maxims, a part of me now believed that she was trying to only irk me. Simply because I wasn't chosen by them.

When the time to leave had come, I was in the vicinity, putting Amanah's and Zain's coats and shoes on. My mother-in-law was deliberately difficult while my father-in-law seemed to be an oaf all the time. As he put his overcoat on, he said to his friend, 'I had always wanted to make Parvin our daughter-in-law. But I guess, it wasn't meant to be.'

I was fuming. I tried very hard not to let the tears roll down my eyes. It was so humiliating.

It all felt planned. I wanted to grab the car keys and the kids and drive off. It was even more frustrating because every time my in-laws cooked up something, Yasin was always somewhere else. I looked for Yasin when Abba spoke about his "wish" but he was too busy talking to Parvin's brother. I felt like taking it out on him. After a long, tedious journey back to our flat, I stormed into the kitchen despite Yasin calling after me. I rummaged through the cupboards for the medicine box. I found a leaf of paracetamol and popped two in my mouth. Yasin followed me to the kitchen and asked me why I ignored him. I knew he wouldn't let go of this easily but a part of me wanted a fight.

'I'm sorry and thank you,' I said.

'What's the matter? Why are you talking like this?'

My eyes welled up. 'I wanted to thank you for taking me on this trip where your parents insulted me in front of everyone – everyone except for you. How ideal.' I summarized the incident for him.

'That doesn't justify you misbehaving so sarcastically with me,' he said. 'I was calling you and you just walked off. You could've waited for a bit. Offered me tea and then told me this. You always say the wrong thing at the wrong time. You have no courtesy or intelligence.'

I was crying and my head was pounding. I didn't want his mum to see us arguing but she did see it all, thanks to the size of our flat.

'Stop arguing, Yasin. You shouldn't talk like that to Kolsum,' Yasin's mum said. Then looking at me she added, 'Your father-in-law is a bit naïve and doesn't understand when not to say certain things. I'm really sorry.'

'You don't need to be sorry about anything, Amma. I'll talk to her about this later.'

I could see an impish glee in her eyes. I excused myself and said I needed to lie down for a bit.

Abba went to the mosque to do his Asr prayers while Ranya and the kids were in the sitting room. I dozed off for forty minutes or so and only woke up due to faint conversations that were audible through the window on the wall that separated the kitchen from our bedroom. It was blocked with books though. So perhaps my mother-in-law couldn't distinguish that it wasn't a bookcase against a wall. I could hear her telling Yasin that it was justified that he was angry with me. That as a wife I shouldn't be talking like this to him and that had he married a younger woman, then that wife would've had the penchant for obeying him.

I was so angry. She had the gratuitous audacity to instigate my husband against me in *my* house. Just then I entered the kitchen, gave a polite salutation to both of them, and started to prepare dinner. I cooked a mixed vegetable bhaji, a chicken curry and a tomato *tenga, soup,* with fish.

Yasin went out without telling me. In the meantime, his mum came and asked me if I needed any help.

Couldn't you ask that when I started to cook? What's the point of asking when I have finished?

Yasin gave me the cold shoulder even the following morning when we all went to see them off. After we came home, I offered to make tea for him but he refused it.

'I see Amma succeeded in convincing you that I am not worthy of being your wife?' I said.

'What are you talking about?' I told him how I had been able to hear their conversation yesterday and he accused me of eavesdropping.

'My mum was right. You are so disobedient. You think you have become a martyr because you took pity on me? It is *you* who's lucky that *I* married you. You lied about your age. Don't forget that I overlooked it when I found out after our marriage.' I was crying very hard now.

'Stop crying. You look even uglier when you cry!' Yasin hollered.

'If my age and looks bother you so much, then fine. You can end this marriage,' I managed to utter between sobs.

'You will not tell me what to do.'

'Can you please not shout? The kids can hear. Ranya has been exposed to Amma's and Abba's fighting all this time. Do you want her to see the same thing here as well?'

'You don't need to teach me that. Go to your parents' house for the weekend. I need some time and space to myself.'

I packed my things and fed the children some food before we left. Ranya came and asked me if I was okay. I smiled through my tears that everything was fine.

'I feel bad for you, Bibha. I really wish I could do something. I'm really sorry.'

She came and hugged me. I hugged her back. I felt bad for Ranya too. I knew she had a hard time back home. My heart wanted to make sure that she got a better life here but my mind speculated something else – to teach Yasin's mum a lesson. I would make her regret for creating the rift between Yasin and me. Big time.

***

I thought it would get easier. But it didn't. I tried my best to be nice to Ranya but she didn't seem to use her initiative at all. Her brother made it clear to her that she'd have to help out in the house but she just didn't seem to have any common sense.

A few incidents occurred last week. First, Yasin's mum called. She kept talking so I carried on listening. While I was on the phone, Ranya kept saying to hang up as soon as possible, in a callous tone.

Finally, when I did, she quipped, 'Why are you being all polite with Amma? She has been horrible to everyone including you so don't talk to her so much.' I knew what she meant but who on earth was she to *order* me as to what to do and what not to do? I found her attitude brusque: she had already on two occasions made remarks about my weight. She was getting a bit too lippy with me and I wouldn't have that in *my* house.

Yasin came at nine and I told him what happened. He called Ranya straightaway and questioned her. With fake candour, she said that she didn't try to be impolite. Yasin didn't let her finish. He admonished her for being rude to me.

The second incident was the day Yasin told Ranya in front of me that for some of the days in the week, she too would have to do the cooking. The following day, Ranya was supposed to cook dal after she came back from college. But just as I had thought, she found some excuse to escape the chore.

'I'll have a bath and then make it,' she had said.

I suggested that she cooked the dal before her bath, but she insisted on taking a bath first. Frustrated, I cooked it myself. She was given only one thing to cook and she couldn't handle even that! I could imagine that after the bath she'd say that she was tired and had a lot of studying to do.

I was relieved that Yasin came home while she was still having a bath. He asked me why I was cooking the dal when Ranya was supposed to do it.

So, I told the truth. I said that it was getting late and that I wouldn't want to cook after I had a bath. Yasin was fuming to witness the ad hoc plan. The minute Ranya came out he lashed out at her.

I felt sorry for her. I really did. But she deserved it. It's not that I'm being a typical "evil sister-in-law". Yasin's mum was satanic. And she sent her daughter to live with us. So naturally, I had to be very circumspect in this situation. It was a question about my marital life after all. I only did what any sensible wife would do – nip it in the bud.

***

I saw my good old friends today, almost six months later. We met up at my place for a change. It had been raining for the whole week and my friends almost cancelled last minute. Rumaisa's still the same skinny girl that she was, even after two children. Zeenat and Hawa looked a bit bigger than before but they ranted like they were obese. They told me that I had put on a bit of weight and that it was still early days. So, I shouldn't fret too much about it. I agreed with them too. But I had a feeling that I'd keep piling it on unless I joined the gym.

A few days ago, we all had gone shopping at Debenhams. I chose a nice crimson gilet for Ranya. Yasin wanted to spend the money Abba gave for Ranya but I insisted that we bought it for her. Instead of thanking me, the little prick remarked that it would fit me better since I was bigger than her.

I retorted back by saying, *'Thank you for calling me fat.'* She didn't even apologise.

I told Yasin about joining the gym and stressed that I had to lose weight. He said that he'd think about it. I just hoped that he'd allow it. He has made it clear that I shouldn't carry on pursuing further education or work since it was more important that *he* completed his degree so he could get a better job. I knew that I should've been okay with that as I was now a wife and a mother of two children. So, my priorities were now different from before. But somewhere in my heart, it ached.

'I'm going to start my PGCE in the Institute of Education in November,' Zeenat said.

'I completed mine straight after marriage. I've applied for jobs so please pray that I get something,' Arifa said.

'I'm loving the lazy lifestyle. Hubby wants me to start work because financially we're struggling a bit.' Hawa said, 'Hanna starts nursery this September and we want to send her to a private school. So sooner or later I'll have to quit this comfort.'

Everyone looked at me as it was my turn to say something. 'To be honest, I'm fed up with changing nappies day in and day out. I'd love a change in life,' I admitted.

'You can once the kids are old enough, can't you?' Hawa said. I was making tea so as I was already standing, I thought I might as well demonstrate my situation to them.

'You see, I have invisible shackles around my ankles. Every time I want to move forward, they pull me back.'

My friends were quiet for a bit. Perplexity, empathy, and consolation followed one after the other from them. The fact that I had a somewhat insular life partner, was something I shared only with a trusted group of people.

'Meet my sister-in-law, Ranya, Yasin's sister. She lives with us now,' I said as Ranya, who seemed to have a habit of making unwanted entrances, appeared.

Ranya looked reserved; I waited on tenterhooks and my friends looked a bit worried too. So, I added with an obvious wink, 'I have to be careful about what I say to you lot as sister-in-law here may report to her brother about me,' I joked. Ranya looked confounded now.

Phew.

Reverse psychology always works. I did major in psychology after all.

RANYA

My first day at Coral Reef College did not get off to a very good start. As I stepped inside the shower cubicle and turned the knob on, the water didn't heat up enough. It felt as though ten thousand icicles had jabbed into me.

I was running late so thought I'd skip breakfast. But when I went to the kitchen to have a glass of water, I found Bibha had already made me breakfast: two hot buttered crumpets with peppered scrambled eggs and tea.

'For me?' I asked.

'No, it's for me since I'm running late for college. Of course, it's for you,' Bibha joked. I ate silently. Bibha sat there the whole time and that made me self-conscious. I wasn't used to such pampering. I really appreciated it and thanked her but also told her that she didn't need to go through the trouble. Serving breakfast to a pauper was just as overwhelming as *not* serving breakfast to a prince. As I left, Bhaiyya muttered something under his breath for closing the door a tad bit too loud. Then I jumped on the wrong bus to college, missed the second bus as I had to cross over to the other side of the road to catch the right one. When I finally did manage to get on the third bus, I realised that I should've got off the stop before. And just when things couldn't get worse, it began to rain. *Hopefully it'll only be a drizzle.*

I was pretty much drenched by the time I arrived at my destination. I quickly went to the ladies' restroom to dry and fix my hair. It was still damp from the shower that I had before leaving home and the rain only soaked the little that had dried. I parted my hair in the middle and combed the rest of the length back. My light brown eyes looked hazel in the light – something I had noticed for the first time. Black eye liner usually made my eyes pop out but as I wasn't ready to wear the hijab yet, Bhaiyya forbade me to wear it. Without wasting any more time, I headed straight for the reception desk where I had to wait for two minutes. After checking my details on the system, the receptionist said, 'You need to go to the other site for your induction. It's called Coral Reef New Site or CRN for short. This is the old site – CRO.'

'How long will it take? Could you also give me directions please?'

'Cross the road and either walk through the park or take the pathway after the junction, then cross the road again and you'll see other students heading for that site. You can't miss it. Show this paper to the security guard though as you haven't got your student ID yet. It'll take about five to six minutes to get there,' the receptionist directed. Having thanked the lady, I dashed for the door. While I walked briskly I chided myself for running so late. I chose the path after the junction and from a distance, I saw four boys about my age, walking on the other side, in the opposite direction. As they neared, I looked at one of them in particular because he happened to look at me too. He had very thick, straight jet-black hair, casually parted in the middle. That, along with his caterpillar-like eyebrows and pitch-black eyes, stood out in stark contrast to his alabaster complexion.

Did he know me?

Momentarily, I looked away but sensed him looking at me intently. I looked again to confirm that this sense I felt was wrong.

I was wrong.

He wasn't looking at me. He was staring at me! I honestly didn't realise how long this stare lasted. I withdrew my gaze by the time we were almost parallel to one another. I generally loathed guys who stared at girls. But this time I didn't feel like that. I felt weird in the pit of my stomach. Luckily, I managed to reach CRN in one piece. I was five minutes late for the induction.

Probably that's how long I was staring at the mysterious person.

I sat next to two girls who introduced themselves as Ambreen and Lilly. My feet ached and I could feel blisters forming already. Perhaps wearing three-inch high heels wasn't a bright idea. But then, being barely five feet two and almost seventeen, I had to resort to that as I didn't want people to think I was still a primary school kid. I heard someone laugh and it came from a rather handsome boy sitting next to Ambreen – Ambreen was all over him, flirting, and even touching him, "accidentally". She wore washed out jeans and a crimson top with a provocative slit across her chest. Her original black, wavy hair had blonde highlights and her eyebrows were plucked and tinted. She had no makeup on yet looked ravishingly beautiful. Lilly was svelte and dressed in a salwar kameez that looked custom made. They both seemed taller and prettier than me even though they mentioned (which I reckon was out of politeness and for conversation sake) that I was very pretty.

I looked at my own clothes; I wore an off-white boyfriend blouse with a black mermaid skirt and a grey cardigan. The only adornment was an amber necklace. I felt my clothes didn't represent their cultivated urbanity. 'Hamid – Ranya, Ranya – Hamid.' Ambreen introduced us briefly, in a whisper. The induction seemed to last for ages. Eventually it ended our misery and we all made our way upstairs to the library. We all placed ourselves along the two sides of a rectangular table. A constant murmur from all the students filled the air.

'So, do you have a girlfriend?' Ambreen asked.

'No.' Hamid looked ever so slightly uncomfortable.

'You might lose him before you manage to get him.' Lilly laughed. I nudged her to be quiet despite laughing out loud. Ambreen didn't hear any of that as she was too busy studying Hamid. Indeed, Hamid was drop dead gorgeous.

'Where are you from Hamid?' I asked, which I believed to be a decent question, comparatively.

'Egypt. What about you?'

I noticed he had very white teeth. 'Same as the others here – Bangladesh.'

'Seriously?' He looked genuinely sceptical.

'Why, where did you think she was from?' Ambreen asked.

'I thought you were Arabian or Pakistani.'

'I'll take that as a compliment.' I laughed. A weird feeling began to nest in my stomach; for it felt like I was being watched by someone. I casually looked all around the vast library with its colossal amount of neatly placed books. *Di*

would've devoured this place had she been here back then.
And then my eyes locked into his; I found that person who I'd
seen on my way here sitting right across our table, watching
me. I looked down and a few seconds later looked back at him.
I repeated this step a few times and was sure that his gaze,
unlike mine, was uninterrupted. I suddenly went through that
awkward moment when you decide to look at someone and
they're already looking at you. Every attempt I made to check
this person out was a total failure, so I gave up.

Hamid was in my biology, English, and tutorial classes. So,
over the first few weeks, Hamid and I began to get quite
friendly; not the love-kind of friendly, just friend-like friendly.
He was very attractive, all right. But there was something
about him that was uncanny. At lunch break, Hamid,
Ambreen, Lilly, and I went to the chip shop. Owing to the
inclement weather, our fingers were almost numb from the
cold. The paper cone containing curry sauce on hot chips was
not only delectable but warmed our hands too. As we spoke,
the subject suddenly turned to *husbands*. Ambreen wanted five
very rich husbands so that each could provide her with a
diamond ring before she dumped one for the next.

'Why don't you marry just one very rich guy who can get
you five diamond rings and more instead?' Lilly suggested.

'Oh yeah, that's a good idea,' Ambreen said. We couldn't
stop laughing. 'Oh well. I'd love to have a rich husband but
mainly a handsome and loving one.'

'Yeah, me too,' Lilly and I agreed.

'And me,' came Hamid's affirmation.

RANYA

I was running late for home and was getting nervous because I didn't want to face Bhaiyya's wrath again. He seemed to get upset about almost everything I did. The very first "big" trouble I got in was the *Garnier* hair dye Lilly had given me. It was a plum shade. She loved the colour but wasn't sure if it'd suit her or not. She requested me to try it so she could have an idea and I didn't mind.

When I got home, I asked Bibha to check if I mixed the colour and activator properly or not. She said I had but looked apprehensive.

'I don't think your brother will approve of this.'

'Isn't it allowed to colour your hair in Islam?' I asked.

'It's allowed but, since you don't wear the hijab, it's not right that you get extra attention.'

'The colour probably won't show up on my hair anyway.'

Bibha didn't say anything. I dyed my hair anyway since it was going to be wasted otherwise. I was washing my hair after applying the colour when I heard a frantic knock on the bathroom door. I turned the tap off and asked who it was. It was Bibha. She said to come out as soon as I could. I came out with a towel wrapped around my head in a turban. I went into the living room; it was also the room I was staying in. There was a sofa bed on the left-hand side with Bhaiyya's desk and chair opposite to it. On the right side was Amanah's and Zain's

196

old toy boxes in bright red and blue. But instead of toys, they had my clothes in them. Bibha had helped me to sort my clothes out in them as there was no spare wardrobe. I wished she didn't help me for she kept deriding the clothes I had. Every time something looked bizarre to her, she would guffaw and run to the kitchen to show Bhaiyya how ridiculous it was. Pretty much everything looked peculiar. I wanted to tell her that they were all hand-me-downs from Di but feared that she would start rolling on the floor with laughter.

I found Bhaiyya sitting on the sofa bed, which had been turned to a sofa now. Bhaiyya was sitting up straight. This indicated that the matter was serious. He acknowledged my presence through lowered eyelids. Bibha was standing next to the desk while Amanah and Zain played in the room. Bhaiyya told them to go to his and Bibha's room and play there.

'Sit.' Bhaiyya pointed towards the swivel chair.

The situation could've been described as a staid meeting had the towel turban not been on top of my head. Bhaiyya was fuming. He elaborated on what Bibha had predicted. All throughout his lecture I kept my head down; not out of deference but out of the sheer farce of the situation. I was restraining the urge to laugh at what he was saying. He jumped to the conclusion that having my hair coloured would gain me attention. As I was attending a mixed school, it could lead to boys talking to me and then I'd end up having a boyfriend, which could lead to the possibility of me getting involved in an illegal sexual encounter. At this point my towel turban fell off and I burst out laughing. Bibha grinned too but quickly regained her self-composure. It was an edifying sight and so Bhaiyya's countenance increased only in seriousness. I knew that I was going to be done for disrespect now but I just couldn't control my laughter. Bhaiyya left the room and came back with something in his hand. It was his wallet.

'How much was the hair dye?'

'Six pounds.' He got out a fiver and a one-pound coin and left it on the desk.

'Give it to your friend.'

I felt bad. So, that evening I decided to wear the hijab. Abba and Amma were keeping me here for only as long as it'd take me to complete my GCSEs and A Levels. For that time period, I surmised that I might have to abide by my brother's rules. I announced this later that evening and to my surprise they were very joyous at my decision, especially Bhaiyya. His earlier anger had vanished. Bhaiyya explained the importance of the hijab, which represented modesty. I felt like a hypocrite.

I was highly ignorant about the religion but I felt a good character was by far more essential to exercise than the hijab. I prayed five times daily and fasted in the month of Ramadan and I always tried to be honest.

Wasn't that enough? If true beauty emanated from the inside, shouldn't piety be the same?

At the weekend, we went to Bibha's mum's place for dinner. Although the entire London city was dotted with our paternal and maternal relatives, we either went to Bibha's mum's house or to her aunt's.

Bibha's little sister, Kimi, was two years younger than me and for some reason she adored me. She regretted the fact that I wasn't staying in their house. I told her that it'd look weird if I stayed with them and not with my brother.

'I just wish you were my sister too. You're so much fun. Affa is so strict all the time. I have to cut my hair to the length *she* prefers, wear the hijab 'cos *she* says that we should.' Kimi sighed stroppily. 'Why? *She* never wore it till she was at uni. Ugh. She's so suffocating!' Kimi crossed her arms and blew a strand of hair that had fallen on her face. She veiled her petulance in front of others with a more couth attitude though.

'Aw, don't say that. Your sister's telling you that because she doesn't want you to make the mistakes she's made.' I said this without conscious volition.

'She's uptight about who I'm friends with. I can't be friends with boys, or girls who have boyfriends.'

'She only wants the best for you.' I didn't know what else to say. Bibha had gone out to her aunt's place with her mum and the kids so Kimi and I were home alone.

'I'll be right back.' Saying that Kimi dashed upstairs. She was holding a burgundy moleskin notebook when she came back.

'What's that?' I asked.

'It's my sister's diary. She used to keep it when she was at uni. I found it in the attic last summer.'

I saw a glint of malevolence in her dark eyes. She sat next to me and flipped the pages till she found the page she wanted me to see.

'Kimi, you really shouldn't be looking into it. You should give it back to your...'

'Here.' She gestured me to read. It was a joint written piece in black ink.

My adorable, soon to be wife, Kolsum. I fell in love with you the very first day I saw you. Your beautiful smile struck me like lightning. And I knew that I wanted to marry you one day. And that day isn't too far. Wish you all the best in your life.

Love, Robert.

The diary seemed to contain random insertions from well-wishers and fellow students. 'Why are you making me read this?' I asked Kimi. I was feeling disturbed.

'I want you to see how Affa has been. I even remember her going out with this Robert. I was very young then but I remember them holding hands in the park, talking away. My point is, she is wearing the hijab and doing what Islam tells us to do out of her own choice, and that's what Islam tells us, that there is no compulsion in religion. So, my problem is, why is she making me do all the "right things" just because *she* now realises it? No one told her off when she was making mistakes so why am I being penalised? If Abba was alive then she would've never been able to do this to me. Amma just agrees to whatever she says because she is her golden child. Besides, I keep this diary in secret so that if she tries to be too much of a control freak then I can show this to her. And that will put her in her place.'

'Don't do that Kimi. She's your sister…'

'Half-sister.'

'That's not the point. She's older than you. Okay, so you're not ready but you need to get that across to your sister in a polite and acceptable manner.'

I lectured her for five minutes or so and she remained silent throughout. I, treacherous as I was, merely collaborated with a posse of indoctrinated individuals.

'Yeah, okay. I know. I just get really angry at times.' Then after a pause, Kimi held my hand and asked, 'Promise that you'll never *ever* mention this to Affa?'

Kimi had put me in a very addled state of mind. If I ever mentioned this to Bibha, Bhaiyya, or Amma *(the terrible)*, then great devastation and ignominy would follow. But I wasn't the type to harass people. Moral ethics and principles were my first and foremost beliefs. I never compromised with that, no matter what.

'I promise,' I said.

Bibha, her mum, aunt, and cousins were back a bit later. While Bibha was downstairs with her mum, Kimi and her cousins played some music on the computer. 'Khala, please guard the door and warn us if Affa comes.' But before any of us could say anything, Bibha opened the door. Kimi quickly shut down the computer.

'What were you lot doing?' Bibha asked. Kimi's and her cousins' faces looked blanched.

'Oh, I just wanted to check something and pressed the wrong button, I guess, so Kimi just sorted it out,' Khala lied.

A couple of days later, I was summoned to the living room again where I was ordered once again to sit on the swivel chair. This time Bhaiyya looked far more vexed. His hands were at his sides, in tight fists. His lips were pursed, his eyes bulged out, and his eyebrows were affixed in a frown. Bibha was standing next to Bhaiyya this time. *Perhaps as a precaution?*

'I have come across something very disturbing today,' Bhaiyya began. 'Supposedly, you have been spending a lot of time in college with a particular Egyptian boy. Is that true?'

At first I was baffled. Then I realized that he was talking about Hamid. But the phone rang before I could clarify anything. He took the cordless phone and left the room. Bibha asked me if I was seeing this boy. I laughed and said that I wasn't since I wasn't that type at all.

'I may not be as practising as you lot are but I adhere to certain cultural practices – no free-mixing before marriage. Besides Hamid is gay. Ambreen was looking forward to asking him out when he…'

'What?' Bibha looked at the door to make sure Bhaiyya didn't hear her. 'Don't say this to your brother. You'll be in more trouble otherwise.'

Bhaiyya came back with his distended fury. He was adamant on getting me to admit the clandestine affair I was having with Hamid but when a decorous response failed, I had to refute this notion of his with effrontery.

'Why won't you admit it, dammit?' Bhaiyya shouted.

'Why won't you believe me that we're only friends?'

Bhaiyya just stared at me. Then, looking at Bibha he said, 'I feel like slapping this girl.'

'Hang on, how do you know all this? I mean, are you spying on me?' Bhaiyya and Bibha looked at one another, tacitly acknowledging the invidious position they had just placed themselves in.

'Your brother's only trying to protect you,' Bibha said. I arched an eyebrow.

'A friend of mine works there and I asked him to keep an eye on you. You came from Bangladesh so you don't know how things are here, Ranya. You are seventeen now and it's a dangerous age. Hormones will be playing up. You can't make a boy your friend. One thing will lead to another.' Then looking at Bibha again, he said, 'I told Abba that he should get her married off. If I had it my way, then I would've stopped her going to college.'

I felt violated and humiliated as my innards convulsed to make me feel sick. However, despite internal contradictions, I accepted that Bhaiyya was only looking out for me, and this was all being done in pure edification.

I went to the kitchen later on to help Bibha set the table for dinner. Bibha began to tell how it was vital that as Muslims we didn't free-mix. I explained to her that I've never had that sort of intention. Our culture didn't approve of this and I wouldn't do anything that would shame my elders. But for some reason I felt that she was trying to imply that I was that kind of girl who, if given the scope, would get involved in an illicit relationship. Her infallible air prickled my skin. Then it dawned on me; I recalled telling her about the boy I had seen in the library. And perhaps she felt that I would swoon over forbidden territories.

I was annoyed. It felt like an accusation and before I knew it, I opened my big mouth which I regretted straightaway. 'Look who's being all righteous now. Are you telling me that you never *ever* spoke to a boy during your college and uni days?'

'Yes, but I never had a boyfriend,' Bibha defended herself. I was shocked that she lied.

'Oh, yes you did.'

Bibha's facial expression changed to a serious frown and her deep voice sounded sterner. 'What are you trying to say?'

'Nothing.'

'You shouldn't talk like that to me, Ranya. I am very disappointed.' Reluctantly, I apologized. I couldn't break my promise after all.

***

Within eight months I'd have to prepare and sit for my GCSEs, and because of the dwarfed hiatus between the studying period and the exams, I'd only be able to do five subjects. The education system was very different in London compared to Bangladesh and two months had passed before I could make any sense of the pedagogy. I was left with six months now and instead of being erudite in my subjects, my mind was saturated with tension. Bhaiyya was still taunting me about my lifestyle and the potential dangers of my inveterate habits.

I hated to admit this but I felt an urge to hear my parents' voices. After college, I came home straightaway as Bhaiyya didn't approve if I was late by more than ten minutes. I went to the kitchen where Bibha was serving Bhaiyya tea and some toast.

'Can I call Abba and Amma?' I asked.

'I need to make a phone call but if its urgent then you can call them now but don't take too long.' Bhaiyya was incisive. The novelty of me wearing the hijab died down after a couple of days and Bhaiyya reverted to his taciturn and truculent nature.

I used to hand over the phone to Bhaiyya to speak to our parents the first few times, to which he used to look disinclined. After a while, he'd indicate that he was busy or send Bibha to speak instead. It was a ritual for Bhaiyya to reproach our parents' parenting skills in comparison with Bibha's sophisticated parents' etiquette maxims. And all the while, sycophantic Bibha would nod her head to show appropriate subservience at the opportune moment. What used to make me take umbrage was that Bhaiyya did this *every* time after this kind of a long-distance phone call. He'd dart his smart criticisms on me till I was pitted.

Abba and Amma reminded me about the purpose of my stay – that I'd have to study medicine; so, I needed to get straight A's in everything. Being love-struck amidst the myriad of complications I had wasn't getting me anywhere either.

Mahi. That was his name. And finding this information was as hard as extracting gold from an ore. Until then I referred to him as Adidas jacket.

A couple of weeks ago, I was in the CRO site. I was in front of the vending machine paying for a packet of crisps and a can of coke.

'Hi.' I heard a girly voice as I collected my snacks. I turned around to see a dainty girl in a beige coloured cardigan and a matching scarf sitting in one of the chairs with desks.

'Hi.' I smiled back. As I approached her I noticed that she was quite pretty. The kind of pretty that makes you feel a bit intimidated. She was all smiles and didn't have a single bit of makeup on yet the radiance of her beauty shimmered in the massive, gloomy room. Seeing all the faces and people here was reducing my once extrovert persona into a diffident one.

'I'm Panna. What's your name?' she asked.

'Ranya,' I said. I was still standing so she asked me if I'd like to take a seat next to her. I was happy to be in her company.

We chatted for the entire lunch break. She happened to be in my maths and tutorial class too so I was eager to be her friend. I met her almost every day for that week and I saw *Mahi* pretty much every day after school too. It was through Panna that I gleaned his name. He always stared at me till his bus came or a friend joined him to speak to him. On Friday, I confided to Panna about him. I didn't know his name then so I referred to him as *Adidas* jacket since he wore it every time. Panna told me that he definitely liked me or else he wouldn't have stared at me. I didn't believe her at all but liked the comfort of it. Suddenly a non-Asian girl appeared and signalled for Panna to come aside. She looked flushed from crying. Panna left her bag and told me to keep an eye on it while she went with her friend.

As I waited, I saw a boy approaching the area where I sat. I recognised him to be the boy who usually hung about with Panna. He was attired in sports clothes and looked a bit scruffy.

He gave me a quick hello and asked if I had seen Panna. I filled him in and so he asked me if I could look after his folder and give it to Panna when she came back. Although he seemed friendly and easy-going, I couldn't help but be cautious. After Bhaiyya told me that his friend was spying on me I studied every bloke around me; a cynical trait became dominant in me. Panna introduced him as Adam but never mentioned if he was her cousin or brother. She came back shortly and told me that the crying girl she went with was her primary school friend.

She was Moroccan and was going out with a Bengali boy who was now, to her utter dismay, breaking up with her. When she finished, I told her about Adam.

'Oh, your cousin gave me this folder and said to give it to you,' I said. I would've said brother but she was too pretty to be his sister.

Panna looked somewhat uncomfortable.

'Your cuz seems to really look out for you. My brother is very strict,' I said.

'Oh, my God. Look at the time. I need to go to CRN. I've been late for my social science class this entire week already. See you soon. Take care.' She hugged me and left. I found her departure a tad bit abrupt.

Was it something I had said?

My next class was in CRO. I walked just a few minutes before class started and found Hamid standing there alone. Some other students were nearby talking to one another.

'Hello, Ranya.' Hamid put his hand out.

'Erm, I'm sorry, I can't shake hands with you,' I said.

'Why?'

'Apparently, it's not allowed for a Muslim girl and boy to do so,' I said.

'I am Muslim. But we don't follow such a rule.'

I couldn't help but laugh here. 'You don't follow a lot of rules, Hamid.' Hamid shrugged and suggested that I wrapped the scarf of my salwar kameez around my hand and then shook hands with him. I refused all the same and laughed again since he was actually serious. He sat next to me in class and I felt very uncomfortable.

What if Bhaiyya's spy friend is one of the students and sitting amongst us here? Maybe the teacher is the spy. Or maybe, even Hamid himself.

I was thinking of all sorts of possibilities. Lilly and Ambreen were fifteen minutes late for class. I got up and told Ambreen to take my seat. This way I was relieved that Bhaiyya's spy wouldn't report anything about Hamid and me.

Oh. If only Bhaiyya knew that we were no more than students sharing a few classes. We weren't even proper friends.

After class, Lilly gave me a tape in which she recorded all the best Bollywood film song tracks. She said that it was a gift and I was touched. She felt bad for the trouble I had got into due to the hair dye.

I waited at the other site as Bhaiyya told me that morning that he'd pick me up. As I waited. I saw *Adidas jacket* walking past with his friends. He looked at me again, but this time briefly.

*Maybe Adidas jacket himself is none other than **the** spy.*

A chill ran down my spine and I was convinced that he kept staring at me with that purpose. Bhaiyya came on time and told me to sit at the back as he was going to collect Bibha from the nursery along with the kids. He drove for some time in silence and glanced at me in the interior mirror a couple of times before asking, 'You're a bit quiet... everything okay?'

'Hmm,' I said. I wondered if he remembered how close we used to be. Bhaiyya asked me again and my eyes watered this time. He pulled up the car and told me to tell him what the matter was.

'Is anyone troubling you at college?'

I wished that I could tell him that his over-protectiveness-turned-into-paranoia was creating more insecurity for me; that his morose attitude was corroding me like acid while Bibha's louder than necessary sarcasms harassed me. That his proclaimed surveillance on me was more insolent than me not seeking his permission to enter his bedroom in broad daylight, while the door was open.

'I'm fine. I just miss Amma and Abba,' I lied.

'You girls vacillate so much. You're worse than the weather.' Bhaiyya smirked.

My *salt and pepper* surmise was that it would've been incongruous had I expressed my true feelings. I ruminated that I'd have to mask my thoughts most of the time while I stayed with them.

The kids were thrilled to see me and I them. They demanded that their dad put *Nasheed* on. I asked Bhaiyya why he always listened to *Nasheed*.

'Music is not allowed and we should abstain from it.' He elaborated on this and I felt more and more uncomfortable at the thought. In fact, the irony escalated since Amma was a singer and I had grown up with music. I wasn't fanatic about it but neither would I refrain from listening to it all together. I told Bhaiyya about the gift I was given. He said to return it to my friend when I saw her next and forbade me from listening to it.

'Is it the same girl who gave you the hair dye?' Bibha asked.

'Uh, yeah,' I said.

'I think you should keep your distance from her,' Bhaiyya stated.

I agreed with a decorous 'yes'. My walkman was completely broken now but I recalled seeing another one in the room I was staying and a cheeky plan formed in my head.

At bedtime, I saw that Bhaiyya's walkman was still in the drawer of his desk. When all was quiet, I prowled about the room. Once I was certain that everyone was asleep, I took the gadget out as quietly as I could and slipped in the cassette Lilly gave me; it had some of the best tracks I knew.

The dark room was iridescent with lights that shone through the chink in the curtains. And then suddenly I saw the door open slowly. I jumped up. Frantically I took the earphones out.

'Who is it?' I asked. It was Bibha. She asked if she could come in.

'Hold on,' I said. The earphones had been neatly coiled around the walkman but I was in great danger of being discovered so I quickly gathered the wires and stuffed them back in the drawer with the intention to wrap it around neatly afterwards. I opened the door and let Bibha in who briefly apologised for coming at this hour. Had it been the other way round, oh well, another meeting would've taken place. But as this was their house, I supposed that they were free to do as they pleased.

'I just came to take the walkman for your brother,' she said.

I froze. My insides seemed to curdle from still digesting food and it made me want to retch. The cassette was still inside and there was no way I'd be able to take it out without getting caught. I had to tell Bibha the truth.

'Please don't tell Bhaiyya,' I implored. Bibha didn't say anything. I was waiting on tenterhooks when she left. Within a minute, I found Bibha back in my room.

'Your brother wants to see you.'

'Why?' I squeaked.

'He wanted to know why the wire was all out and I told him the truth that that's how I found it.'

Presently Bhaiyya knocked on the door. I turned the light on and grabbed a shawl.

He looked at me with an edifying sight. He asked me a straight question and I gave him an honest answer. This was followed by a ruthless barrage of criticisms towards me. I was declared uncouth, immature, and irresponsible to be deliberately indulging in western decadence. He gave me a full one-hour lecture for this misconduct.

'But Bibha's sister, aunt, and cousins listen to music. They were listening to some Indian songs the other day at Bibha's mum's house,' I said. I wondered if she even knew that they lied to her due to her strict regimes.

'My family *never* listens to music. They know it's *haram* and they'd never indulge in something like that,' Bibha stated. Her over-confidence almost gave me a rash.

'Don't worry about what other people are up to. You worry about your actions, do you understand?' Bhaiyya growled.

I was in tears throughout. I didn't know what to do. I recalled how I used to laugh at his initial chastisement. But now it dawned on me that this was the make-up of his character. Every little thing about me bugged him. I was having to conform into a claustrophobic trait of conscientiousness. Every day I was stressed out thinking that

Bhaiyya would have a go at me in front of everyone if I didn't close the doors silently – day or night. Or if I didn't make my bed as soon as I woke up. Or if I didn't raise my sleeves when I ate.

Once I tried to get something next to the wardrobe while he was praying. I went behind him and acrobatically took what I needed. When he finished praying he was enraged at my audacious attempt. But he was like that with everyone. His pugnacious demeanour was practised on his wife and children too.

One thing, however, was getting clearer; I was mistaken. I had thought that leaving my parents and coming here would solve all my problems but I was so wrong.

The following day, however, something strange happened. After I came back from college, I saw Bhaiyya and Bibha in the kitchen. I gave Salaam lest I was admonished for having bad attitude added to my list of flaws. I left straightaway when Bhaiyya called me. I was petrified. I didn't want to hear anything any more as his dogmatic tutelage was more of a shroud than shelter. But Bhaiyya didn't lecture me. He asked me if I had returned the tape or not. I said that Lilly was not in so I'd return it tomorrow if she came. To that Bhaiyya said that I didn't need to do that for he now felt that I needed time to adapt to moral etiquettes. And on that note he pardoned me and ruffled my hair as a brotherly gesture. This brought unwanted tears to my eyes again for it was a reminiscent of the long lost Bhaiyya I used to know once upon a time.

I excused myself and went to the bathroom to take a shower. Crying in the shower was just as convenient as crying in the rain. As I rinsed shampoo from my hair, I noticed something I had never noticed before. My hair was falling out in bunches and I cried even harder.

RANYA

Unrequited love is like lung cancer that attacks a person who has never smoked. I was in love. But I didn't want to profess my love to him since in the past I had broken a few hearts and I knew that I'd break his too if he reciprocated. I didn't know why I did that.

I thought of him always. In class my mind was always off to *Adidas jacket land.* Ambreen had had enough and said that today I'd have to ask him out.

'I don't know. I can't do that. And I don't want to exactly "go out" with anyone. It's not right.'

'Oh, stop being all religious.' Ambreen laughed. She was wearing a black leather jacket with faded blue jeans that were ripped on the knees.

'Fine. If you don't then I'll tell him.'

'You will do nothing of the sort,' I said. But I had a feeling that Ambreen meant what she said. It was a bleak day in late autumn. The days were getting shorter and colder. I was wearing a white salwar kameez and so was Lilly. But hers was a straight cut one with *churidar,* leggings. She made her own salwar kameez. She could watch any Indian film and imitate the salwar kameez design the heroine was wearing. My A-line suit was nice but dated.

Ambreen was chiding me for being coy in this matter but I knew I wasn't. I didn't want Ambreen to do what Yaara had done in the past. But with a few encouraging words from her and Lilly, I mustered the courage to talk to Adidas jacket. And then he walked past with his friends.

'There he is,' I said.

'Go,' my two friends said in unison, as they pushed me.

'No. I can't.' My tummy was churning like it did whenever I was going up and down in a lift.

'That's it. That's my cue.' Saying that, Ambreen dashed off following Adidas jacket to the atrium. I pulled her jacket and it almost came off her. She didn't care but I did, since the red top she was wearing was strapless. I let go of her jacket to save her dignity but regretted instantly since I set her off to lose mine. My hands and feet felt cold and numb while my cheeks felt hot and red. I didn't know what to do. I didn't want to create a scene. It felt like déjà vu and a part of me in a way wanted to find out what he thought about me.

'Hi there,' Ambreen said to him. He was sitting at a table with his friend. His friend was trying to hide a smile. I was standing next to Ambreen. And wished I was invisible for she blurted out, 'My friend here has a huge crush on you.' I decided to take it easy. If I refuted this straightaway, then they'd know that it was the truth. So, I remained calm and looked baffled. Adidas jacket acknowledged my presence but didn't look at me.

'I'm not into dating. It's haram in Islam to free-mix,' he said. His voice was serene. I admired him each second as I had never stood this close to him before. He looked beautiful. Ambreen grimaced and gave me a hopeless look before leaving.

'Erm, don't worry about what she said. She's a bit crazy.' I said just beforeI ran after my friend. I felt relieved that it was over. But it felt bad. I loved him more now. He was a good and decent person for a sixteen or seventeen-year-old. From then onwards I did two things. I dedicated myself to do research about Islam as that seemed to have gained Adidas jacket's love and commitment. The other thing I did was drink *Ribena*. I hated the taste since I was a kid but made an effort to love it now since he only drank *Ribena*. I knew it was a stupid idea but that was my way of getting close to him without affecting his feelings. True love didn't mean that you'd have to gain your loved one's love. Or kill yourself. Rather it meant that you'd respect their feelings of not seeing you that way, yet live your life in the memory that you loved him or her.

It was hard and depressing. I couldn't stand anyone else's love for me. I was asked out by a few boys in college but they seemed as repulsive as mould on a fruit. I just hoped and believed that one day, if he was meant for me, then destiny would unite us.

RANYA

After the music debacle, I mistook Bhaiyya's pardoning gesture as an overnight decision to be gentle and coaxing. He told me that it was fine if I wasn't ready to wear the *abaya* but that I should wear baggy clothes; if I wore trousers then it would have to be baggy and the top had to be below the knees. This was because it was not appropriate for a sister who has come of age to wear revealing and tight clothes even in front of her own brother or *mahrams*.

I was okay with all this but then a few weeks later, he began to object to that too. He wanted me to wear the *abaya* now. By now I was tired. I had enough of disputing with him so I acquiesced to his order. I began to notice that Bhaiyya's moody behaviour was affecting Bibha too although she didn't protest. At times a light humorous remark she'd make towards him would become a misnomer for a malicious and disrespectful insult.

One Saturday, Bhaiyya returned from the gym and took a quick shower while Bibha and I set the table for lunch. As she served food on his plate, Bhaiyya sniffed the air and asked what the weird smell was. 'Has something gone off?' he asked.

'No. I cooked everything today. Maybe it's coming from you.' Bibha giggled.

Bhaiyya's face twisted in rage. 'How dare you say this to me when you can see that I just had a shower? Are these the manners you learnt from your parents? Is this how you speak to your husband?'

Bibha tried to mollify him by even saying that she had made a mistake in saying that, but he carried on accusing her of her thoughtless behaviour. To sum it up, all the good she had done ever since she entered his life was erased and forgotten. He did all that in front of me, and their two young children, and he did that pretty often too.

Privacy was not of a high standard in a one-bedroom flat but nevertheless Bhaiyya couldn't be excused. His attitude was savage even towards Bibha. I felt more embarrassed because Bibha was mortified. Bhaiyya usually left the house, after an argument with Bibha, and I'd find her doing her normal chores with puffy, red eyes and nose. I'd try to give her space by not talking about the matter. I also used to fear that she'd take it out on me as I was the sister of the person who was harassing her. But she didn't do that. Rather she would smile at me through teary eyes if I came in front of her. This smile was a copy of her original one, a backup smile for hard times.

I felt quite bad for her so one day I asked Bibha directly if my brother ever hit her. She replied in the negative.

'Your Bhaiyya has a very a bad temper but it's not his fault. It's hard to deal with him.' Her voice broke here and so did my heart. 'He can be very insulting at times. He doesn't see other people's point of view.'

I agreed with her. I was sad but I was relieved to know that I wasn't the only one bearing the brunt of his words.

One cold morning, Bhaiyya informed us that Abba was coming over. Not for good but that he'd be staying for some time. I was happy but worried at the same time.

How would we all fit in here? Bhaiyya then told us that Abba had decided that he'd had enough; that he'd divorce Amma this time. I told Bhaiyya that he didn't mean it. He only did that to get some respite from her and, during that period, Amma would come back to her senses: would do her normal wifely chores again as an apology.

'Give it another month or so and things will go back to normal – she will slack in her household duties and start swearing at Abba and his family. Abba will be patient for a year or so before pulling the leash of divorce again,' I said.

Bhaiyya didn't ignore me but neither did he disregard what I said. Then he told us, 'No, I think Abba is serious this time.' Bibha brought up the subject of accommodation. They explained that they'd tell Abba to sell some of his properties and gather some money to put down as a mortgage for a house in Luton as properties were cheaper there. I was surprised that Abba agreed. Perhaps he was dead sure this time.

Three weeks later Abba came. We had dinner straightaway and after that Abba handed Bhaiyya a cheque for thirty thousand pounds. In a way, I was glad. Who knew, perhaps severing one relation would unite another?

I slept on the floor in a sleeping bag and Abba slept on the sofa bed in the living room. I felt very uncomfortable but what else could be done? Abba brought clothes for his grandchildren, shirts for Bhaiyya and two suits of salwar kameez for Bibha and I. A purple, fluffy fairy-tale dress for Amanah and a three-piece suit for Zain. They were very happy but the look on Bibha's face portrayed the opposite. She smiled her back-up smile. She later told me that that she abhorred Bangladeshi clothes. I knew what she meant but would've preferred her not telling me all the details, like the fabric was cheap, the sewing was ridiculous, and that Bangladeshis adopting a western fashion sense was a pathetic mimicry.

On a small scale, Bibha reflected the broader picture of our propensity for ridicule. We lack the etiquette to encourage and applaud our own people. Instead of appreciating their efforts, we slate them. We criticize the result and ignore the struggle behind it.

The first week went smoothly. We went to Bibha's mum's place for dinner as usual, and the following week we went to her Khala's new house in Croydon. It was a long drive and that was a bad thing. Bhaiyya's sense of humour was not as profound as Abba's, Bibha's, and mine. He got frustrated when he couldn't find the right direction to their house. Abba was sitting next to him and joked at his folly for going around the same roundabout three times. Bibha squeezed my hand as an indication that she feared Bhaiyya retorting back to Abba. He didn't. Instead he blanked anything Abba said or suggested.

The air regained tranquillity after he got back on the right track. Bhaiyya started to talk with Abba about more general things. Like the appropriate age a girl should get married. This talk soon turned into a heated altercation. Abba brought me here to pursue a career in medicine. Therefore, it was disturbing when Bhaiyya kept stressing the importance of a girl, who had come of age, to get married as soon as possible.

'Define "come of age",' Abba said.

I could feel Bhaiyya rolling his eyes at this. 'It's when a girl and a boy has reached puberty. The law of this country, however, doesn't allow girls to be married at twelve or thirteen but by sixteen, with their parents' approval they can.'

'So, what are you trying to tell me?'

'I think you should get Ranya married off. It is your duty after all.'

'She's only seventeen.'

'She's old enough. That way you will be allowing her to have a relationship in an acceptable, Islamic manner. I know *I will* get my daughter married off when she comes of age.'

In a more authoritative tone, Abba then asked Bhaiyya how old his wife was when he married her. Bhaiyya quipped that if his in-laws knew any better then they would've got her married earlier.

This argument was like the roundabout my brother was struggling to get out of earlier. The air was now tense and heavy with languor. Abba being the calmer one decided to rest his case. He was quiet for the rest of the journey but had a reticent aura about him even though he spoke with everyone in the house of our host.

That night when I was tucked up inside the sleeping bag, Abba asked me if I was asleep. I replied in the negative.

He asked me to tell him the truth about how Bhaiyya had been treating me in the past few months. I was thankful that the lights were off, or else he would've seen the lie printed on my face like the scarlet letter. Later when I contemplated it, I realised that Abba's cheerful demeanour, earlier that evening, was no more than a façade.

For the next whole week, there was a cold war between Abba and Bhaiyya. Bhaiyya would pick on Abba, mock him almost, impervious to the fact that the rest of us were feeling embarrassed. I'd study his face intently every time he did that, so that I could come to a conclusion whether he was being nasty or naïve.

Did he feel piqued that Abba was funding me, his daughter, under Bhaiyya's roof, yet he had stopped funding Bhaiyya, when he was here, homeless?

Bhaiyya was now putting Abba under duress with his purist values. He was correcting Abba in front of everyone. He didn't have the common sense that he should either overlook or find a more suitable way to get his point across to a venerable father. Bibha would often laugh it off but I began to have an inkling that this would soon lead to something grotesque.

And it did; and when it did, it precipitated a crisis.

It was like a string of beads. The beads were the rifts while the string holding them together was the thin ice on which we all tiptoed. And then the string snapped. I prayed that Bhaiyya would not do or say anything to snap it. But destiny had something else in store. Of all the people, it was me who cut the string. I had a moment of myopia when Bhaiyya was ridiculing Abba behind his back in front of Bibha, and me.

Once evening, I was boiling some water in a pot for Abba who didn't like the boiling water from the kettle due to limescale. Bhaiyya was guffawing at this. He kept questioning me why I agreed as it made no sense. I was standing in front of the cooker waiting for the water to boil while Bibha was cleaning the worktop, laughing away like a sycophant. I wished she had told Bhaiyya to let certain things be, instead of being facetious about it. But Bhaiyya was mulish on top of his aggressiveness and kept asking me despite my cold answer that I was only doing this as it was polite to do as your elders

221

told you to do so. Bhaiyya looked at Bibha and burst out in peals of laughter. Bibha grinned more now. I looked down and tried to stop the annoying tears that flowed whenever they wanted to.

'Yes, but what is the *difference* between boiling water in the kettle and in a pot on the hob?' he asked again, shaking his head in absolute disbelief this time.

I looked at him. He was laughing and waiting for an answer.

'I *told* you that it's because *Abba* has asked me to do so. What's your problem anyway?'

'What's up with your tone?' Bhaiyya was serious now and that was a ghastly portent in itself. A chill ran down my spine. It seemed as though he had a penchant for impertinence. I turned the gas off and stormed out nevertheless. My limbs were functioning against the order of my mind. For the first time, defiance overpowered my docility.

I went to the living room to tell Abba that I had lied to him that night about Bhaiyya being fine with me. But Abba was offering his Maghrib, dusk, prayer so I sat behind him, crying silently. He finished praying sooner than usual and at once looked at me with great concern in his eyes.

I hugged Abba and started to complain when he patted the back of my head, saying, 'I knew you were hiding the truth that night. I heard everything. Don't worry. I'll take you out of here.' He held my hand and took me back to the kitchen.

I stopped crying and was engulfed with more anxiety now. 'N... no I'm fine, Abba. It's nothing. Please don't!' But it was too late. I had snapped the string and no one could stop the beads from scattering now.

I had a gut *salt and pepper* feeling that Abba not only wanted to avenge me but also wanted to enact revenge.

'Yasin.' Abba's voice had the same nuance of terror in it, which he had shown years ago – when my earth had stood still. Only this time, my worry was for Abba, not Bhaiyya. 'I need to have a word with you. Sit down.'

'Why don't you sit down?' Bhaiyya almost ordered.

'Don't argue. I'm your father and I have told you to sit down. As my son, you should *not* be ordering *me* to sit down.' The day when Bhaiyya would've had the effrontery to challenge our father had come.

Bhaiyya raised his voice and said that he was just being polite and so offered him a seat. To this Abba said that he wouldn't be able to fool the man from whose loins he came from. Abba and Bhaiyya were both shouting and talking at the same time.

Bibha was next to me and asked, 'Ranya, what did you tell Abba?'

'Why are you asking her that for? She had this all planned. She thought she'll be clever and get some sympathy. Little did this birdbrain think about the terrible misunderstanding she'll be creating.' Bhaiyya spat the words at me. I saw pure hatred in Bhaiyya's eyes for me.

I was upset but at the same time couldn't deny everything Bhaiyya said; I didn't realise that Abba would take such a drastic step. Abba went to the living room and I followed him. He was packing his bags. A moment later he went back to the kitchen and demanded that Bhaiyya return the cheque he had given him.

Without a word, Bhaiyya went to his bedroom and was back in a jiffy with the slip. He slammed it on the dining table, in front of Abba. 'I'm not after your money and neither am I in need of it. Thank God I am doing well. I only asked you for it because *you* wanted to come and stay with me and my family.'

'Oh really? So, who gave birth to you? Who looked after you? You were self-sufficient from your mother's womb, eh?'

Hearing this, Bhaiyya came up to Abba; so close, that his face was only centimetres away from Abba's. At six feet, Bhaiyya was five inches taller than Abba. This was pretty much the same height difference they had when Bhaiyya had come Dubai as a young teenager. Bhaiyya's hands were in tight fists, his shoulders seemed to have bloated in anger and Abba appeared to cower. I gave out a loud gasp but Bhaiyya ignored me. Bibha went and pulled Bhaiyya away from Abba.

'Don't you dare talk about my mum. What have *you* done? What did you used to do? I haven't forgotten anything.' He rasped the words at him. Abba stared at him in disbelief. Bhaiyya shrugged off Bibha's hands and flounced out, leaving Abba riveted to the spot where he was standing.

Tears flowed uncontrollably from my eyes. Abba quietly walked back to the living room and sat on the sofa bed. He still looked like he was in shock. I stood next to the door and Bibha came and sat next to Abba. She apologised on Bhaiyya's behalf and then unexpectedly Abba broke down into tears. Bibha hugged him and cried too. She seemed more useful as a daughter-in-law than I did as his own daughter. I was shattered to smithereens.

***

It was six when Abba left and he came back two hours later only to collect his belongings. He told me that Fupa was waiting in the car for him and that he'd be staying at theirs till Fupa found a suitable place for us to rent.

'Where will I be staying in the mean-time?' I asked.

'You need to stay here but no more than a week.' And for a week I stayed, in continual humiliation. Bhaiyya ranted just that day between the time Abba had left to when he returned. After that he fell silent. Bhaiyya simply ignored my entire existence. He communicated with me only twice through Bibha and, even then, he referred to me as "that girl in the living room".

I think Bibha felt sorry for me. The kids would play with me from time to time but I couldn't join in with the merriment I used to have before. Albeit unsaid, I understood that I shouldn't be at the dinner table when Bhaiyya was around. Bibha would therefore bring my food to me in the living room. Her words were limited too. I guessed that she couldn't betray her husband's dignity.

College was closed due to the winter holidays so I felt even more claustrophobic. But I did manage to get some respite in that unbearable week; on three alternative days, Bhaiyya went out for his evening classes. Luckily, he was studying part-time for his first degree.

But sadly, each class was only an hour long and the commute wasn't too long either. Those were the times when Bibha would speak to me. We'd talk about recent as well as past events. I confided in her how Amma was towards me and

225

that was the reason why I had come here. Bibha agreed and filled me in with how Amma mistreated her when she went back home. I was ashamed of myself and wished that I hadn't heard of it.

At length, Bibha surmised that it was, in fact, Abba's fault. 'But then again Abba only reacted to what you told him.'

I reminded her of Bhaiyya's obnoxious behaviour towards Abba but she demurred. I found that weird since she had indicated in the past few days that he should address Abba in a more honourable manner. She agreed but kept stressing that I shouldn't have exaggerated to Abba the way I did.

Every now and then she'd sigh and say, 'I'm just grateful that your brother didn't deposit the money in the bank. It would've been so embarrassing and complicated to get the money back otherwise. It would've seemed like he was after the money the whole time.'

RANYA

Fupa's friend whom we referred to as Jabir's dad, had a two-bedroom flat where he lived with his wife and three-year-old son called Jabir. They wanted to rent out a room in their flat and we were the perfect lodgers. We moved in a couple of days later as Abba had to buy some essential stuff for us. He bought two of everything: cereal bowls, dinner plates, spoons, forks, butter knives, kitchen knives, cooking pots with lids, frying pans and two wooden spoons. He also bought two bed sheets, a blanket, a sleeping bag and two pillows.

While Fupa did the grocery and supermarket shopping, Abba took me to the bank, opened an account in my name and deposited £1500. Abba, however, used the debit card, not me. After that, he bought a mobile in my name; he used the phone and said that he'd give both the card and phone to me once he left.

We went to "our new place" and put the things where they needed to be. That day, we had dinner at Fupu's place and when we left, she gave us some food. While Abba and Fupa spoke in the living room, Fupu and I spoke in their bedroom. She advised me not to blame myself. 'Take this as an experience in life. Hardship makes us stronger so don't feel weak.'

I broke down into tears. I told her how Bhaiyya was so uptight and strict about everything. Fupu consoled me that things like this happened.

'But Bhaiyya wasn't like this all the time. He stayed with you when he was a young teenager, didn't he? Wasn't he nice and normal then?' I asked. I expected a nod from Fupu but instead she remained silent. I insisted that she told me how Bhaiyya was then.

'Well, he was a kid after all. He's very feisty and hot-headed like his mum.' She gave a little chuckle before continuing, 'I remember after dinner, he used to refuse to take his plate to the sink. I had to be firm with him to which he retorted, *"I'm not bothered to take it to the sink."* It's funny how people change. He used to also refuse to take his shoes off when inside the house. Yet now when we visit him, he emphasises the importance of not wearing the same shoes in the house which have been worn outside.'

I didn't know what to think any more. At seventeen, I was already too depressed and for the past few months I'd been struggling to breathe. I ignored this at first but, after a while, I felt the need to see a doctor.

I booked an appointment in the morning on the way to college. I couldn't wait to see Panna. There was a happy and peaceful air about her, which I needed as a passive mask to breath in. But I didn't see her in any of the classes I shared with her. So, I met up with Ambreen and Lilly and tried to keep my distance from Hamid.

But when I was waiting for my bus, I noticed Panna in the distance. She was hugging someone, and then locking her lips with that someone. That someone was Adam. I was shocked.

She wore a headscarf. How could she do that? But during my three years in Coral Reef College, I got used to witnessing girls doing that. While some girls in hijabs smoked in public, others fell pregnant out of wedlock.

What they were doing was their own choice and God has given us free will. But wearing a hijab on top of that gave it a perverted look. Their actions didn't define hijab and neither did hijab define them. Hijab was just as normal as dyeing one's hair.

And then I looked at myself in the mirror. I was deceiving everyone too. I wore the hijab making everyone believe that I was pure and pious, when I knew that I didn't want to wear one yet. So, I told Abba that I didn't want to wear a headscarf until further notice. I didn't want to wear it for the sake of it. Character was more important and I wanted to improve that first. I confronted Panna a couple of weeks later.

'So why didn't you tell me that you're seeing your cousin?' I asked.

'He's not my cousin. We used to go primary and secondary school together.'

'You didn't have to lie that he was your cousin then.'

'I didn't lie about anything. You assumed that he was my cousin and I didn't correct that as I felt that you wouldn't approve of that.'

'And why did you think that?'

''Cos you also wear... erm, *wore* a headscarf.' Panna looked down.

'Listen, I'm not a highly religious person. You wear a headscarf if *you* wish to wear one. If you're not ready, then don't wear it. The point is, adhere to good character. I have no intentions of having a boyfriend before marriage. But just because I don't wear a scarf, it doesn't mean that I have or will have a boyfriend. People may not agree and guess what? I don't care,' I explained.

'No, you're right.' Panna looked serious. 'I know I shouldn't do this too, but...' We hugged and decided not to judge each other. We met Adam and I teased him for not telling me anything before. He was blushing and getting annoyed and I was loving it. I felt free. I told Panna how my dad and I had to move out. She was sympathetic but noticed that I looked happier.

'Oh my God. It's him, there,' I said. My heart skipped a beat.

'Him who?' Adam asked.

'The guy Ranya digs.' Panna nudged me with her shoulder.

'Him? That's Mahi. We used to play football together.' This little bit of information felt like spiritual revelation. And this was how I had gleaned his name and other details about him, from Adam.

'You *know* him? Tell me more. How old is he? Does he have a girlfriend?'

'I'm tellin' ya nuthin'!' Adam teased.

I implored him but he refused to tell me anything at all. Seeing my frustration and desperation, Panna coaxed him. So he offered me a forfeit-he demanded an apology for teasing him earlier and in return he'd tell me whatever he knew about Mahi. I rolled my eyes and as a result had to apologise twice.

'He's sixteen. He doesn't have a girlfriend,' Adam said. 'I'm not that close to him any more so I don't know anything else.'

'Oh no. I'm older than him, then.'

'Academically you're in the same year,' Panna said.

'Why aren't you friends with him any more?' I asked.

Adam looked uneasy but spoke anyway. 'Last year he became religious and all that. He started lecturing me that I shouldn't hang around with Panna as it's not allowed and blah blah, blah.' He raked his fingers through his hair and as he said this he glanced at Mahi briefly. 'Yeah... so I stopped hanging around with him.' Panna looked at me and I understood why she didn't want me to know about her and Adam. But this made me like Mahi even more as I couldn't believe that he thought in the same way as I did.

Maybe we'll get married one day...

I couldn't stop thinking about Mahi. I saw him everywhere I went. In the meantime, my breathing problem was escalating and recently it was also accompanied by insomnia. I saw the doctor three times in three weeks. In the first week, she asked me general questions like how often and for how long I had been experiencing this phase. In the second week, she suggested that I took a lukewarm shower before sleep and had a warm milky drink. By the third week, Abba was intrigued by this appointment ritual I had. He insisted that he came along with me to the doctor's surgery. I felt uncomfortable at this but it almost felt like an adamant decision.

Dr Nicola, who resembled Gwyneth Paltrow, came out and called my name. Abba got up as well and followed me. She asked me who he was but Abba was quick to reply, 'I'm her father.'

'Oh okay. But you don't need to come.' Abba smiled and said that he was a doctor too. Dr Nicola said that in that case

231

he should know that he didn't need to be inside the room with me. Abba looked a bit taken aback. I felt he deserved it.

I was asked if my problems had improved or not and hearing a negative answer, she performed a particular test on me.

'For three minutes, I need you to close your eyes and not think about anything, at all.' I obeyed her. Exactly three minutes later, her stopwatch rang and she told me to give an account of what I'd been thinking of in those minutes.

'You told me not to think about anything so I didn't think about anything all.'

'Yes, but you must've drifted off to some random thought at some point, even something like, "Will I be able to do what the doctor has asked me to do"?'

I reiterated again and again that I hadn't thought of anything. She was sceptical and then surprised.

'How were you able to do that?' she asked as she typed on the computer.

'I'm kind of used to it,' I said. She wanted to know how frequently I practised this.

'Since I was a child. When something bad happened, I'd just block everything from my mind. And I still do it, sometimes.'

'And how "bad" would you describe this thing which makes you block your mind?' Dr Nicola looked at me this time. It felt like I was being studied under a microscope.

Should I tell her about what has been happening to me so far? What about reputation? He's my brother after all...

'N... nothing. It's not that bad. I just do that, like a game.' I withdrew my gaze. But Dr Nicola didn't.

'Tell me the truth. You have nothing to worry about,' she assured me. I managed to convince her that I was fine for she stopped asking me anything else. She said that it wasn't something she'd be able to diagnose so she made a referral for me at the Royal London Hospital.

'You should receive a letter within a few days. Make sure you call up to confirm a suitable day for your appointment.'

I walked the way home from college as it was a rather warm day for February. A quaint smell of the seaside pervaded the air momentarily and reminded me of the good times in Dubai.

Every Friday used to be a holiday and if Abba and Amma were not fighting then we used to go to the beach. Amma would make egg and cucumber sandwiches while Abba would make a spicy tuna and *harisa* mix to eat with freshly baked *khubz, baguettes.*

He used to also pick up plenty of soft drinks, and ice-lollies from the campus supermarket and put them in a big cooler bag. Those were the wonderful days. I used to wish that they'd never end. When I used to step out from the car, the hot sand used to feel like hot coals under my feet. Di and I used to stomp as we laid the picnic mat. The azure sky used to reflect its beauty on the sea, which in turn used to kiss the hot sand with lazy waves. As I matured, I came to realise that perhaps good times were no more than a tantalising mirage to a desperate drifter, like me.

I came home and Abba told me that he had done some shopping so I could start cooking.

'I just cooked a chicken curry yesterday,' I said.

'Yeah, it was so nice that I couldn't help myself. I ate all of it for lunch.'

I had tons of reading up to do but that'd have to wait now. I prayed and started to prepare dinner. I cooked a turnip and fish curry, lentils, another chicken curry but with potatoes this time, and boiled some rice. I cooked more than usual so that it'd last for two days. But this curry too came out very nice and Abba ate more than half of everything just by himself. He got up whilst eating and kissed my forehead.

'You cook really well. You've got the magic touch of my mum's culinary skills. I'm so proud of you.'

I smiled Bibha's back-up smile for the first time. Any other time I would've gloated with merriment but right now it irked me. This only meant that tomorrow I'd have to cook again. After washing up the dishes, I went to the bathroom to wash our clothes which I had soaked earlier with detergent and water.

I saw Fupa's friend, his wife, and son, Jabir all ready to go out. The nice lady, whom I called Apa, told me that they'd be back quite late so we should lock up.

I went to the room to hang the clothes on the radiator. The carpet, which was midnight blue with repetitive orange-coloured diamond shapes on it, looked like it needed to be hoovered. There was a double bed with a funny looking pink headboard at the end of the wall and next to it was a window with red curtains and a white net, split into two. A pine wardrobe and a desk were next to each other opposite the bed. Abba slept on the floor in the sleeping bag and I slept on the bed. I placed the hoover downstairs and, having finished all my chores, I came back to the room. I was exhausted so I flopped on the bed and reminisced about Mahi. I cherished the brief moments of seeing him that day and it was awesome. He was staring at me for so long that he didn't notice his friend looking at him blankly. His friend followed Mahi's gaze, which was directed at me and then back at Mahi again. He blushed when his friend waved his palm up and down his face to distract him. It felt great to know that he knew I existed.

'You seem quite happy today?' Abba said. I jerked up and fixed the top of my nightdress.

'I'm just too tired and don't feel like studying.' I said. Abba came and sat down next to me. He brushed my hair and traced my oval face with his fingers.

'Suck my tongue,' Abba said. He got on top of me as he said that; just the way he used to do back home in Kakongonj.

'No... I don't want to do that.' I was feeling weird all over.

'Then stick your tongue out and I'll suck it.'

'No... I don't want that either,' I said and tried to be as polite as possible. A part of me remembered films where an angry refusal led the rapist to rape his victim. Abba brushed my hair off my face and tucked it behind my ear. He started to kiss me softly around my neck, face and lips. These incidents were occurring more often than ever before. I tried to think of nothing while it happened and, in the process, I'd stop breathing. I so didn't want the fast rate of my breathing to be a welcoming gesture to carry on. I pursed my lips tight and remained frigid.

'It's okay. Don't worry. It's pretty normal for a father to show love to his daughter like this,' he whispered into my ears over and over again.

He said this every time he encountered me like that. It never felt right but as he was my father it made no sense for him to harm me. But despite this passive solace, the sodden stirring of past incidents effervesced in my belly, creating tidal surges through my veins, followed by cold perspiration drops on my temples. A frisson of acute anxiety erupted as the words, *"I always loved you more than Megha. I'll make you feel very happy. Tell me, are you happy?"* were whispered, and an affirmation was tacitly demanded.

A particular memory came flashing back to me. A memory of that horrendous evening when I was just a little girl. I was playing with my beads with Abba when Amma hollered, 'Ranya! You need to have your shower, *now*!'

I got nervous and hurried like crazy; yet I never got to have a shower that evening. From the bathroom, I let out an ear-shattering cry. Within seconds, although what felt like a lifetime, Amma and Di, my elder sister, ran towards the hallway where they now found me standing wide-eyed, perplexed and terror-stricken. They looked relieved though, to see Abba already there, next to me, trying to calm me down.

'For God's sake! What's the matter, Ranya?' Amma and Di asked for the umpteenth time.

But I only chanted, 'I'm scared! I'm scared! I'm scared! I'm scared…' in delirium. For all their heartfelt entreaties, I could give no answer, not even another word, no matter what or how they asked me. I just didn't know what to say or how to say it.

'Now take off your knickers,' Abba had said. He too had taken off all his clothes save for his underpants. 'We can't have our clothes on when we take a shower. I'll make you feel very happy.' And that's when I screamed, nonstop. As I screamed, he gradually put his clothes back on. He opened the door and I ran out to the hallway. Amma and Di were already

there by then and kept asking me what the matter was. Amma looked concerned and asked Abba as I gave no answer whatsoever. 'You know how little children sometimes get overtired on days when they're really hyper and don't get enough sleep? Well, that's just what's happened to Ranya.' Amma nodded in agreement while Di put my clothes back on.

RANYA

It was a Saturday and I wasn't expecting anything in the post. But when Abba handed me a letter addressed to me, I remembered what it was. He enquired about it and I filled him in with the details about my breathing issues.

'I've been referred to a psychiatrist as my GP said that all physical anomalies have been ruled out.' Abba was drinking black tea and this news shocked him so much that he almost choked on it.

'Why do you need to see a psychiatrist? You're absolutely fine. You're just stressed... because of studies and all that happened at Yasin's place. Just try and relax. Trust me. I'm a doctor too. Do you know what? We should go somewhere today. What do you say?'

'I don't know, Abba. There is something I need to tell you. You may get angry but I need to tell you this.' Abba looked concerned but assured that he wouldn't get cross. I broached the topic about Mahi and how I was infatuated with him; that I knew it was a phase but it was inhibiting the normal progress of my life, especially my studies.

'Have you been going out with him?' he asked.

I answered in the negative and suggested that it'd be better if I changed colleges but he said I'd have to simply ignore this. He also said that I wasn't guilty of anything, provided I didn't speak to him or have any kind of relationship with him. With a sceptical look in his eyes, he thanked me for trusting him to tell him this.

Over the next week or so Abba's behaviour was rather erratic. It seemed that the news about Mahi was troubling him but he didn't want to quite express it. The following week he came home one day and said that he had booked his flight to go back home.

'I thought you wanted to stay away from Amma and do some medical research while you were here?' A part of me was excited that he was leaving; I never really wanted to share the room with my father in the first place. 'Weren't you supposed to leave in the summer holidays?'

'No, I spoke to your Amma and she said she's missing me. I'm missing her too and I don't like the cold. It's bad for my arthritis.' Abba was smoking more often these days. I'd told him that he should quit but he just said, 'Smoking helps with depression. Besides, I've switched to *Mayfair*. It's not that strong. Women usually smoke this brand.'

Abba left within that week. I wanted to accompany him with Fupa who drove him to Heathrow Airport but he said that I ought to concentrate on my studies. I felt bad for him.

Who will cook for him now?

I felt wretched that I hated to cook everyday while he was around. The old man only wanted some good food, that's all. And I was moaning for nothing. I opened my chemistry book but couldn't concentrate on it. I couldn't fathom that I used to be the same person who used to love education, and spend hours studying. I felt like an airhead now. There was a wealth of books in bookshops, school libraries, and public libraries and the internet too. But my mind was prone to wandering all the time. I was failing in my tests and homework and as a result Mr Abbas told me to see him in his office after class. Mr Feroz from my tutor form group was also there for some other reason. I entered his office with no idea of what I was about to hear. Mr Abbas returned me my chemistry mock exam paper along with a piece of his mind. I had to endure a ruthless diatribe from him regarding my poor performance and concentration during class hours. The height and width of my embarrassment was expanding and I wished the ground would split for me to hide. Mr Abbas used to be Bhaiyya's teacher more than a decade ago.

'Your father left both your brother and you in the hope that you'd study hard and become doctors but both of you have wasted his money and shattered his dreams.'

My chemistry teacher didn't realise that by ranting like this, he put my form tutor too in the same bracket of discomfiture. Before leaving, he commented that my father was dismayed at Bhaiyya's unfulfilled promise and knowing that, I shouldn't repeat the same as that would be similar to picking on a fresh scab. I knew where he was coming from and he was right, but I didn't know how to make amends. I wanted to pay attention to my studies but I just couldn't concentrate. I was lost in my infatuation.

But why did it make me feel so bad? Why did it feel like there was some underlying cause behind my depression?

I had questions but no answers. I picked up a *Mayfair* on the way home.

***

When I was younger, I used to always pray to Allah that my exam results would be good through a miracle. I knew that it depended on how hard I had studied and ultimately it was that which had an impact on my results; nevertheless, I prayed like crazy on results day.

Today was no different. I wore a red salwar kameez, a black denim jacket, and black pumps; and I prayed to Allah that my GCSE results were decent. But they weren't. My subjects were English, mathematics, biology, chemistry, and physics. And I got *B, B, C, C, C* in them respectively.

Abba will kill me! My mobile rang. Lilly sent me a few Bollywood themed ringtones. This one was:

Thora sa Pyaar hua hai
(A bit of love has blossomed)
Thora hai Baqi
(A bit more is left)

It was my favourite ringtone. But the ringtone didn't flow the sweet tune as it usually did and the person calling was also not who I wished it to be. I switched it off hoping to buy some time. I got on the bus and rehearsed what to say till I arrived home.

My landlord's toddler greeted me with a hug. He was adorable and loved me to bits. But today I didn't want to see him; I just wanted to be by myself.

As usual, the house was smelling of yummy food. Apa cooked every day. At times, I felt like telling her that I'd pay her extra if she could kindly cook enough for me too since it was a bother for me to do shopping, cooking, cleaning, and washing my clothes by hand. She told me to use her washing machine but shyness prevented me in both the cases.

She looked out for me and always advised me to come home before dusk. She was cooking hilsha fish curry today, my favourite. But I was too stressed to think about food. My mobile rang again for the fifth time.

'Assalamu alaikum, Abba.'

'Walaikum salam.' There was pause before he said, 'So?' I wished Abba asked how I was first. I told him what I got and in which subjects. He didn't say anything positive or negative about it. I told him that our form tutor said that this GCSE was in fact the standard of O Level and so *C* was equivalent to a *B*, and *B* was equivalent to an *A*.

He didn't say anything to that and I had a feeling that he felt I was making excuses. He asked me if I wanted to speak to Amma. I said no so he hung up. With Abba, silence was often a presage for disapproval. I got a notepad out and penned a letter.

Dear Abba, I hope you and Amma are well. I am okay. I know how you must be feeling. All I can say is that I am extremely sorry for letting you down. I should've concentrated more on my studies. I know I have no excuse for justifying my poor results. But I promise you, Abba, that I will perform a lot better in my A levels. Please pray for me.

Yours truly, Ranya

I posted the letter but never got a reply. And neither did I have the courage to ask Abba over the phone if he had received the letter or not.

RANYA

Ambreen, Lilly, Hamid, and Panna, along with her boyfriend, left the year I commenced my A Levels. I felt quite lonely. A lot of new faces appeared in my classes of my forcefully chosen subjects, chemistry and biology. One girl in particular, called Azufa, befriended me. She was tall, slender, and dark with striking features. She wore a hijab but was one of the decent hijabi girls. There were girls who wore hijab but smoked, took drugs, snogged and frolicked with their boyfriends' privates, in public. And then there were girls like me who didn't wear hijab but abstained from such indecent acts.

Azufa seemed to be nice girl. She seemed to know the other students and soon I got to know that they all went to the same school. We started to hang about a lot especially since we shared our tutor group, biology, and chemistry classes. She used to always save a seat for me next to her and I for her. Often, I found her sitting by herself during lunch hour, reading. I hardly ever saw her eating.

'You know what? There won't be any more of you if you keep on skipping lunch,' I joked. She smiled and looked uneasy.

'Is everything all right?' I asked. She looked tense and I wanted to help her in any way possible.

'Erm... I don't have any money to buy food,' she said.

'Oh.' I felt really bad for her but didn't want her to see me pitying her. 'Well? What am I here for?' I grabbed her hand and took her to the vending machine. I got her favourite flavour of crisps: cheese and onion, a chocolate bar, and a can of coke. For myself, I got a Ribena. Azufa thanked me for the rest of the day till I told her that I'd quit being her friend if she didn't stop. On the way home, on the bus, she explained that her parents were struggling financially since a lot of their benefits had been cut.

A few days later, Azufa asked me about a particular off-white salwar kameez I had worn at the beginning of the year. I told her that Lilly had made it for me. She asked if she could use it as template. I agreed and brought it for her the following day. We went to the girls' bathroom and she tried it on to see if it would fit her. It fitted her perfectly. She admired the way she looked and I couldn't help but tell her that she could keep it.

'Are you sure?' Azufa asked.

'Yeah. It looks nicer on you anyway since you're taller,' I said. She thanked me again for the rest of the day. On the way home, as usual, we waited together for our bus. She usually got off three or four stops before me but the distance wasn't close enough for her to walk it home. I asked her why she decided to walk today especially since it was raining too.

'I don't have any money for the bus fare.' I scolded her for feeling shy and not asking me to give her some change for the fare. 'And please save me from your thanking lecture,' I finished.

This was often the case with her but I didn't mind since I knew the pain of not having enough money for one's basic needs. Over the year, Azufa and I became very close. I told her about my unrequited love and she told me about some playboy type of guy in college, on whom she'd had a crush since primary school. She pointed him out to me in class and her eyes welled up when she saw him flirting with one of his girlfriends.

'He's not worth it, Azufa. He probably has a girlfriend in each of his classes.' Azufa nodded and later I bought her cheese and onion crisps to cheer her up.

Initially, she used to wear a headscarf but by the end of the year, Azufa wore the *abaya* too. We weren't in touch over the summer holidays and when I met her after college resumed, she was a completely different person. She didn't look like before and she behaved rather strangely too – sort of... *radicalised,* like Bhaiyya. I had no solid proof but she seemed to avoid me. She didn't save seats for me, and refused to sit next to me even if I saved a seat for her. She didn't travel home with me any more, didn't wait for me when classes were over, didn't talk to me during break times, and never asked for any money for food or bus fares.

After six months, I mustered the courage to confront her. After our biology class, I went up to her and asked her what the matter was.

'It's just that you don't wear the hijab. You wear western type of clothes and makeup. Don't take me wrong... you look absolutely stunning, but it's not right for girls to display their beauty.'

'So how come this wasn't an issue before?' I asked. I was struggling to control my anger.

'Well, you seemed like you were in need of a friend so I was hoping that you'd change and start to wear the hijab soon but you didn't. And I'm sorry but I don't want to be seen hanging around with you since people will comment that I am a hijabi but I hang around with non-hijabis.'

I wanted to correct her that it was she who was in need of a friend and not the other way around. But I didn't want to provoke her and neither did I want to stoop low by reminding her of my favours. Without further comment, I wished her well and swore to myself to never befriend people who judged girls by the piece of cloth they wrapped around their head. For such girls were better off wrapping those pieces of cloth around their mouth for uttering such foul-smelling verbal shit.

**

I wasn't able to keep up with my promise to Abba as I still couldn't concentrate on my studies. Due to poor grades, I had to retake a lot of the modules, on top of the new modules. I knew it was solely my fault for all I did was daydream about Mahi. I didn't see him around college any more and then I had a revelation.

When I was doing my GCSEs, he was in his first year of A Levels. When I was doing my AS Levels, he was doing his A2 Levels. So now that I was in my second year of A Levels, he was at university. I had no idea as to *which* university he had gone to. Except for the stunt Ambreen had pulled, I never spoke to Mahi and neither did he ever speak to me. We shared no lessons together and the closest distance between us used to be at least twenty yards, if not more. In those two glorious years of college, the only thing we both did was look at each other till some kind of a distraction turned up. I only dared to dream or imagine of speaking to him. I convinced myself that Mahi was someone my mind had created, just like it had created other things before. The characters, settings, and themes were conveniently, to my liking. Probably he was one of my oddest imaginations. So odd, that I believed he did and didn't exist – both at the same time. His presence was somewhat surreal. I always felt his aura whenever he was around. Often, I'd scan the place around me, among other people, for I'd feel his eyes watching me; and before long, my eyes would meet his and this way I used to know that he was looking at me first, that he knew I existed.

The last time I saw him was more than six months ago. I also acknowledged that I'd probably never get to see him again. And this doleful thought made me break down to tears. For the first time, I cried and wailed for someone; for someone I ardently loved. That my love was not reciprocated made every single ounce in me, ache with an ineffable pain which I could neither cope with nor comprehend. I cried till I became delirious. Subconsciously I prayed over and over again, *Please let me see him – just once, just a glimpse.* And just like a lullaby, I murmured this till I fell asleep.

***

I'd never forget that morning. It was a cloudy and windy day, and wearing an overcoat had become necessary. I walked through Whitechapel market like I did every Saturday, and bumped into one of the girls from college. As we shook hands,

I remembered why I always avoided that with her. Her hands were coarse like a wire scourer. We spoke for a while, when suddenly I felt that surreal feeling I used to feel whenever Mahi used to stare at me. I looked on the right, left, front, and even behind me. My friend asked me if I was looking for something. I shook my head. There was no sign of him. And why would there be? *Silly me! As if my prayer would come true. But why am I sensing that funny feeling?*

I felt guilty for not paying attention to her – she had to ask me something twice as my mind and eyes kept wandering. 'Your eyes, they look puffed up. You okay?' she asked.

'Yeah, I'm fine,' I lied. I couldn't avoid that dreamlike feeling of Mahi's presence. Like a radar signal, it kept getting stronger, and like an approaching siren, it kept getting louder in my head.

And then my heart stopped beating. Mahi was there, in person, walking from the left with his sight fixated on me. He was wearing a beige jacket and a pair of khaki trousers.

Was my prayer really answered? That "funny feeling" proved to be right again. I wanted to carry on looking at him but decided to look at my friend instead. I was so happy. A stupid grin was affixed on my face. I just couldn't stop grinning. Like a zit, it seemed to stay on for ages. A few seconds later I looked to my right, but by then he was gone. Lost in the crowd. Minding his own business. And that was the last time I ever saw Mahi. This unbelievable moment lasted me a good few months till the novelty wore off. *I ought to have asked God for something more substantial.*

RANYA

Amma and Abba were very meticulous about the way we spoke. We were taught to speak in the proper Bengali language. This was the vernacular amongst the ethnic community when we were in Dubai, Hayapur, and Kakongonj. But it put me out of place in London since most of the Asian/Bangladeshi community were from Sylhet and spoke *Sylheti* – a dialect that was linguistically not considered to be part of the Bengali language. This speech also varied in nuance considering the diverse parts of Sylhet that people came from. Panna, Ambreen, Lilly, and Azufa often took the mickey when I sometimes spoke in my way in Bengali. As Azufa became estranged from me, I came across another girl from my biology class called Chini. Chini meant sugar in Bengali, and indeed she took after her name. She was brought up in Hayapur and came to London a year ago. We shared the same lingo and childhood memories – well, almost.

Chini was shorter and bigger than me, but neither of these adversely affected her. She too fancied someone but unlike me, she was confident when it came to talking to him. Chini loved her life and accepted herself just the way she was. I realised that I was the total opposite.

Her parents were also back home and she was here with her brother. They stayed with their aunt in Romford. I used to spend the days of Eid by myself but since I befriended her, I spent the festivals with her. Her family was very cordial so we used to hang out often. We used to go Trafalgar Square, to the cinema, eat out in McDonald's, eat endless numbers of ice creams and get facials and our hair done at parlours. It was therapeutic and helped me come out of my depression. Her parents visited her during the holidays and I noticed that her mum was nothing like her. She was tall and lithe.

'As you can see, I haven't been blessed with my mum's genes.' Chini pouted. Before I could say anything, her mum hugged her and ruffled her hair saying that she was perfect just the way she was and that she made her very proud.

On my way home by train, I figured out the secret to Chini's confidence. Her mother's support and love as to how she was, made Chini love and accept herself. On the other hand, my mother's scorn led to increasing self-doubt in myself. My shame to accept myself for how I was, was no more than a reflection of my mother's attitude towards me.

One Friday, Chini called and told me to meet her the following day at our college, at nine a.m. sharp. She was very outgoing and made plans for us to go to Chessington. We met up and that weekend was both the best and worst weekend of my life. We rode on the roller coaster, which almost gave me a heart attack. Chini couldn't stop laughing when she saw my state after the ride.

'Here you go, ride that virtual reality rocket instead. It's more suitable for chickens like you,' Chini said.

I told her to shut up as I wiped tears from my eyes.

It was over ten p.m. when we finished watching a Bollywood film at the cinema. I expressed my concern of travelling back to my place this late. Chini, on the other hand, wasn't scared to travel even further than me.

'Tell you what? Come and stay over at my other aunt's house. They live in Tottenham and I'm staying there over the weekend.'

'N… No, I can't do that. I don't want to be a bother,' I said.

'It won't be a bother. It's just for one night and one day. You can leave tomorrow while it's still daylight. And don't worry, my aunt's son stays in another place close to his Uni and my brother is with him.' I still looked sceptical so she added, 'Uncle stays at his restaurant during the weekend. So, it's only my aunt and her daughter in their house.' I thought quickly. I never travelled this late from an unfamiliar place before. I was scared. Besides, Jabir's mum didn't approve of my late arrivals so I accepted Chini's offer and thanked her. On the bus, I messaged Jabir's mum about my whereabouts. It was eleven forty-five p.m. and Chini was cracking jokes. I didn't find them funny as more than two stoned people were on the bus. Chini called me anal retentive and I was too anxious for a comeback.

I wanted to leave after breakfast but Chini's aunt and daughter insisted that I stayed a bit longer. They ordered some Turkish food for lunch, which was very nice. It was almost four p.m. so upon my prompt, Chini, her cousin, and I set out to leave. They suggested that we viewed the fleet of speedboats and yachts on the River Thames, as it was on the way to the bus stop.

It was summer and the days were longer but for some reason, I was getting butterflies in my stomach. We arrived at the bus stop around five. Chini's cousin bid us farewell and left. It occurred to me then that Chini and I were not going to be taking the same bus. We were waiting for almost an hour. In my mind, I prayed that my bus came before hers.

'My bus is here. See you soon, ta.' With a peck on the cheek and a hug, Chini left.

I was feeling nervous now. I began to think of Mahi and soon half an hour passed by without me even realising. It was half seven and still there was no sign of my bus. I'd also have to get off after six stops to catch another bus, which would take me to my college; from there I'd have to get my usual bus to get home.

The bus stop was getting scarce of people. I noticed a very tall family of three on my left and a middle-aged man on my right. The latter seemed to look at me in a discreet manner. On a second glance, I recognised the man from the harbour where Chini, her cousin and I had been a few hours ago. The tall family got on the next bus and there was still no sign of my bus. I was hoping that the middle-aged man would get on that bus too, but he didn't. The bus Chini rode on came again and so did another bus. The man boarded neither of them. I noticed that he wasn't trying to be inconspicuous any more when he looked at me. He was wearing a burgundy blazer and jeans, and had a bit of a pot belly. He looked South Indian but I couldn't tell for sure. What I was sure of though was that he was bad news. And it felt that he was a lot closer to me in distance now.

It was just over eight p.m. and hardly any people were around now. My heart rate increased and a cold shiver ran down my spine. I began to recite *Ayatul Kursi*. Bhaiyya had taught me this long time ago when he had come to Hayapur.

He told me that this was the longest verse in the Quran and it should be read for protection. I recited the verse like crazy in my mind. I felt conscious of myself and wished that I wasn't dressed the way I was. I wore black leggings, a blue/green mini mermaid skirt, a black top, and a slate denim jacket. I wore my hair in a high ponytail with large loop earrings. My three-inch-heel ankle boots began to hurt my feet and my conscience, as they portrayed me as the perfect victim for perverts. I tried my best to not look scared but I knew that *he* knew that I was.

My bus finally came at quarter past eight and I was utterly grateful. I got on the bus and so did the man. The bus was not completely empty so I felt assured. The man sat right at the back and I right at the front. The bus halted at Aldgate East and I got off thinking that I was getting scared for no reason at all. But then, to my horror, I saw the middle-aged man get off at the same stop as me. A scarlet sun was waving its rays, indicating that I would be on my own very soon. There was not a single person in sight other than the man and myself. I was dreading the worst.

This is it. I will be dragged in some alley and raped and killed maybe. And it'll be all my fault. The man was looking at me with confident menace. He had a hidden smile, which only I could see. It was the smile of a predator and it was reminiscent of Abba. I stood at the bus stop waiting frantically for the bus. I looked down and could hear footsteps getting closer to me. I carried on reciting the verse of protection. I sought forgiveness too from Allah.

Please save my honour. From the corner of my eyes I saw a man appear from a newsagent's shop. He was wearing formal trousers, and a white shirt. He was carrying his blazer and a briefcase in his left hand and was studying the post for bus routes. He looked Indian too. He had a big moustache and looked around fifty. Without thinking, I approached him and started a conversation.

'Are you waiting for the bus?' I asked.

'Yes. My bus should be here soon. Are you waiting for the fifteen too?'

'Yes.'

'It should be here in about two minutes. Ah there it is.' Saying this he got on the bus and it was then that I realised that he was none other than the bus driver himself. The bus was quite full. As I got on, I looked around, but the creepy middle-aged man was nowhere to be seen. Like a rain cloud, he was a vampire that got vanquished once the sun shone.

I arrived safely at home that night after all. I had a shower, ate pot noodles, brushed my teeth, and went to bed. The following morning, I did something I had never done before. I took out the Quran from a suitcase I had kept it in, indefinitely. It included a translated text. I didn't know why but I had to find out why and where hijab was mentioned in this Holy Book. I looked in the glossary, which referenced Chapter 33, verse 59. It read, *O Prophet, tell your wives and your daughters and the women of the believers to draw their cloaks close round them (when in public). That will be better, so that they may be recognised and not annoyed. (And withal), Allah is ever Forgiving, Merciful.*

I got goosebumps when I read this verse. Never ever before did I connect like this with the Quran. This verse seemed to speak directly to me, as though it was waiting to be read by *me.* Hijab was mentioned but no coercion was evident in its recommendation.

It wasn't to be worn by just any woman. It was specifically for the *believing women.* God could've said *beautiful women* but He doesn't say that either. Hijab is to be worn so that we can label ourselves as "decent women" and not be disturbed.

I felt guilty too. I recalled a memory of nine eleven.

I was at Canary Wharf with a couple of friends when we watched the news on the TV in one of the cafés. I had recently taken my hijab off and was feeling awkward about it. The tragedy gave Islam the connotation of terrorism. People were discussing how hijabis would be harassed by non-Muslims as a result of this. While my friends reflected their concern, I rejoiced secretly. It gave me the perfect alibi as to why I decided to take my hijab off. God knows about such flaw in people like me, hence He added the part that He is forgiving – when we err.

I couldn't stop laughing for only yesterday I had advertised myself, with my dress-code, as a "come-and-get-me-you-perv-out-there". Jabir's mum wasn't religious but culturally informed and so used to advise me to not stay out late. All these bits of information were fitting in like a jigsaw puzzle now. Hijab was not just a piece of cloth but rather a modest appearance that didn't provoke sexual predators. With a sigh, I made up my mind that I'd wear the hijab. I wasn't doing this for anyone else. I was doing it for myself. God tells us to wear hijab for our own protection and not because He wants to oppress us. It's like how a government body would issue certain rules if there was an epidemic or endemic disease breakout. For our own good they advise us to follow certain hygiene regulations. Perverted men were the likes of such fatal disease and the hijab was simply a prevention measure.

When college resumed, a lot of the girls didn't recognize me. It was funny but I was glad that I was doing this because I knew the reason behind it.

Suddenly I felt a hug from behind me.

'Oh my God. You look so nice with the hijab. One of the girls from my history class told me that you were wearing one now and I couldn't wait to congratulate you.'

It was Azufa. She went on and on about some gibberish. She wanted me to join her circle of friends.

'It's okay. I don't want to be part of the cliquey Venn diagram you are in.'

Her eyes showed an expression between hurt and confusion, and I left her to it.

***

I had worn the hijab for three months now and it felt good. I always wore a black or a coffee brown cotton pashmina and that particular day I wore a brown scarf. I was returning home from work one day around three o'clock. I worked at Euston Square, in a bakery and usually brought back some freshly baked baguettes or naan breads, which I used to eat with a meat or chicken curry. I didn't know how to cook the conventional way so I used to cook the proteins by adding curry sauce out of a store-bought jar. I loved lentils but I could never cook them right and I missed a proper home cooked meal. Abba used to tell me off for making pot noodles, doner kebab, and chicken and chips, my staple diet, but he didn't understand that it wasn't easy buying food, dragging it home and then preparing and cooking it, which often didn't turn out as good. It was also lonesome to eat by myself and the stress of my studies was also inhibiting my appetite.

I stopped by the corner shop to buy some red chili powder on the way back. I thought adding a teaspoon of it would add some extra flavour; I didn't find the jar of curry masala hot enough. I was just a few feet away from my humble abode when I noticed the roads to be rather empty and silent for that time of the day. No sooner had I thought that than a car zoomed from my left and slid into the right. I couldn't see the driver and kissed my teeth for their reckless manner. I just turned into the street I needed to go in when a tall Asian/Bangladeshi boy aged around eighteen or nineteen walked straight up to me asking for my number. I noticed that a car was parked not too far away where some other similar-aged boys were inside laughing and smoking. They were looking at me and smirking; I noticed that it was the same car that sped before. I felt defiled and angry.

I'm wearing hijab. Why am I still being annoyed, God?

I wasn't scared for I wasn't too far away from home, but as no one was around, I felt some anxiety. My first thought was to rip open the chili powder packet and flick its fiery powder into the odious, putrid-smelling character in front of me. But then a girl emerged from inside the car. It was Ambreen. She wore a ripped pair of denim shorts and a white, see-through, off the shoulder blouse that showed her padded bra. She wore lime green converse trainers with ankle socks. Her bleached hair had copper and brown tones to them. Unlike the current trend of straight hair, Ambreen had tousled, wavy curls in a messy bun – her signature look. She chided the boy who was pestering me and apologised on his behalf.

She looked a bit out of it and smelt a bit weird too.

'Where have you been all this time?' I asked.

'I went back home. It was all a trick. My mum forced me to marry my cousin. Ugh. It was horrible. I had a whole packet of laxatives and made myself sick till I was brought back here. I contacted the social services and told them that I wasn't going back to that motherfucker – erm, sorry. I know you don't like swearing and stuff.'

'It's okay. What are you doing now?'

'My mum kicked me out of the house when she knew what happened. I'm staying at this place for homeless girls. It's quite nice actually.' A guy walked next to her from the car. 'Meet my boyfriend, Baz.'

He smelt strange too. Ambreen explained to her boyfriend that I didn't look it but that I was a very spiritual but down-to-earth kind of person. He left after a bit and I asked her what that smell was. 'Marijuana,' Ambreen whispered. I looked at her with an arched eyebrow. She got defensive and told me that she had had a very troubled life so it was all fair. 'For God's sake, I was even molested by my *own* uncle when I was thirteen. Can you believe that?'

'I'm sorry to hear that,' I said.

'That's why I'm all messed up.'

Am I messed up too? Is that the reason why I feel angry and scared every time a boy likes me?

After saying goodbye to her, I went home and studied myself on the mirror. Other than wearing a headscarf, I wore light-blue bootcut jeans, a white top and a black leather jacket.

My hair was covered but the rest of my body was still sending out invitation cards to be sexually assaulted. I looked up in the Quran again and this time I read the same chapter and verse, and noted the part about "the cloaks". Modesty was to be observed entirely. Perhaps one was better off to not cover the hair but wear baggy clothes than to wear a headscarf with tight-fitting clothes. In both cases, one could be the subject of innuendo.

Perhaps Bhaiyya was only looking out for me. His approach was not the best but his interests weren't evil. I had their landline number memorized and after deliberating a bit, I dialled their number and waited on tenterhooks as the phone rang.

'Hello?' it was Bibha.

'Assalamu alaikum. It's me,' I said. Bibha couldn't figure out from my voice so she suggested a few of her friends' names before giving up. She was quiet for a few seconds before exclaiming joy at hearing my name. I spoke to Bhaiyya after her. He sounded happy to speak to me again.

I loved time. It was the best healer of all times.

RANYA

I received Abba's email one morning. He explained that my chemistry teacher would arrange for my ticket to go Bangladesh over the summer holiday. It was a one-way ticket. It struck me as uncanny since I'd need to return again in a couple of months to start university. Mr Abbas pointed that out too. Nevertheless, I was deferential since I believed he knew what he was doing.

The time came for me to leave and Bhaiyya drove me to Heathrow Airport. On the way, he said that he would've appreciated it had Abba asked him himself to drop me off at the airport. I didn't say anything for I didn't want him to know that Abba was resentful that I had spoken to him again after the way he behaved with Abba.

Soon after I was in Kakongonj, I found out the reason behind all this. In the airport, Abba casually asked me to join some dilapidated, private university at some point.

'But I've already been offered a place at Queen Mary University.'

'It's not a proper medicine degree. Besides Mr Abbas doesn't think you'll get the required grades.'

'I know, but after the first two years of medical engineering, on the condition that I get a 2:1, I can jump into the third year of medicine, hence the term "Access to medicine". My grades were not good enough for medicine since I had studied here, in Bangladesh, where the school I went to didn't even follow the British curriculum. You then sent me to London where I first stayed with Bhaiyya, then stayed by myself and sat for my O Levels within eight months. It took me six months to just figure out what a coursework was!' I defended myself, albeit my heart said that he'd make a facetious remark.

'You should've worked harder for your A levels as you would've known the drill by then.'

Abba's voice was calm his words, stolid. 'What's the guarantee that you will get a 2:1 at the end of the two years? You're terrible at interviews so what if you muck up the one which you'll have to attend afterwards for the "jump into the third year"?'

I fell silent and my heart sank.

***

My parents were didactic when it came to decide our careers – Di had said that it was an Asian trait. Abba was renowned for his largesse when treating his patients, while Amma spent her days gloating about her presumed youth, beauty, and pursuing her singing career in the media. Her oft-repeated motto was: *Media is not my profession but my passion.* It was a tacit acknowledgement in our entire family that she was desperate only for the attention and money. Amma, however, didn't allow any of us to embark on her path of career since it was generally condemned in Asian society when one of your own was in the realm of media. They told me to study medicine, as Bhaiyya and Di both decided not to choose that career, a long time ago. I knew that being a doctor was impossible for me because I was terrified of blood! But I never told them this. I didn't want to disappoint them, especially Abba. But then, an incident occurred once with our servant boy.

'*Apamoni*, sister, can you please help me... I have a little cut on my head.' As he spoke, blood trickled down his right temple He called me *Apamoni*. Servants weren't allowed to call their master and his family members by their name.

'Yeah, erm... sure.' I hesitated.

I wished that I hadn't seen the sight of blood dripping and soaking his white T-shirt. I tried to wash the deep cut in his head but couldn't carry on for the smell of blood was making me nauseous; and then I threw up. Eventually, it was our injured servant himself and Abba who had to come to my aid. It was a long time ago but perhaps that made Abba realise that I too wouldn't be able to follow him in his footsteps.

When I went home, it brought back bitter-sweet memories. Amma was lying on the sofa watching Indian dramas on Star Plus. A servant boy, with his two legs amputated, was massaging her legs.

Aww, my baby's here. Come and give me a hug,' Amma said.

I hugged her reluctantly. 'You've lost a lot of weight,' I said.

'Yeah, we've been struggling a lot.' She gave out a long sigh and then with a quiver in her voice she said, 'Three children whom we raised with so much care, yet no one to look after us in our old age. Go and eat. I've cooked for you.'

I washed my hands and went to the kitchen. Abba was there already, heating up the rice in the microwave and placing two pots on the stove. One of them was a chicken curry and the other was a fish curry with Indian olives from our orchard, two blocks away. It was a new plot of land, abundant with vegetation. Abba had bought it recently for two hundred thousand takas. Amma boasted that this was the sixth piece of land to their name.

Abba added water to the fish curry to increase the quantity.

As I served myself, I remembered how Bibha's mum would cook at least eight curries whenever she'd turn up. She'd serve her daughter lovingly and ask if the curries tasted according to her liking or not.

After lunch, I went upstairs and rested a while. I woke up drenched in sweat as there was a power cut for an hour. Amma told me that Abba had already left for his surgery. The electricity was back and I thought of taking a shower. I went to the bathroom next to my room but the state was appalling. I guessed that no one used it so that's why it hadn't been cleaned. I went to Abba's room, the en suite, with my toiletries and clothes. That bathroom looked okay but when I saw the toilet, it made me retch. I looked for cleaning products and found a bleach bottle that had hardly been touched. In fact, when I looked closely, I remembered that it was the one I had last used before I left.

It was a massive bathroom so it took me over two hours to clean it and I scrubbed it inside out till the entire bottle of bleach was spent. I was just finishing off when there was another power cut. I sighed. I could never get angry with someone or something I couldn't count on.

After two months or so, Abba told me that as I was almost twenty, I should mentally get ready to get married since my older siblings got married around that age. I couldn't contact Di, as the house phone restricted calls outside Kakongonj. For a year, my days in Kuraishi Villa became those of the living dead. But one day I picked up the phone, which was ringing just after the dawn prayers. I had an intuition that it'd be Bhaiyya from London.

A week later, Bhaiyya came from the airport to our haunted mansion of a house. Amma and Abba didn't know that he was coming – only I did. Bhaiyya had told me not to tell them as he wanted it to be a surprise.

Amma fainted when she saw him. Abba maintained his usual calm persona; however, I noticed the whites of his eyes turn watery behind his black-framed glasses. Amma never liked cooking but Bhaiyya, being her golden child, was the only person who could make her cook properly. She asked Bhaiyya if the kababs tasted good or not since she knew that this was his favourite. Bhaiyya remarked that the ginger was a bit too much. Amma apologised and I could tell that she was hurt.

After a late lunch, I gave Bhaiyya a tour of the property. We first went into the garden.

A rich earthy smell welcomed us. Even in November, the air was humid. A neat pavement surrounded the green garden. Leaves and vines of several bottle gourds and luscious pumpkins laced the edge of that pavement where we ambled. A coconut tree stood tall and proud amidst the garden and just next to it, the light scent of a henna tree lingered. A short papaya tree was opposite to those trees and bore just one ripe, half-eaten papaya – most likely by a bird. The cauliflowers and tomatoes looked ready for harvest. The back of the house had a narrow four-by-eight-foot allotment where Dad grew all kinds of green and red leafy vegetables. He was proud of his organic crops. More than of me, as a daughter, at least.

'Ahh. I just love that soil-like smell in the air,' Bhaiyya said as he cupped some earth into his hand. An earthworm wriggled away. I grimaced.

Clapping the earth from his hands, Bhaiyya suggested that I gave him a tour of the house now. It was a three storey one with acres of greenery around it. A pond surrounded with Kans grass could be seen from the distance. It was also perhaps the only source of water for the local indigent people. Albeit only five kilometres away from the main town, our area still seemed to be rural. Electricity was a privilege for those who had it and to find local transport was a commute in itself.

After the tour, we came back to the patio on the second floor. This allowed some privacy and I confronted Bhaiyya while I had the chance.

'Bhaiyya, why are you here?' With my mobile confiscated, no access to the Internet, phone, or the post office, I was reduced to counting on merely God's mercy that Bhaiyya would come and sort out the peril I was in.

'It's high time I saw Amma and Abba. You, too, haven't been in touch since that one email you wrote after you came here last… July was it?' I nodded. 'So, your Bibha and I were worried for you,' he said.

I filled Bhaiyya with all the details – about Amma verbally abusing me and slandering me in the most immoral of ways. Bhaiyya wanted to know exactly what Amma had said for he needed to know the truth. I told him that Amma had always been odd and there was no point confronting her for she was worse than an animal. I refused to repeat what Amma had been saying to me as it was unspeakable. Bhaiyya looked sceptical.

'There's one more thing. I asked a friend at uni, here, to exchange some pounds for me. With that I bought a mobile. I used to call Di with that. Di passed on my number to her husband, who didn't know that Abba was unaware that I had that mobile. After he found that out, he confiscated that too. And from that mobile he discovered my plan.'

'What plan?'

'When he told me that he was getting me married off to some geezer, I planned to get into this "contract marriage" where you just marry the guy but upon arrival to the UK, the marriage is nullified.'

Bhaiyya kissed his teeth.

'I was desperate, Bhaiyya! What kind of a life is this? I just wanted to get out of here. I have been forbidden to go out of the house since Amma and Abba found this out. I just want to go back to London.'

'Hmm. I'll see what I can do.' That evening Bhaiyya had a long talk with Amma and Abba.

Later on, he knocked on my bedroom door. Immediately I asked, 'So?'

'They refused to let you come back to London.'

I didn't say anything. I went downstairs and saw Abba going to the mosque for the evening prayer. The minute he was gone Amma turned around and started to rant, 'You slut, you whore. Who will want to take a fucking bitch like you? I'll tell everyone that you fucked your own father and then got an abortion once you found out that you were pregnant with the child of an immoral sin. Burn in fire, you prostitute. Why do you wear a headscarf? That's why I hate Islam. This is what hypocrites like you do. I curse you. You will never have children. You fucking cunt. You are just jealous of me because I am still young and beautiful. You are nothing compared to me.'

Amma was extremely nice to me during the first week I came here. Really nice. I forgot all the hard feelings I had. And during that time, she told me sincerely that she didn't care how ill she was. She just wanted me to be happy and go back to London to finish my studies. I couldn't believe that Amma had changed into a nice person. My dream finally came true so I told her that I only wanted to stay with them, that I wouldn't leave her. To prove my word, I handed my passport to her. She took it and gave it to Abba. The next morning was the day I wished that it had been only a nightmare; but it was reality in every inch and ounce. Amma was back to her normal self. She accused me of depraved and unfathomable deeds just like old times. And this time, she even stole all my salwar kameez suits.

I shed silent tears day and night. Life became more miserable after my escape plan failed. During the day, I cooked and cleaned, for both my parents claimed that I'd have the right to food in return for housework. This was the last thing they had also said to Di before she ran away.

As I cried and mopped the massive house by hand, Amma would often spit and tell me that I had missed a spot. This would build up anger, which I'd dissipate with heartfelt tears during the night prayer.

But today I wasn't crying. I smiled secretly instead. For as Amma shouted, she didn't realise that Bhaiyya was right behind her. Usually Bhaiyya also went to the mosque but he got delayed, and Amma thought she'd slip into something more comfortable like delivering me a shameless tirade.

Bhaiyya heard every single word and he looked more outraged than ever. The gentle façade Amma had displayed for the sake of Bhaiyya, was lifted to my benefit. Bhaiyya faced Amma and questioned her. The face Amma made was unforgettable. She was trapped now. But this scenario precipitated another crisis.

Being back with Amma meant massaging her legs once again. My hand was not hard enough so she told me one day to use an iron mallet. She was dead serious so I obeyed. And since then she kept it in her room. Amma got hold of that mallet and with that she aimed to hit Bhaiyya but his reflexes were too quick for her. Bhaiyya was horrified at what I'd been going through.

'You're not staying here! I'll make sure of that,' Bhaiyya promised. He waited till Abba came back. He spoke to him until five in the morning. I was praying the morning prayer when he knocked on my door. Bhaiyya looked tired.

'I spoke to Abba again. Amma is a lunatic and I've taken the onus on myself. I'm not letting you stay here. You'll be staying with me. I will be your guardian from now.'

'But will you let me go uni?' I queried.

'Of course, in fact, you should take your driving lessons once we get there next month.' I felt a surge of happiness. My brother had not changed. He was still the loving brother he used to be.

I was so relieved and happy during the last month of my stay here, that I willingly cleaned the house more often than necessary. One day I went to the kitchen and found Amma cutting fish with a *boti,* a Bengali sickle-style cutting tool. Her hands were shaking. I felt bad for her so I asked if I could be of any help. She gave a snort of disgust and I expected that. She started to rant that she was glad that I was leaving again since her blissful married life had only been disrupted by me.

'Amma, why on earth would I have a problem with you? You've always accused Di and me, saying that we are envious of you when we were the ones who have cried our eyes and soul out in prayer that you two never split. If you and Abba are still together then it's because of our prayers,' I said.

'Shut up, you bitch. You are the reason behind my miserable life. Your Abba is so nice to me when you're not around. You're always coming between us. I hate you.' I left. I had my mobile back so I called Di and told her what Amma was telling me. She advised that I tried not to annoy Amma.

'I'm so glad that I'm leaving,' I said.

'You know how she's always been insecure. It's not really her fault.'

'Oh, come on Di...' I started but she interrupted me.

'No Ranya. I mean it. Amma went through a lot in her life and she's demented now. We just have to be patient. Haven't you seen how she's become so weak? Abba expects her to cook but she's too ill both mentally and physically. In fact, I would've advised you to stay here and look after her.'

'What? Are you crazy? Is this the same person speaking who left us all at the break of dawn? Who thought only about herself then? You shouldn't be telling me this.'

'My case was different, Ranya,' Di defended herself.

'So is mine. You were lucky that you had someone. I don't have anyone so your solution is that *I* look after Amma.' I was shouting by now. 'What do you think? That I never noticed that Abba and Amma preferred you over me? You made out with a distant uncle and instead of beating the crap out of you, you were told to keep it a secret and find someone to get married to. And when I tried to find someone to merely escape these two monsters in my life, I get threatened and imprisoned. Why? You hardly even come here to see me…'

I couldn't say any more as Di hung up on me. But I was fuming; she was being so unfair. I went to Abba's room and began to tidy up. Cleaning the house always mollified me so I spring cleaned his room. He had an emperor-sized bed. As it was an en suite, the bathroom itself was the size of a single bedroom in London. There was a walk-in closet adjacent to the bathroom and a mahogany three-mirrored dressing table next to the closet. Abba's PC and printer were next to the bed where he slept by himself. Amma never used this room. She made the downstairs guest room and bathroom her room. It'd been like that all the time. Over the years, normal parental behaviour became peculiar for me.

I moved the bed with all my might as I wanted to dissipate my frustration and clean things that could've been kept untouched. And this led me to unearth something beyond mere dust – a Tesco brand A5 notebook. I hadn't seen a foreign item in a year and seeing this brought back nice memories. I picked it up and wiped a thick layer of wood debris from it with the back of my hand. I turned the paperback front cover and smiled as I recognised the English joined handwriting.

The date at the top right-hand corner went back two years. It was the time Abba and I were renting out the room in Fupa's friend's flat.

It's a diary. I shouldn't read it.

I glanced quickly and flipped about ten pages, filled in blue writing, when my name caught my eye a couple of times. I couldn't help but read that part.

...Ranya has come of age now. I am finding it very difficult to keep myself away from this sin. It's wrong but I can't help it. I got away with it before but she's old enough to understand now. And I'm scared that she is seeing this boy and maybe she's told him everything about our secret. I managed to rip and throw away the referral letter that came in the post for her. At no price, would I let a psychiatrist in London, see her and backtrack her issues to me. Before things get any messier, I need to leave. She was in the dark before but being here she's learned about the dynamics of relationships. I can't sublimate her any longer.

RANYA

Bhaiyya picked us up from the airport promptly and I beamed to see him. He had lost a lot of weight and looked better than before. He handed me a coat that belonged to Bibha as they thought that I mightn't have any with me. I was touched by this but I had my denim jacket on so I didn't need it. I held the carrier bag in which he brought it though. I was wearing a teal blue jilbab. I had purple, navy, black and olive-coloured ones too which I got made back home. Amma took me to the tailors in the market to make them along with a few salwar kameez. Any other time, I would've thanked her but because of the way she had been treating me, she deserved no gratitude.

I inhaled a good amount of British air when we stepped out in the cold, bleak afternoon. The icy cold air prickled my face and hands but I loved it. I was elated to be back and to be away from Amma. I didn't even look at her nor speak to her, let alone hug her when we left. Abba hugged Amma and kissed her and I knew that he had no intention to leave her as he had made it seem like to Bhaiyya.

I couldn't wait to see Bibha, Amanah, Zain and their new addition, Yusha. My throat felt sore but I didn't mind. I was the first one to enter their flat. It was a lot more spacious than the old one. Bibha was carrying Yusha and her other two children ran up to me to hug and kiss me. I gave Salam to

Bibha and walked up to her. She smiled but didn't try to hug me. Her smile resembled her back-up smile.

We had an early dinner of pilau, korma, meat curry, a fish curry with potatoes and a salad. I couldn't taste anything due to my blocked sinuses but complimented Bibha anyway. Afterwards, I lingered in the kids' room where Bibha brought in some duvets and pillows. She said that she'd make my bed for me.

'Okay...' I said. 'Where will I be putting my clothes?' Back home, Bhaiyya had told me that as they had a bigger house now, I could have the spare room but when he saw me at the airport, he mentioned that that wouldn't be the case anymore.

'You can put them in Amanah's wardrobe.' She added after a pause, as though she heard what I was thinking, 'It's because during the day, the third room is used as a reception room for the brothers when guests come. And by night, it's Yusha's nursery. It'll be odd if men came into your room where you'll be putting your clothes and stuff. You'll have no privacy. Abba will be sleeping in that room though for the time being.' I nodded.

I had £1.49 as credit in my mobile and I used that to text my friends that I was back for good. They were very happy to hear that. I was looking for Bibha to speak to her but she said she was tired as she hardly slept these days. My throat felt very sore so I went to the kitchen to have paracetamol but then I heard Bibha's voice from their room, *'Yusha's routine will be all disrupted now. It's going to be so hard to tiptoe in our room once he's asleep.'*

RANYA

I was feeling a lot better the next day. After a breakfast of eggs and buttered toast, I showed Bibha the bangles I had bought for Amanah and the earrings I got for her. Bibha always liked my choice; whenever I wore an outfit or any jewellery she'd compliment me and try them on at some point. So, I thought she'd like the earrings as I liked them a lot.

But later in the evening, holding the pair, she asked me, 'Have they been worn before?'

'The earrings? No. why?' I was a bit taken aback at what she said.

'I don't know, they just look a bit cheap and seem like they were worn before.'

She examined them from all angles. 'You keep them. I don't really get to wear earrings anyway 'cos of hijab.' Saying this Bibha put them in my hand. I was going to refuse but I noticed a wry look on her face so decided not to say anything.

Two weeks went by and then Bhaiyya began to get annoyed about petty things.

One night, Bhaiyya muttered something under his breath. Abba asked him what the matter was to which he said nothing.

Later he asked me a set of questions. 'Has Abba been looking into that box where I put all my DVDs? Why is he watching DVDs every single day?' Then looking at Bibha he said, 'Someone doesn't need to worry about asking me if they can see them.' His words were saturated with sarcasm. I didn't say anything. I just wished that he didn't say it in front of Bibha. I could see her sneering from the corner of my eye. I didn't feel sorry for Abba this time. I seemed to be the black bin liner where anyone and everyone dumped their rubbish.

***

The following day, Amanah asked me where I was going. I told her that I was going Oxford Circus with Abba. She got really excited and asked if she could come too. I told her that she'd need to ask her parents first. It was quarter to nine in the morning and a Saturday too so Bhaiyya and Bibha were still asleep. I could hear Amanah knocking on their door asking if she could come with us. I had an odd feeling that this would take a bad turn. Suddenly I heard the door open, followed by a slapping noise. Then Bhaiyya shouted at Amanah for saying that she wanted to go with us. I was feeling an unfathomable sense of awkwardness. I felt responsible for that slap. I found Bibha in the sitting room and told her that we were leaving and should be back late afternoon.

'Did you tell Amanah that you were taking her with you?' Bhaiyya asked. I almost jumped. I couldn't tell when he came up behind me. I told him what I said to her. I could see Bibha's eyes watering a bit. I felt wretched. Bhaiyya immediately picked up Amanah and gave her a ten-pound note, apologising that he had misunderstood the whole story. I felt a bit nostalgic when I saw this. It sort of reminded me of how Bhaiyya used to be caring towards me when I was younger. On the bus, I kept thinking: *Will Bhaiyya remain the same or change his attitude towards Amanah when she grows up?*

I hated to acknowledge this but I felt that the sooner Abba left the better it would be. This was for two reasons. Firstly, Bhaiyya was still trying to change Abba's inveterate habits and beliefs; Abba wasn't agreeing to his suggestions and nor could Bhaiyya compromise without them, and as a result, this was thinning the safety barrier between them. Secondly, my intuition was ringing like an alarm clock these days.

I was near Sainsbury's, finishing my meeting up with college friend, Lilly, when I saw Bhaiyya, Bibha, and Yusha in their car. They were parking and just getting out.

I approached them and asked, 'Are Amanah and Zain at their Nanni's?'

'No. Abba's home and they're with him,' Bibha said.

'Okay, I need to go home,' I said. Bhaiyya said that if I loitered around for half an hour then I could go home with them but I said that it was urgent.

'They do have toilets here,' Bibha joked.

'It's not that. I just remembered something so I need to dash. See you soon.' I took the bus home and ran the rest of the way like crazy. I rapped on the door, which felt like ages. I was panting and struggling to catch my breath. Abba opened the door and I wondered if he saw the panic that had engulfed me. I tried to study the look on his face but got distracted by Zain's crying. I went inside and he ran up to me. Amanah smiled and I recognised that smile. I plastered that kind of smile on my face for most of my childhood. Zain was crying incessantly and Amanah looked distressed. Abba was carrying Amanah and she looked uncomfortable. I took them to their room and distracted them by reading storybooks and playing board games. I told Abba that I'd babysit them and he could do anything else he liked. Abba and I were noticeably quiet with each other for the rest of the evening; my mind declined the ominous possibility but my heart pounded with intense surety.

Abba left a month later. I was sad but no tears ran down my cheeks; I was relieved too but no smile adorned my face.

***

I wore my favourite dark blue, denim skirt today. It was the skirt that had fitted me three years ago. I had put on a bit of weight but due to the past events, I had lost a good few kilos and was happy to wear it without sucking the life inside me with my belly.

When he first saw me wearing this, Bhaiyya had told me that it was not allowed to wear tight clothes even in front of your brother and father but this skirt was okay since it was baggier than usual. I wore a baggy lime green top with it and finished the look with a forest green eyeliner.

'Is that a green eyeliner?' Bibha asked when she saw me.

'Yes.' She made a face so I told her that a lot of people told me that it made my eyes look hazel.

'I'm sorry but Asians look ridiculous in any other colour other than black.'

'Oh well, I like it.' I was frying some vegetable pakoras for tea which I made before.

'By the way, Ranya, you should change that skirt,' Bibha said. She explained that it was not appropriate in front of my brother. I told her that Bhaiyya had allowed it before to which she said that she'd have to speak to him again.

After ten minutes or so, Bhaiyya came out of his room and told me in a restrained manner, 'Uh, Ranya, maybe in future when you are married, you can wear this in front of your husband.' I looked at Bibha who was behind Bhaiyya. She arched an eyebrow and shrugged her shoulders in a gesture of *"I told you so."*

'Also, you don't need to wear so much eye makeup at home. You can save that for you husband too,' Bhaiyya added. Bibha smirked and didn't try to sound discreet.

Feeling dejected, I went to the bathroom to change and wash my eye makeup off. I recalled this splenetic incident with utter dejection and avoided the consideration of heading towards a bigger mistake.

***

A couple of days later, Bibha said that we were going to some seminar. I was getting ready when she came into the room I shared with Amanah.

'Erm, Ranya, can I borrow that green eyeliner you wore the other day?'

'I thought you said that Asians—'

'I know, I know. I just wanted to see if it complements this black eyeliner I have.'

The next week, Bhaiyya and Bibha went to her mum's for dinner. I was invited too but I refused. I felt awkward to go to Bibha's mum's or aunt's place every now and then. We had lots of relatives from both Abba's and Amma's sides of the family.

Once I asked Bhaiyya if we could visit our maternal aunt – the one with whom he stayed with as a kid. He sort of changed the topic. Another time I asked him about Fupu's place and he changed the subject again. Then one day we got a wedding invitation card from our maternal aunt. I was very excited. But neither Bhaiyya nor Bibha showed any interest or indication of attending it. The morning of the wedding arrived and Bibha told me to do the cooking for that day.

'But the wedding is for lunch time, isn't it?' I asked.

'What wedding?' Bhaiyya asked. I reminded him although I could tell by his tone that he had no intention of going.

'Nah. We're not going there,' he said. I told him that it was necessary to attend since we hardly ever visited them anyway.

Without looking at me he said, 'Nah, they're too secular and I'd rather keep my distance.'

I felt very upset. This was one occasion where all our maternal cousins, who were now married and settled in various parts of London, would unite. I was eleven or twelve the last time they saw me. In the evening Bibha told me to cut onions and grate ginger and garlic for her. I asked her why.

'Your brother didn't like the cauliflower and fish curry you cooked for lunch so I need to cook something. Clean the chicken afterwards, cut up the tomatoes, and then grate them.'

RANYA

Bibha had already fed the kids and put them to bed. I shared their older two children's room: Amanah's and Zain's. The two children slept on a bunk bed and I slept on the floor with a couple of duvets as a mattress and another as a cover. That was not a big problem but Amanah who was gradually developing a habit of kissing her teeth, was turning out to be quite obnoxious.

Bibha had set out the rule to me at the very beginning that under no circumstance was *I* ever allowed to admonish their children. And should a problem arise then either Bhaiyya or she should be informed and they would deal with it. I agreed but it turned out that they'd taken the matter very lightly. Like the time when Amanah used the F word for the third time. I complained to Bibha who once again told me not to tell Bhaiyya.

Another time, I ironed all of their bedding, on Bibha's order, and made their beds too. Just when I had finished, Amanah kissed her teeth. I bit my tongue for I didn't want to apologise to a ten-year-old like I had to do last time upon Bibha's decision. But then the little girl took all of the bedding off and undid all the buttons of the duvet, all the while moaning that I didn't know how to make a bed properly. Bhaiyya was at work and Bibha had gone out first thing in the morning with Yusha.

It was twelve p.m. and there was hardly anything cooked. The house phone rang and I picked it up. It was Bhaiyya. He called to tell me to prepare lunch as Bibha would be picking him up from work. After everyone had eaten, Bibha came to the kids' room and showed me all the clothes she had bought for herself. She also bragged about how she washed, dried, and ironed a white linen top she had bought, melted the plastic tag and reattached it to the label of the top and returned it.

'The lady goes, "it seems like it's been worn." And I'm like,, "Really? So, I was wearing it with the price tag attached to it the whole time?" The manager came as the lady was so confused. They had no choice but to give me a voucher for £20 with which I bought this gorgeous skirt.' Bibha held the skirt against her waist. 'It's beautiful, isn't it?'

It was beautiful. In fact, it was exactly the same green checked Maxi skirt that I had shown her, proclaiming my adoration for it, only a few days ago. My only allowance was the £250 per annum grant I used to get from my uni. With no income, pocket money from Bhaiyya, or benefits, all I could do was hope that I could buy something like that one day.

To change the topic, I told Bibha about Amanah's attitude.

She waved her hand in the air saying, 'Amanah is almost eleven so her hormones are playing up. Ignore these things.'

I wanted to say something but Zain interrupted me. 'Mum, Yusha was very brave to be in the car all by himself when we went Sainsbury's, wasn't he?'

'Shush,' Bibha warned him. 'We don't want your dad to know this.' Zain nodded his head, obediently.

***

I met up with some of my friends today. I was seeing them after a long time. I had just about enough credit to send one message so I informed Bhaiyya that I'd be a couple of hours late. When I got back, the atmosphere in the house was intimidating.

'How was your meeting with your friends?' Bibha asked.

''Twas cool.' I felt awkward having dinner with them as I could sense that Bibha was upset with me about something. I poured some milk into a bowl and got some shredded wheat out. I scooped two heaped teaspoons of sugar into it. I was between a size ten and an eight, and didn't mind being that size.

'So, what happened to your timing?'

'Huh?'

'You were two hours late. You were supposed to help me cook dinner.' I looked down and apologised. I felt that I had to. A brick wall seemed to be emerging all around me.

Bhaiyya drove me to Coral Reef Sixth Form College a few days later. I had to obtain a reference from my ex-tutor from my old college. I somewhat imagined Mahi walking past.

'Apply as soon as you get the reference. That three-year B.Ed. degree at St Agnes University will be the best thing for you as it's just around the corner and you'll be able to teach in a primary school straight after you pass your degree. One of yours and Kolsum's, I mean your Bibha's friends have done the same degree and they recommended it.'

'I was thinking of re-applying to the Access to Medicine course at Queen Mary.'

'No don't do that. Being a doctor is not a woman's job.'

'There is always a high demand for female gynaecologists.' My voice came out as a whimper.

'You don't have to be one. Someone else can. It is very difficult for a woman to be in a medical profession after marriage. You can study but I'm also looking to get you married off by next year if someone suitable turns up.'

My world literally whirled. I heard the devil in me scoff.

Three weeks later, I received an interview letter from St Agnes University. I was elated and told everyone in the house. Bhaiyya was excited and wished me the best but later that night, Bhaiyyah knocked on the door. It was very strange of him to do so as he'd never do that. I checked the time. It was past midnight.

'Yes, Bhaiyya?'

'Erm, I need to speak to you about something.'

'Okay?'

'Islamically, it is not allowed for young women to attend a mixed university, especially if an alternative is available. So, you should join a university that allows distance learning.'

'Study from home?' I asked though I knew it.

'Yes. I am doing my degree like that too.'

'But I went through all that hassle with the application, I mean, you were the one who wanted me to do this.'

'I know. But we, I mean I, didn't allow your Bibha to do her PGCE after marriage for the same reason. So, it won't be fair if I allow you.'

'No offence but Bibha is like thirteen or fourteen years older than me. She's also a mother of two kids. She is your wife. I am your daughter-like sister since you're my guardian.

Besides, she was still in her final year of uni when you two got married.'

'But you *are* still my sister in reality. So, that's why it won't be fair. And frankly, I don't trust you completely after you, as well as Abba, told me about your failed plan to run away with some stranger.'

'You can't use that against me! You knew my reason.'

Bhaiyya was quiet. Then he said, 'I am your guardian so it will be wise if you don't argue. You can attend the interview but decline it even if you're offered a place.' I cried silent tears. I knew I had no choice but to be acquiesce..

I was offered a place at St Agnes. And for the second time I was made to decline an offer from a university.

One morning, I needed Bhaiyya's assistance when I was filling out the application form. He was still eating his breakfast.

'Don't do full time. Do sixty credits – that's part time,' he said as he spread some raspberry conserve onto his buttered toast.

'How come? I've already lost a year of uni. It'll take me six years if I don't do one hundred and twenty points each year.'

'Ranya, expect to get married any time. You are going to be twenty soon. Your Megha Di and I got married before that. You need to get married while you're still young. After marriage, you'll be someone's wife, daughter-in-law, and sister-in-law, maybe. You will have to study part time then. You will have other priorities.' Bibha reminded Bhaiyya that his tea was getting cold so he thanked her and took a sip. 'It's better that you get into the habit of balancing household chores and studying. Your aim as a woman is to be a good, responsible wife and mother – not a career-orientated woman. Look at your Bibha. She should be your role model. She probably loves you more than your own sister does.'

Hearing and digesting over-exaggerated, misogynistic words, brought tears to my eyes.

'You are lucky, Ranya, that your brother is doing all this for you. We treat you just as we treat our Amanah,' Bibha said. She was at the sink in the kitchen.

Bhaiyya got up from the chair at the dining table and said, 'You should also help out more with the household chores, like, you know, putting the dirty clothes in the washing machine. It's not fair that Kolsum always has to do that.'

I do all the preparations for Bibha before she cooks or I cook. I change dirty nappies by default, babysit your children, give them baths, brush their teeth, make their school lunch, hoover and mop the house three times a week, and clean the bathrooms. I am not allowed to go to uni, or work and so, conveniently, I can't take driving lessons as you had promised. I sleep like a traveller and am given no pocket money. And you two are saying that I am lucky? That I ought to help out more?

I felt like punching my eyes for the non-stop tears that kept flowing. A tornado was engulfing me with a preternatural speed and there was no stopping it.

RANYA

I didn't know why but about six months later, I felt as though a mean plan had been executed. I had to sit for a difficult exam in Epping. I was supposed to come home at six p.m. But as the train broke down halfway, I arrived home around eight p.m. I wasn't allowed to pray the maximum four-minute Maghrib prayer as the white lady in charge had closed the premises by five p.m. sharp. I was furious at the impudence but I let it go. By the time I reached home, I was cold and famished. I made ablution and combined both the dusk and evening prayer. I couldn't wait to eat. I went to the kitchen and Bibha asked me why I was so late. I explained myself but she looked indifferent. Then I noticed that she was just getting things out to start cooking. I checked one pot that had a little bit of lentil soup left. I had cooked it two days ago and was also mocked that it tasted weird..

'You haven't cooked yet?' I asked.

'I had a lot of things to do. Besides you were supposed to arrive by five.'

Every Saturday, after our Islamic circle, which finished at one p.m., Bibha would take the children for extra-curricular classes, which didn't finish until six. Bhaiyya had therefore told me to come home straight after the circle so that I could sort out lunch and dinner every Saturday. "Don't forget to cook my brown rice. And make sure it doesn't become soggy like last time," Bibha would remind me every Saturday.

I didn't say anything but it must've been obvious that I wasn't too happy about this arrangement for they told me that the onus is on them to train me to be a good homemaker. So, I did it. But what I couldn't believe was that of all the days, today, my sister-in-law didn't have the common sense to get dinner ready.

Controlling my frustration, I helped myself to some rice and that remaining bit of lentil soup, microwaved it, and was about to eat when Bibha said, 'Feed Yusha along with you. Dinner won't be ready until after two hours.' Yusha ate it all so I made myself a butter and honey sandwich.

As I ate it, Bhaiyya went past and said, 'Ranya, change Yusha's nappy after you finish eating.'

***

It was crucial now that I no longer stayed with my brother and his family. Bhaiyya just didn't seem like the person he used to be. I stared out the window and remembered the day my study materials arrived. I was so excited. I was scared too to ask Bhaiyya myself so I got Bibha to ask him on my behalf; I wanted to seek permission to go to the local library once a week in the morning, for studying purposes.

The following morning, as Bibha was getting ready to go out with the older kids, Bhaiyya called me to their room. Since I started to live with Bhaiyya and his family, he only spoke to me when there was a need for admonition. Even at meal times, he never acknowledged my presence. If he ever got a film to watch, he would call everyone's name out save for mine. Once I decided not to see the DVD he had brought. I wanted to see if he noticed my absence. He didn't. I felt my invisibility was selective. His aloof behaviour increased so much as so that I saw him as my sister-in-law's husband rather than my brother.

'Your Bibha was saying that you want to go to the library?'

'Yes.' I had that feeling that this encounter was going to be an unpleasant one.

'You are only studying part time. You don't need to bring home a first-class degree. That will not gain you a good husband. After your household chores, there is more than enough time for your studies.'

Desperation spread to my insides like an infection. The corners of my eyes were smarting already. An unwanted tremor in my voice was inevitable now. 'But I need internet access for my studies. And there's no computer at home.'

'Why are you whimpering? Can't you talk in a normal voice?' From the corner of my eyes I saw Bibha grinning.

I cleared my throat to which Bhaiyya rolled his eyes. In a more conscientious tone I said, 'On second thought, as part of distance learning, the Uni can give me a grant.' Bhaiyya looked interested so I carried on, 'Erm, you could pay for the internet service so this way we all can share the computer?'

'Hmm. That sounds like a good idea. What do you think?' Bhaiyya faced Bibha.

'Yeah, I think it's a good idea.'

A week later, I handed the cheque over to Bhaiyya when I received it in the post. He thanked me curtly but I felt glad that I was able to contribute in some way.

A computer was purchased within a week. But I was hardly allowed to work on that computer which was kept in their bedroom. Bhaiyya was very strict with everyone's use of the Internet.

I told Bibha when Bhaiyya was out that it was unfair what Bhaiyya was doing for I had paid for the computer. That it was a deal I had made with him and she had witnessed it too.

'Three hundred pounds would only go so far to buy a computer. We had to add another four hundred pounds to it,' Bibha explained.

***

The following morning, after breakfast, I sat down to read the Quran. I could hear Bibha having a go at Amanah and Zain for not tidying their room properly. Yusha was crying quite loudly and I felt very uncomfortable. I got that sinking feeling that Bibha was annoyed with me and taking it out on her children instead.

'Ranya, can you go and chop the onions and get a couple of chickens out of the freezer.' Bibha sounded terse. She was looking at the floor which she was brushing. She avoided eye contact whenever she was angry with me.

'I am just finishing my chapter.'

'You should do that after the household chores. From now on don't start studying or reciting first thing in the morning.'

Later in the afternoon, I folded the clothes from the dryer. I didn't want to do it but I also didn't want Bibha to boss me around or complain to Bhaiyya that I hadn't been using "my initiative". Bibha had a habit of stuffing lots of clothes in the washing machine and this was a massive load. I tried to do it quickly so I could get on with my studies. Amanah and Zain wanted me to play Scrabble with them too so I did that while I folded the clothes.

A while later, Bibha got up from her siesta. 'What are you three cheeky monkeys doing?' It seemed that her grumpy attitude from the morning had subsided. Nowadays, I found myself on tenterhooks with regards to Bibha's moods. I spoke a bit too soon for a bit later she mocked me. 'Who folded these clothes?' I turned my head from the Scrabble board and saw her examining them before tossing each item of clothing to her left and right. Soon all the clothes lay in two piles, unfolded.

'I did it,' I said.

'What? You call this folding? Even Amanah and Zain can fold better than you!' she harrumphed here. 'You need to do things properly. I'm a perfectionist. And this is how you fold clothes.' She held out a neatly folded T-shirt for me to see. Bibha was being sarcastic but not angry.

So I said, 'At least I'm a perfectionist when it comes to brushing the floor.'

'What do you mean?' Bibha's tone suddenly sounded serious.

'I move the sofa when I brush the floor. You don't do that. I can see the bread crumbs under it from where I'm standing and you swept the living room today.' It was a great comeback. But a chill ran down my spine. For she was silent. And that meant bad news. I resumed the Scrabble game with Amanah and Zain and, as expected, Bibha shouted at the kids, this time for not doing their Quran instead. They left the living room to fetch their books. I decided to follow them but it was too late.

'Sit down here, Ranya. I need to have a word with you.' Bibha was sitting already, with her legs crossed, and instructed me to sit opposite her.

'Oh my God, Bibha. Don't tell me you took all that seriously. You were being funny and so was I. I don't know why you always do that. You have the licence to make jokes about me but when I do the same, you take it all personally.'

'I did not take it personally. I am a lot older than you and therefore you should not be sarcastic with me. You were being very rude with me. Once your brother's back, we can ask him.' Bibha sounded very calm as she said that. It almost felt deliberate. And that's when the bathroom door, adjacent to the dining area, opened wide.

Bhaiyya stormed into the dining room and asked hastily, 'What's the matter?' I was confident that once Bhaiyya heard both of our sides, he'd deal with it justly. But then Bhaiyya's next words came across as a big fat slap. 'I could hear Ranya talking way too much, more than she should. You explain to me first, Kolsum.'

Bibha maintained her self-composure as before. She was still seated cross-legged on the very sofa under which the breadcrumbs lay and began, 'I was just telling Ranya that she should be respectful when she speaks to her elders...' I felt like blocking my ears. The partiality stung like a paper cut.

'Okay. Ranya? Is that true?'

'Yes. But my point is, Bibha says that she has a good sense of humour so why did she take it personally—'

'You should not talk back when you are being told to do something. You are lucky that you have someone like her to teach you etiquette and good manners. Things that our mother was supposed to teach you. You ought to be grateful for the favours your sister-in-law does for you. You will not be sarcastic or question her. Is that understood?' Bhaiyya's eyes looked like they would shed lava any second. I nodded as hot tears rolled down my cheeks. I had lost my voice too. 'Now apologise.'

I turned towards Bibha and said, 'I'm sorry.'

'It's okay.' But don't do that again. Amanah and Zain will get negatively influenced otherwise.' Triumph rang in her serene voice.

RANYA

A couple of weeks after the "clothes folding fiasco", I went to the library with Amanah and Zain.

I wanted to go shopping for some personal things and I didn't want to bring Amanah and Zain along as I had to buy sanitary pads. After allocating two spots with computers for my niece and nephew at the children's section, I popped out to a pound store which was just in front of the library. I got back to the library within fifteen minutes and having chosen some books, Amanah, Zain, and I made our way home. Something told me that Bhaiyya and Bibha wouldn't approve of this little act I had done, so I hesitantly asked my niece, 'Can you two, do me favour?'

'Sure Fupumoni, what is it?' they asked.

'Don't tell your mum and dad that I left you on your own to do this shopping, okay?'

'Okay.'

But that very evening, Bhaiyya asked me to go to the kids' room and wait for him. Bibha asked Amanah and Zain to leave their room and gave them some activity to do in the dining area. Bhaiyya wanting to see me indicated a predicament on my part.

I tapped on Bibha's shoulder.

'Is everything okay? Why does Bhaiyya want to see me?' Am I in trouble?'

Bibha shrugged her shoulders. 'Let's see what he wants.'

They both sat next to each other on one of the single beds (the bunkbed by now had been split into two single ones and so my floor bed space was confined even more). I sat on the other bed. Their body language spoke out louder than words that they *both* were against *me*.

Bhaiyya spoke first. 'Amanah said something this afternoon which has shocked us quite a bit. I know you can be absentminded at times but this news has terrified us.' Bhaiyya looked sinister. Bibha looked even graver.

'What are you two talking about?' I asked.

'I don't want to know where you went or who you may have met up with – what strikes us with utmost concern is that it happened while you took our children to the library, and left them, unattended.' Bhaiyya paused for a bit. 'Are you aware that I could turn you in with the local authority for this?'

I was gobsmacked. I looked at Bibha but she avoided eye contact. I recalled the incident where she had left Yusha unattended in the car and forbade Zain to mention it to Bhaiyya.

'Amanah and Zain were terrified when they told us this. She was scared because apparently, you told her not to say this to us,' Bibha put in.

'Oh yes of course. How dare you tell our children to keep secrets from us?' Bhaiyya glanced at Bibha before continuing, 'Seriously, I'm regretting that I took on the burden of your guardianship.'

'You ought to show more responsibility. Such immaturity will not help you in your married life,' Bibha added.

I wanted to finish my studies before I got married but at that point only two things mattered. Apology for my reckless behaviour to save myself from further accusations and getting married to the next available person as soon as possible. I'd have to relieve my brother and his family of their misery.

KOLSUM (BIBHA)

I couldn't have been happier the day Yusha turned six months. Because that was the day a miracle took place. The council offered us a three-bedroom house. So many people have to be cramped with six plus children in a one-bedroom flat yet I've been so lucky – so damn lucky – to have been given this privilege. I prayed and thanked God for this. We saw the flat and were much taken by its location and the fact that it was a new property. After my family came around as a house-warming party, I called up Rumaisa and asked her to visit me. I was in the same area as her now and couldn't wait to show off my new three-bedroom flat to her. She used to always brag about her two-bedroom flat when she used to visit me before; now it was my turn – and now I had the upper hand.

She came around at eleven o' clock. Our children attended the same infants' school so we had pizza for lunch and chatted till it was time to pick our children up. We expressed our concern over the 7/7 incidents that occurred only a month ago. Rumaisa said, 'Wearing the hijab is going to become such a problem; 9/11 had the same impact. And so many sisters took off their hijab – some out of fear and some deliberately since they never wanted to wear the hijab in the first place.'

'I know. Tell me about it. It makes me sick how some girls wear all these fashionable hijabs and are total airheads,' I said as I bit into a generous slice of tuna and jalapeno pizza.

'They have no idea about the *Deen,* religion, whatsoever.' Rumaisa scoffed.

'I mean look at my sister-in-law. She was wearing a denim skirt once with full makeup on. Why on earth is she dressing up at home like that?' Rumaisa said that there was nothing wrong with doing that at home. But then I reminded her that she shouldn't be doing that in front of her brother. I knew more about Islam than her after all. 'Some people just don't understand what is appropriate and what isn't.'

Rumaisa sipped her coke and asked, 'So how's life with your husband's sister?'

'Ugh, don't even ask. I mean it's not as bad as some people have it. Yasin will *never* allow her to take advantage of me. I had made it very clear to him that *he* can do or say whatever he pleases but not at any price should his *family* ever bully me – *again.* But then there are times when he makes certain decisions without consulting me.' I paused to sip on my coke. 'Supposedly, Ranya had a hard time with her parents. Remember what their mum did to me when I went that time?' Rumaisa nodded and shuddered. 'This time when Yasin went there, he saw it for himself and on the spur of the moment, decided to become Ranya's "guardian". I mean, he doesn't realise this but I know that it's exactly what his mum wanted. It was all planned. Her dad didn't want her to come back here so her mum intentionally mistreated her and in turn Yasin felt sorry for Ranya and took her along with him. Get it?'

Rumaisa echoed her surprise but then said how lucky she was at having a white revert for a husband. 'Saves me from such hassles. So, what about Ranya's parents? What did they do to their own daughter?'

'Oh, they may be all educated and rich and from the famous "Kuraish" family but they are the stingiest and worst of people.' For an hour, I filled her in with all the details.

'I feel so bad for you to have such horrible in-laws. But what about Ranya? Does she help you around in the house?'

'Ah, that's another topic altogether. She just seems to be a daydreamer. Say I tell her to keep an eye on the rice or curry; the next thing I know, she's brushing the floor or cleaning the bathroom and has completely forgotten about the rice or curry. Or if I tell her "make sure you brush the floor when you wake up". You'd think that she'd remember to do this every day, but no. I need to tell her this every single day. She just doesn't seem to take the initiative, like you and I do. We just do things that need to be done. We don't need to be told all the time, do we?'

I helped myself to another slice of pizza and cringed inside for the weight I was piling upon 'The other day, Yusha did a poo. So instead of telling me this, why didn't she just clean him? I told her to clean him anyway.'

'And then?' Rumaisa was well engrossed.

'You won't believe this! To spite me, she didn't clean him properly. And then I noticed that his top was half wet. I asked her how that happened and she goes she doesn't know. What a liar. I don't know if she does this deliberately or she's just stupid, honestly.'

'My older brother's wife used to run away from chores too. Eventually she succeeded in taking our brother away from us,' Rumaisa said.

'Well, they're lucky that I'm not like that. I did so much for Yasin. They should be grateful to me. Yasin can be so insulting to me at times. If it wasn't for my children,' my voice broke here, 'I would've left him ages ago.'

Rumaisa touched my hand and expressed her sympathy. 'We all have problems, Hun. Look at me. People think that I married a white guy so I must be so lucky and happy. Little do they know what I'm going through.'

'What do you mean?' I had no idea what Rumaisa was about to reveal. Rumaisa fought back tears. She explained how she wanted more children but she couldn't have any. She lied to her mum that the doctors said that she'd developed some rare form of infertility. But the truth was something else.

'Him and I are living together for the sake of it. We don't talk any more. We don't even sleep together any more. I just can't stand him.' She paused here for a bit and I gave her a hug. 'If it wasn't for Sheila's divorce, we would've divorced by now.' Fiddling with the corner of her scarf, she explained, 'My sister's divorce has shaken my parents badly and if I break this news to them then they'll die.' I hugged Rumaisa again and couldn't help crying with her. I felt fortunate that the problems between Yasin and I weren't as grave as those between Rumaisa and her husband.

The doorbell rang. It was Ranya who was back from the library. I told Yasin last time that it was okay to allow her to go to the library at least twice a month. But little would the little twat be grateful about that. She gave my friend Salam and I told her to eat the pizza. She asked if she could have it in the kids' room and I allowed it. I didn't want her to be here anyway.

'Hmm. Your sister-in-law is obedient. She's quite pretty too.'

'Yeah, I guess. But she's nothing compared to her sister. Megha is stunning,' I said. It was the truth after all.

'Yeah, it happens sometimes. In your case, it's the other way round,' Rumaisa said.

'What do you mean?'

'Well, I guess that's what people say when they see you and Kimi.'

I felt like slapping her. Served her right that her marital life was falling apart.

Later that night Yasin broke some very interesting news to me. I made him his peppermint tea which he usually drank after dinner.

'I met Ahmed today in the mosque. We spent some time talking and, incidentally, I mentioned that I'm looking for someone suitable for Ranya. Then he told me that his wife – your buddy, Rumaisa, is looking for someone for her younger brother, Fahim.'

'And?' I said. Yasin had an annoying habit of starting a conversation and then stopping midway.

'And so, after exchanging some details…' Yasin paused again to chew a piece of vanilla and apple cake I had baked earlier. He complimented me on the dessert before sipping some tea. I prompted him again so he carried on, 'It turns out that Fahim and Ranya may be suitable prospects for one another. What do you think?'

I didn't know what to think let alone what to say. After what I had said about Yasin, Ranya, and their mum, I didn't think Rumaisa would be interested any more, even if she ever was in the first place. 'Erm, don't you think Rumaisa's family is a bit of a low class from us? I mean their family isn't that educated.'

'Yeah, I thought about that too but then though my parents are highly educated and come from a reputable family, only you and I know how they really are.' Leaning back on the armchair, he continued, 'Fahim's parents may not be educated and neither are they from a high society like my parents but at least that makes them humble. They are very generous and open-minded. They even allowed two of their children to intermarry. Besides, Fahim has a degree and a good job whereas Ranya hasn't got a degree yet. Nowadays girls and boys are very picky. If one of them has a degree, they want their other half to have one too.'

I wasn't. And perhaps I should've been picky too.

'The only thing I worry is that they have a large family. I don't know if Ranya would be able to cope,' Yasin speculated.

I never wanted a big family. Staying with the whole family of your husband can be very difficult. As the daughter-in-law, it will be expected that you do all the cooking and cleaning. And fancy doing all that with hijab on all hours. That's why I chose to marry Yasin since I knew that he had practically no one in this country.

'I think a big family would be perfect for Ranya. She always says how she missed out on not having similar-aged siblings. So perhaps this is her second chance to live that moment. Rumaisa's younger sisters are all of a similar age to Ranya too,' I said.

'Hmm.'

'Well, I should be expecting a call from Rumaisa tomorrow,' I said. I couldn't believe that Yasin was convinced.

This was a golden opportunity to get rid of Ranya. But I also knew that Rumaisa, being the snotty person she was, would never accept this alliance. Especially after I confided in her everything about Yasin's mum. How I wished that I hadn't.

RANYA

In Asian culture, when a girl gets married, she has to be attached more to her in-laws than her side of the family. In a weird way, it felt as though Bhaiyya was the weaker sex and Bibha, the dominant one.

A few days later, they went to Bibha's aunt's house for lunch. I refused politely. I had a feeling that Bibha was starting to suspect me. After they came back, Bhaiyya went to his room. He always spent time on the computer – *my* computer. I was in the living room reading a book when Bibha started the conversation.

'A distant relative came around at my aunt's today. She was saying that she was in the same year in school as your mum.'

'Oh.' I didn't want to speak about this anymore. I had a gut feeling about what it would lead to. And I was right.

'So, I was saying to her that Amma looked really young compared to her. So, she said, "when people have the time to colour their hair and hide their age then obviously, they will look younger".'

'And the point is?' I asked.

'Well, Amma accused me of hiding my age when I wasn't. I'm thirty-five but in order to bring a cousin of mine to this country, my parents had to increase my age by three years.'

I told Bibha that she was telling me this news for the sixth time in three years. And vouching for this fact, I even argued with my ferocious mother. She even asked me what year was written on Bibha's passport. 'And without realising, I said your actual date of birth, which was three years less than that which was printed on the passport. Since you are telling me the truth, technically, I didn't lie,' I finished.

I expected Bibha to thank me for this since any sister-in-law would want to harass their brother's wife in such a situation. Instead, Bibha seemed lost in some thought. Amanah came in that time complaining that she didn't find the dress Bibha's mum had given her, comfortable.

'Stop whinging. Your nanni's side are the only ones who will ever give you anything decent, if anything at all. So, appreciate it.'

The following week, we went to Bibha's mum's house for lunch. Again. Bibha's mum was very happy to see me. She cooked a lot whenever we came. Surprisingly, Bibha never cooked the dishes her mum cooked. Unsurprisingly, Bibha forgot me when she was at her mum's or aunt's. No one ever talked to me in their house except for Bibha's mum and Kimi, who had become a bit distant recently. Both her twin brothers stayed in that house and were married too.

Kimi greeted us at the door. I felt Kimi's makeup was a tad bit over the top. Had she worn a saree, one would've thought that she was getting ready for a wedding party.

Did her twin brothers object to that?

'Oh Affa, I love that greenish eyeliner you've put on. I thought you only went for black.' We were in her room. It was spacious with a small double bed and a four-door wardrobe. A dressing table opposite her bed displayed lots of makeup items and jewellery.

'Yeah, you should wear it, it's really nice, that's why I got it with me. Here, try it. I bought it yesterday.'

Just then Bibha's older twin brother's wife came in. She was an amicable person who either never got upset or was very good at hiding any disappointment.

'Oh my God, Affa. You look so young. You look younger than your brother even though he's thirty-six and you're thirty-eight.'

'Huh?' I said out louder than I should've. I wanted to explain but thought I'd let Bibha do the talking. But she just said that she'd been blessed with youthful skin. I looked at her and tried to get her attention. But she didn't look at me for the rest of the day. She looked a little flustered but other than that her poise was as calm as an innocent person's composure would've been.

***

Summer was here although the temperature still had a single digit. Once again, we were at Bibha's mum's place for lunch. Soon there was a commotion in the living room. I came to know that mangoes and jackfruits were customarily given as gifts to the husband's family by the wife's family. The younger twin's wife was being harassed for the fruits her parents had given.

'Oh my God. What on earth is this?' Bibha said when she saw the display of diced fruit on the table. 'Couldn't you tell by the skin of the fruit that they were all bad?'

The younger twin's wife, Ginia, was in stark contrast to the older one. 'Your brother was the one who helped us in choosing the fruit,' she said. I could sense the agitation in her voice.

'Excuse me! Don't you now put the blame on my brother. This is supposed to come from *your* side of the family so how does *my* brother come in the equation?' Bibha returned.

I felt sorry for the older twin's wife, Bushra. She was trying her best to change the subject to avoid any arguments. But every time she said something, Kimi responded to it. And it was making the older Bhabi seem nothing less than a tease.

'He's been losing so much weight recently. I mean look at his twin brother. He's healthy—' Bushra couldn't finish her sentence.

Kimi was quick and curt to finish it for her. 'It's because of *you*. You can't cook properly. Boro Bhai, elder brother, had the perfect weight before he got married.' I was shocked to hear this; not because of the content of the statement but rather the attitude Kimi showed. Bibha's mum and aunt were still arguing over the fruit.

Bushra tried again to divert the conversation. 'I like your salwar kameez, Kimi. I wonder if I should get one.'

'Don't, 'cos they don't do sizes beyond XL.' Kimi turned around and shared a secret smile and wink with her cousins.

'Yeah, I know I've gained too much weight since I had the baby,' Bushra said, looking down.

On the way back, Bibha was talking about her brothers' wives to Bhaiyya. She related the events to him and the topic moved on to their children.

'Saleh's kids are better looking than my younger twin's kids. It's because of Bushra as she's fair. Hafiz's and Ginia's son looks like a turtle.' Bibha laughed.

'Amma didn't like Ginia at all. The first thing she said after she saw her was, "she's not as pretty as Bushra".'

I couldn't help but make a point here, 'Fairness doesn't necessarily mean beautiful. It's the symmetry in one's features. Bushra may be taller and fairer but if my mum saw Ginia she would've regarded her prettier than both you and me put together.'

'Oh definitely. I'm just saying how the older generation always thinks that being fair is prettier.'

'I'm sure you believe that that's what you were saying.' It was uncomfortable but I was glad that I was carrying Yusha; it prevented anyone from seeing me rolling my eyes.

I had to, however, admit that Yusha was probably one of the world's cutest babies. He was scrumptiously chubby, with hazel eyes set against a snow-white complexion. His lips were plump and red and his hair was blond and wispy. In a way, he resembled Di.

Like his siblings, he spoke clearly from a young age. By the time he was two, he could articulate his thoughts like a four-year-old.

As I didn't have younger siblings, I lacked the knack for handling young children. When I first moved in with Bhaiyya in his old house, Amanah was only three or four. She wanted to hang on the monkey bar, which Bhaiyya used for his training. It was attached in their porch between two walls. I refused to lift her up saying she was too small but she persuaded me saying that her dad always hung her up there.

Bhaiyya was at work, Bibha was on the phone in her bedroom, and Zain was playing in there. I lifted Amanah up on the bar and stood against the wall, carrying on reading the book I had borrowed from the library. That was the one highlight of my life – reading books from the library. I was deprived of it till I came to London.

'Fupumoni, can you get me down? I think I'm going to let go.' I made the huge blunder of holding her around her knees. Amanah let go trusting that I held her firmly.

I saw her drop face first. A thud vibrated. This followed a painful scream. I turned her around trying to see if she was all right. And then I let out an even louder and longer screech. There was blood on the spot where she had fallen and her entire mouth was covered in blood too. Bibha ran at once from her room with Zain close by.

'I'm so sorry. It's all my fault. But it was not deliberate...'

'What happened?' Bibha asked. She was calm.

I explained everything to her. I was certain that I was going to be kicked out of their house that day and sent to my parents back home. But strangely, neither Bibha nor Bhaiyya said anything to me. They were unusually calm about the whole situation. I tried to study their expressions discreetly but they gave nothing away. Bhaiyya joked with Amanah that celebrities paid a huge amount of money to get the swollen lips she got from the fall. One of Bibha's twin brothers drove her to the hospital and back while he dropped off Bibha's mum to cook for the evening. I explained to Bibha's mum about how sorry I was. I cried for days out of guilt.

Since then I developed a tendency to avoid young children. I didn't want to harm them even by an accident. The burden of this unfortunate culpability was still heavy on my heart.

Perhaps Yusha sensed that I wasn't good with children, for he didn't like me at all. Whenever he cried from his cot, I'd rush to get him out. But he'd smack himself back in it showing that he'd rather stay in the cot than be taken out of it by me. This used to crack everyone up. I laughed too but deep inside I used to feel sad.

If he ever felt that I was about to carry him, he'd screech like a cat splashed with cold water. And he'd speak his mind, crying out, *"Go away, go away."*

This phobia, however, did yield an advantage. Whenever Yusha whined at mealtimes, Bibha would say, 'Hurry up Yusha or else your Fupumoni will never *"go away"*.'

I once overheard Bhaiyya telling Bibha that he and she should go out for a meal. Bibha stressed that there was no one to babysit the kids. 'What do you think Ranya is here for? She ought to make herself useful.' Bibha said something but it was inaudible. Perhaps she didn't like it that Bhaiyya said it out so loud. But whenever they went out without their children, Bibha would call Amanah to look after Zain and Yusha. Amanah moaned that she didn't want to deal with her brothers who fought all the time. To this Bibha said, 'You are in charge when we're not around.'

I got ready quickly and told them that I was going to the library. Bhaiyya was furious. 'Why are you saying such a stupid thing? Can't you see that we are going shopping now?'

'But I thought Bibha just said that Amanah is in charge when…'

'She's not an adult. Don't try to act smart, do you understand?' I nodded. 'Try and do at least one thing to show some gratitude,' Bhaiyya said.

I ought to go to an eye surgeon and have my tear ducts removed, I thought. I heard the word "creature" and was glad that I didn't hear the entire sentence. Then after they left, Zain asked me, 'Fupumoni, what does "ungrateful" mean?'

I defined it and then asked where he heard it.

'I was in the room when Abba was talking and he said "ungrateful creature".'

***

It was getting utterly boring staying at Bhaiyya's place. Sometimes we went to religious talks where I often met girls I had seen at college. I saw Lilly once too. She told me that she had finished her degree and was now a full-time primary school teacher in a school close to her house. I didn't regret that I hadn't accepted any university offers for I was tired of living on my own. I wanted a family: a family that loved and cared for me. I didn't quite feel at home at Bhaiyya's. I felt like an outsider. I felt like a dog that was given food on time but chained.

I did, however, love spending time with my niece and nephews. Even though Yusha disliked me, he didn't complain if I changed his nappy. But I didn't like doing that all the time and I was also too scared to refuse. Bhaiyya and Bibha kept telling me that they were treating me no differently than their own daughter, Amanah. Amma was always horrible towards me but it didn't seem to hurt as much as it did when Bibha said something.

The other day, I changed Yusha's dirty nappy. After some time, Bibha called me and said that I didn't clean him properly. She didn't sound angry but neither was she convinced that I didn't do it intentionally. Sometime after that, I put Yusha on the worktop next to the sink as he wanted to drink some water. I held him around his waist tightly – just in case. But as I tried to reach for a cup, he covered the running tap with his hand and the water splashed on him. I dried him and let him go after he'd had his drink. But within a few minutes Bibha was back demanding why I wet Yusha with water. Her voice was between surprise and amusement – the kind where you know that you have trapped someone.

'I didn't wet him,' I said. I smiled as I said that, for it just seemed funny that Bibha could even think of such a possibility. She entrusted me to change his nappies, bathe him, feed him, dress him, brush his teeth, and even put him to sleep sometimes. And I was doing that meticulously for ten months now, for free. How could she then think something like that?

'Yusha told me that you did it.' Bibha still had an odd smile painted on her face which I felt like slapping off.

'Bibha, why would I wet him like that?' I was serious now. She didn't answer me.

She was changing his clothes in the sitting room. She seemed a bit rough the way she did it. Without looking at me, she said, 'Children never lie.' She wasn't smiling any more.

I felt accused. It was a trivial matter but every now and then, magnifying such petty issues were cumulating into a huge volcano inside me, impending an eruption. Since this episode, Bibha began to toilet train Yusha. He had accidents every time and every day. The carpet in his room had been saturated with his urine at least ten times so far. I told Bibha that perhaps it was too early to take his nappies off. But she said this was the way to do it.

'Shouldn't you put pull ups on him then?' I suggested.

'They're a waste of money,' she said.

And a waste of my energy. I was tired of cleaning and scrubbing the carpet every time he wet it. Sometimes I had to clean it twice or more depending on whether it was according to her definition of "clean" or not. As usual, Bibha assured me that it wasn't hers but rather my brother's order that I did more work in the house.

It was for your own good. Secretly, I lip-synced the last bit.

That night some guests came. I helped Bibha with all the prep work and cooked tarka dal which she asked me to do. It was the only thing Bhaiyya liked better when I cooked it. One of ladies expressed their liking to the dal and that lead to everyone complimenting Bibha as they assumed she had made it. I felt too shy to mention that it was I who had actually made it. I was waiting for Bibha to correct them but she didn't say anything.

Later in the night, after everyone had gone into bed, Amanah asked me if I was asleep.

'No. But why are you still up?'

'I wanted to tell you something. When you went to the bathroom, the aunty in red asked Mum how she made the tarka dal and she told her. But then I told her that it was *you* who cooked it.'

'Oh, thank you. Did you like it?'

She nodded and her eyes sparkled in the dark room. I was still awake for another hour.

Bhaiyya didn't like or allow me to read novels. But that was one thing I wouldn't allow anyone to take away from me. Reading was like water for me. I'd dehydrate if someone deprived me of it. So late at night, every night, I used to take a novel out and read it with the light from my mobile phone. I used to switch it off as soon as I heard any footsteps.

And then suddenly I heard my name. I turned it off and hid the book quickly. I went to the door and was about to open it when I heard my brother mentioning my name. Curiosity got the better of me and I opened the door slightly to hear what he was saying about me.

'*So why are you looking so upset? What's wrong if I let Ranya eat my dessert? She liked it and I had already eaten one ramekin of shemai. So, I let her have the extra one you had left for me. You should take that as a compliment.*'

I waited to hear something else but I didn't. I heard nothing from Bibha's end.

KOLSUM (BIBHA)

It was a Saturday so Yasin and I thought of going to the park with everyone. Ranya was being stuck up as usual and refused to come. I was going to tell her but then she quickly started praying. But two can play the game so I left a note for her on the fridge: *"Ranya, make an egg curry and cook rice so we can have lunch when we get back. P.S Don't make my brown rice soggy."*

I tried to imagine what her face looked like when she read the message.

The cow ate the shemai I had put away for Yasin, so it served her right. I was devastated when Yasin announced that he was going to bring her back to our new flat. But in retrospect, it turned out that this would work to my advantage. Before, I had to be cautious that she didn't report any information back to her mum. But now, she has left them herself. She has no "bodyguard" any more. She is all alone.

At the park, I bumped into Rumaisa. She spread her arms out and hugged me. I wasn't sure if it was a good thing or a bad thing.

'So, it seems like we might be related very soon, ey?'

I didn't know what to say. But was that a hint that they'd consider Ranya? Rumaisa was all smiles. She said that she was hoping to see my sister-in-law. Taking my chance, I said, 'We were telling her to come but she suggested that she'd cook dinner as there was nothing prepared.'

'Oh, I see your hard work is paying off?' Rumaisa beamed.

'So it seems. I must say, she is very obedient.' I prayed that she bought all that crap. And I just hoped that Ranya wouldn't be fussy with this marriage proposal.

'How tall is she?'

'Five feet two-ish.'

'Hmm. Fahim is almost six feet two so I don't know if he'll be okay with it. But she's very pretty so he might consider her. I mean, anyone who's taller than you is tall.'

We were strolling by the river and I had a sudden urge to push her. 'Oh well, at least social status-wise, we are giants next to you.' This was going quite well. We were close enough to not take offence. I told her that we'd speak to Ranya.

On the way back, I told Yasin that I gave a brief gist about Amma and Abba so that they don't think that we kept them in the dark. Also, this way no one would accuse me about gossiping to Rumaisa about them.

'That's good you did that. Saves me from doing all the dirty talk.' He winked.

RANYA

I was well upset. I felt angry with myself for refusing to go to the park with them. But then I pondered as I cooked; I was an outsider. I was an extra, unwanted member in Bhaiyya's nuclear family. Once I was gone, it would revert to being a happy family again.

I loved the way Bibha played her role as a wife and mother. She was always on her toes to serve my brother. An ideal wife. And the children loved her. She was a very loving and caring mother too. Sometimes she could be very nice to me. She would buy me clothes or perfume. When the kids would go to sleep, she would watch a film with me and give me chocolate bars, crisps, and coke. But at times I felt she had a shift in her personality. Like an alter ego, she'd be very quiet or defensive. Perhaps my staying with them was affecting her demeanour.

An hour later, with the cooking done, I sat on Amanah's bed, reading my current novel. From time to time, I looked out of the window, expecting them to return any time. When I saw them, I set the table to avoid being told off that I should've used "my initiative" to set it as they had just come in from outside.

Over lunch, Bhaiyya said that my cooking was getting almost as good as Bibha's. I smiled and hoped that my smile didn't look as fake as it felt. I always sat next to Bibha, who always sat next to Bhaiyya. Then quietly she told me that I should've sautéed the masala a bit more. I apologised.

As I was clearing the table, Bibha started to make tea for the three of us. Bhaiyya always had his tea in their bedroom while he surfed the net. But today he was making a long distant call. I could hear him speak and it turned out that he was talking about me to Abba.

The children were playing in their room while Yusha played with *Duplo* Lego on the carpet, in front of us. Bibha told me to sit down and that she'd fill me in with all the details. Bibha gave Bhaiyya his tea and biscuits and then sat down next to me with a plate of digestive biscuits. I sat upright with my mug of tea.

'Okay.' Bibha cleared her throat. 'Your Bhaiyya has found a few proposals for you but we feel we should go with the one brother Ahmed has suggested.'

I felt shy all of a sudden. I tried not to giggle. My heart sank the minute Bibha said that it was Rumaisa's brother. Rumaisa had this high-pitched voice and a very rural dialect whenever she spoke in Sylhety. Bibha's one was like that too but at least Bibha spoke English more sophisticatedly.

Bibha filled me in with some basic details like his height, name, age, and job.

'Fahim,' Bibha said, 'has five sisters and a brother, who is the oldest of them all.' This gave me the creeps that besides a mother-in-law, I'd have five sisters-in-law to deal with.

But not all in-laws are horrid.

'Are they decent people?' I didn't know if I had worded it correctly. 'I mean, you know how my parents are even though we come from a well-reputed family.'

'I'm sure they are. I mean, I had to tell Rumaisa about the fact that we need to keep Amma out of the whole marriage and everything since she is how she is. And even after knowing this, they are willing to consider you for marriage so I guess that shows some decency.'

Bhaiyya came in and then repeated pretty much the same piece of information. He only added, 'The reason why I chose to go with this person is because they don't have any link back home, which, I'm sure you want to avoid too.' Bhaiyya asked Bibha to make him another cup of tea before carrying on, 'Fahim, is also a newly practising brother so it won't engulf you too much since you are also new to the religion.'

Bhaiyya sounded as though I was a non-Muslim before I came to live with him. Mixed feelings overcame me as Bhaiyya spoke about *Fahim*. The name seemed catchy and got scrabbled in my head... *Fahim Mihaf Mahif Mahi*...

'Are you listening Ranya?' Bhaiyya's voice sliced through my thoughts.

I nodded. Bhaiyya and Bibha started to make all sorts of plans about seeing the groom's family.

An ineffable emptiness formed in my heart. I wasn't sure if it was because I was going to get married or because I was being, politely, kicked out of this place. Bhaiyya explained that I'd be embarking on a new life and that finally it will be my turn to rise on my own. That I will have my own space.

And that I will no longer be salt and pepper.